An Atlas of the Known Worlds

Robert D. Beech

MIDNIGHT DRAGON PRESS

Dedication:

To my wife, Anne,
and our children, James, Abigail and Caroline,
being the (more or less)
true account of how I returned to you
after some adventures
between the pages of a book.

CONTENTS

Chapter One

The Book is Found

"Again, Daddy, read it again," Helen, our youngest child, begs. She has heard the story a thousand times before, but that does not matter. What matters is the sound of my voice in the darkness and the touch of my hand on hers.

"Of course, sweetheart." I pat her head and begin to re-read the story. The dogs settle down at my feet and John and Ruth, the two older children, lean in, caught up in the magic of words, listening to a story they have all heard a thousand times before. Human voices and human touch, keeping away the dark spirits of the night as they have done for thousands of years.

Book time has always been a special time in our family, a sacred hour in which we come together to immerse ourselves in a different reality, one created not on a screen, but in our minds. Tonight, with the noise of a storm howling around us, we seek the magic of books more than ever. Outside, rain lashes the darkened windows, pouring out of the overflowing rain gutters, as the distant booming of thunder rolls ever nearer. Suddenly there is a loud crack just outside the house, and a bolt of lightning—strangely vivid green it seems to me—illuminates the back windows, transforming our backyard into an electrified tableau, sending the cats running for shelter beneath the desk, and causing the dogs to howl in dismay. The house is plunged into darkness—a power failure, I think to myself. We sit for a moment in the blackness, my wife Elizabeth and I, holding each other close, reassuring the children and each other. We listen to the wind outside, whistling softly, and causing the branches of the trees to creak and mutter in unknown tongues.

After a moment when nothing further happens, we begin to relax, despite the sudden darkness. We quiet the anxious dogs, caressing their ears, and kiss the children who huddle together on the couch. Once everyone has been hugged, Elizabeth rises from the couch, stumbling through the dark towards the kitchen where she finds matches and candles to light the living room. By candlelight, we resume reading stories to the children, using the power of words to drive away the fear of the dark.

Despite my hopes, the books do not deter my unease. Instead of the reassuring magic of a story that is "long ago and far away," I sense something more imminent, more intimate, and at the same time, more threatening. The kind of magic that steps out of the book and into the quiet of the house when no one is looking and waits beneath the bed for unwary children. I close the book and set it aside, despite the protesting voices of the children.

"Come on sleepyheads, no more stories tonight. It's time for bed," I say after the last repetition. Taking Helen by the hand, I lead her up the dark stairs. We stumble in the dark bedrooms to find pajamas. I help her to get into them and brush her teeth by candlelight in the dark upstairs bathroom. John and Ruth manage on their own, and then one by one, they settle down to sleep. Elizabeth heads to our bedroom, but I head back downstairs to make one more check of the house before coming back to bed.

Downstairs, I walk in a slow circle that takes me from the landing at the bottom of the stairs, through the kitchen, the dining room, the living room, and back to the stairs, peering out each of the windows that I pass. Nothing stirs outside other than the trees in the wind. I can go up to bed. I should go up to bed. I should sleep, but I cannot. Instead, I take the candle and place it atop the low table in the living room and sit back on the couch, willing my mind to be still.

I hear footsteps in the dark. The cats, no doubt, making their own nocturnal patrols. Their eyes, keener than mine, will surely detect any hidden danger lurking outside the house, but this is a small comfort to me in my heightened state of arousal. Their eyes gleam in the dark, making me jump at their sudden appearances and disappearances. I have never been afraid of the dark before tonight, so what strange instinct is it that keeps me awake, keeps me looking, keeps me listening for I know not what outside the house? I cannot say.

Time has passed. By now, the children must be sleeping, lying in their unusually dark and quiet beds. There are no nightlights or audiobooks tonight, only burning candles that softly light their windows, recalling an older time, a darker time, when candles were left burning in the night to keep at bay those thoughts or spirits that dwell in the dark corners of the world. And so they will do tonight. Or so I hope.

Alarmed by my own thoughts, I go back upstairs to check on the children. John, Ruth, Helen, all are asleep or at least quiet in their beds, the candles beside their beds keeping silent vigil. All is well, the candles say. Elizabeth, too, has gone to bed, the bedside candle blown out, asleep perhaps or lying awake waiting anxiously for me to come to bed. But I cannot. Some strange restlessness fills me tonight. Though the storm has passed, the thunder quieted, and the strange green lightning that filled my wonderstruck eyes so briefly is gone back to wherever it is that such powers go, I cannot make myself rest.

So, I head back downstairs, taking the candle with me, to settle back onto the couch. Placing the candle burning in its sconce atop the low table once more, I sit there, in the unlit house, listening for sounds in the darkness outside and peering out at the night, waiting for the return of the storm, the sound of thunder and the flash of lightning, or perhaps something worse.

The hours creep by. It is cold in the house, colder than I would have expected for a summer night, even after the rain. It is a cold that seems to seep up from the ground and into the bones, a cold that whispers of the ancient struggles of humans against the elements, a cold that says the illusions of warmth and safety are just that, illusions, and that the cold and the dark will go on long after people have vanished from the earth.

Shaking my head to clear these thoughts, I go and kneel in front of the fireplace. I open the screen doors, reach up to open the flue by feel and then, working carefully by the light of my candle, I begin to stack wood from the small pile near the hearth onto the grate, first tiny twigs, then bigger sticks, and finally the log I hope will bring back the warmth that seems to have fled from the house. Some newspaper, balled up and pushed into the stack, serves as kindling. I touch the candle to the newspaper and a flame leaps to life. Blowing softly, I help the flame spread, first to the smaller twigs and then to the larger pieces of wood. Soon a merry blaze is crackling, and I sit back on the couch to watch the fire, letting its warmth envelop me and chase away the terrors of the night.

An hour goes by, the warmth of the fire lulling me into a fitful doze. I can almost let my worries go and sleep, but somehow, I still cannot close my eyes. By the light of the candle, now burned low, I can see that the clock on the mantel says five minutes to midnight, long past time to go to bed. My body feels tired, almost to the point of exhaustion, but still that strange restlessness fills me and my mind is very far from sleep. And so, I stand up, taking up the candle again, and go down the stairs to the basement to search by candlelight among the stacks of dusty books for something to read.

There are books in the basement: old books, new books, books stacked on shelves, books piled on top of bookcases when the shelves have become full, books packed in boxes to be sorted "someday when I have time," and books spilled out onto the floor of what had been the spare room before it became yet one more surface to pile things on. I go down there sometimes at night, tiptoeing down the stairs in slippered feet when the house is at its quietest, when the children are sleeping, the dogs walked and settled down for the night, the cats fed and off attending to the business of cats in the night, Elizabeth upstairs reading in bed or perhaps already asleep.

There are books in the basement. Some of them I have not read since I was a child. Some are from childhoods older than my own. And sometimes, if I take them up to read again, when I blow off the dust that has accumulated over the years, I find there are parts I do not recall and the words do not match my memories of them. One forgets, growing older, or so they say. Or perhaps it is the words themselves that have changed, growing new legs and wings as they lay there between their chrysalis-like covers. Who can say?

The wooden steps going down to the basement are cold on my bare feet. I try to walk softly, so as not to wake my sleeping family, but the treads of the stairs creak in the darkness, echoing the sounds of the trees outside. At the bottom of the stairs there is a landing. On the right side is the door to the spare room, now turned into a vault for hoarded books. The door to the spare room sticks when I go to open it, old wood, wedged in a badly hung frame. Holding the candle with one hand, I use my hip and my shoulder to lever the door open. As I step over the threshold into the room, I hold the candle close to me, fearful that amidst such piles of books and paper any stray spark could ignite a conflagration. Letting my eyes adjust to the near total darkness, I begin to peer about the darkened room.

The books in the basement look different tonight. Without the accustomed glare of electric lights, they seem unfamiliar to me, full of strange and mysterious possibilities. Many of the volumes here I cannot recall ever having seen before, though where else they could have come from I cannot imagine. The dust atop the shelves seems even thicker than I recall from my last trip to the basement. I have lost count over the years of just how many books there are. Hundreds certainly, thousands probably, and certainly there are many whose origins I have forgotten. But that new books, unfamiliar to me, should suddenly appear is an odd thing indeed. It is my basement after all, my hoarded books crowding all the shelves. Is my mind playing tricks on me such that my old books now seem new? But no, these are not new books. These are old books, older perhaps than any I have ever owned. Older perhaps than the house itself, if that is possible.

Atop a pile of books on the tallest bookcase, covered in dust bunnies and cobwebs (surely it cannot be that long since I vacuumed in here?), a strange leather-bound volume catches my eye. It seems out of place, though judging by the thickness of the dust on its cover, it has sat here for a very long time indeed. How did it come to be here? I cannot imagine. I feel sure I would have remembered such a book if I had seen it before.

Puzzled, I reach up carefully, pull down the book, blow off the dust and peer at the cover. The leather binding on the book is cracked, and if there were ever words written or printed on the cover, they are no longer legible. My curiosity aroused, I tuck the odd book under my arm and head back up the stairs to examine it more closely beside the fireplace.

When I reach the fireplace in the living room, the clock above the mantel shows that it is now one minute before midnight. Time seems to be moving at an ever slower pace. As I watch, the second hand sweeps slowly around the clock. I place the book before me and then, sitting cross-legged before the fire with the book in my lap, I carefully open the cover. It is now midnight, exactly. The title page of the book, which looks as though it may have been written by hand, reads, "An Atlas of the Known Worlds by . . ." The lower half of the page is smudged with soot and I cannot make out the remaining letters. The lettering on the title page is surrounded by a fanciful border illustrating ocean waves at the bottom of the page with clouds above, at the top of the page. In each corner of the page a different creature is depicted: a whale, a unicorn, a gryphon, and a dragon. The drawings are tiny but extremely detailed. They almost seem to peer out at me from the depths of the page. The dragon, in particular, seems to focus its eyes directly on mine when I lean in to look more closely at it. There is something almost familiar about those eyes.

Most of the other pages of the book are stuck together somehow, so I cannot turn to the next page, but laying the atlas in my lap again, I find that it falls open near the middle of the book. Leaning closer to the fire to gaze more closely at it, I stare for a time at the lines and tiny writing on the two pages open before me. At first, I can make no sense of them. They seem a random pattern of lines and words or perhaps merely scribbles with no sense to them at all. Peering more closely, I begin to perceive that the image is a map. More precisely, it is a map of my own town where I live with my family. There is my street, correctly labeled, and the streets it connects to, and the great rock formations called simply West Rock and East Rock, and farther away, the river flowing into the city's harbor and the Sound. Why such a map should appear in a dusty volume labeled "An Atlas of the Known Worlds," I cannot say, but that is what it appears to be.

I look up to stare once more into the fire. Though I gazed at the map for but a moment, or so I thought, when I look up from the book it now seems as if the fire has burned lower still, as if hours and not mere seconds have passed. Embers and not flames light the pages before me. And in their dull red light, the ink that a moment before had looked black to me begins to glow strangely, red like the light from the embers, and the lines of the map begin to waver and dance hypnotically, drawing me in. And now, all of the pages that a moment ago had seemed so firmly stuck together, have come loose from whatever spell had kept them in place, and turn freely in my hands. I turn the page. On the next page I see the same map—or rather, a different map, but one that is very similar to the first. There are the same two great rock formations, the river, and the sea just as before, but where the first map had shown a maze of streets and highways there is now merely a curious shaded area labeled, "Old Forest." And where, a moment before, or so I thought, I had read "West Rock" and "East Rock," now I read "Cliffs of the Black Dragon" and "Tower of the White Wizards." I rub my tired eyes, wondering if perhaps they are playing tricks on me, but the image does not change.

Looking up from the book, beyond the glowing embers of the fire, I now see, not the back wall of my fireplace, but a pair of large vertically slit, gleaming eyes of the same intensity and startling green hue as the bolt of lightning that had so spectacularly lit up my backyard during the storm only a few brief hours before. My breath catches in my throat as I begin to perceive the immense outlines of the creature before me.

"Ah, there you are at last," said the dragon.

Chapter Two

The Black Dragon

I WAS SITTING, CROSS-LEGGED, in front of a fire. But not the humble fire I had laid earlier tonight to take away the chill of a stormy evening. This fire, like mine, had burned down to its embers. But whereas my tiny fire had consisted of the embers of a few small pieces of wood, many great trees must have been burned to create this vast bed of coals. The fire pit was girdled all around by a low wall of rock. In the clearing beyond the firepit, I could see the dark shapes of men moving in the night, bringing great armloads of wood to feed the fire, and behind them the dark outlines of trees, while lying in the middle of this vast glowing bed of coals was the largest creature I had ever seen.

Its hide was rough, with great scales the size of shields covering parts of its back, growing smaller and smaller as they ran down the length of its enormous tail until, near the tip of the tail, they seemed no larger than the scales of a common lizard. The beast's tail curled around its body, over and through the burning coals (which seemed not to bother it in the least), and wrapped around its front feet like the tail of a sleeping cat. It had no wings, or none that I could see, such as dragons in story books are sometimes said to have, but four great legs, each larger than the leg of an elephant, but sinewy and sleek with the impression of great speed waiting to be unleashed, and at the end of each leg, three great curved claws extended, longer than any lion's, and (at least on the front feet, which were the ones nearest to me) a fourth claw like a scimitar curving back. The head, which lay resting on the creature's two front feet, was as large as that of a hippopotamus, but slenderer, with a thin pointed snout, like the beak of some enormous bird. Two great green eyes with vertical slits regarded me unblinkingly, and from the nostrils curled faint wisps of smoke.

"Welcome to my hearth," said the dragon in a deep, quiet voice that I seemed to feel in my bones as much as hear. As it spoke I could glimpse a long thin green tongue moving sinuously within the great mouth, writhing like a boa constrictor.

"Thank you," I replied, unsure of what else to say.

"Are you comfortable?" asked the dragon. "I understand that fragile creatures such as yourself have no tolerance for extremes of cold and heat."

The dragon shifted slightly on its bed of coals, and using its tail, which had a small, flat protuberance at the end, like a spade, it flipped a few of the glowing embers up onto its back.

"Ah, that's better," it added, wriggling down into its fiery bed.

"Uh, quite comfortable," I said, eyeing the burning coals nervously.

"Good," said the dragon. "Then we can move on to business."

"Business?" I replied, puzzled.

"Yes, the terms of your employment. You have, of course, come in response to my advertisement?"

"I'm afraid—that is to say, I don't recall," I said. Indeed, I had no clear recollection of how I had come to be here at all. The last thing

I recalled was sitting in front of my fireplace looking at the strange book that had appeared in my basement. It seemed like I had gone from my living room to the dragon's firepit in the blink of an eye. And the book had behaved most oddly. At first it had seemed as if all the pages were stuck together, and then suddenly they weren't, and when I turned the page, I found myself here. But surely, the book was not an advertisement from a dragon? An advertisement for what? I wondered. What would a dragon have to advertise?

"There was . . . an advertisement?" I asked, cautiously.

The dragon lowered its head menacingly, and a great puff of smoke shot out of its nostrils. "I would have thought that the import of my lightning bolt was quite clear," it said. "You can hardly have missed it, as you are sitting less than a hundred feet away from where I sent it, and the bolt should have been visible for several worlds."

I thought about this for a moment and eventually I connected the dragon's words with the bolt of lightning I had seen through my back window earlier in the evening—if it was now indeed the same evening. Had I perhaps fallen asleep? Was I now dreaming? No, surely not. How much time had passed? I could not say, although it seemed to me that no time had passed at all and that the world had changed around me in the time it had taken for me to raise my eyes from the strange book I had been looking at.

Apparently, the strange green lightning had been some sort of a message from the dragon. "Visible for several worlds," it had said. I wondered what that meant and if I was now in a different world than the one I had been in when I sat down to look at the book. I might have sat pondering this longer, but the presence of a large and irritable dragon does wonders to concentrate one's attention.

"My apologies, Sir Dragon," I said. And then, after a pause added, "Or perhaps, Madam Dragon? How should I call you?"

The dragon slowly raked its claws through the coals that it was lying on and leaned forward, bringing its great snout and an uncomfortably large array of teeth closer to me as it answered. I tried to scoot backwards unobtrusively.

"My name is no concern of yours. Or my sex for that matter. You will not trick my name from me as easily as that," said the dragon, testily. Apparently, asking a dragon for its name was something of a faux pas in dragon etiquette.

"Of course, of course," I said, hastily backing away, trying to keep from annoying the dragon further. I decided I would think of the dragon as "he" for the time being, though in truth I had no reason to think of the dragon as anything other than, well . . . a dragon.

"What did it say?" I asked, nervously.

"What did what say?" said the dragon, glowering. The long thin tongue continued to slide in and out over rows of dagger-like teeth even after the dragon finished speaking, as if he were tasting the air, or perhaps contemplating how I might taste. I decided not to dwell on that possibility.

"What did the, um, advertisement say? I, uh, couldn't read it very well. It was dark outside, you know."

The dragon snorted, and flames billowed out of his nostrils for a second, causing me to leap backward.

"It said," began the dragon slowly, as if reluctantly explaining the obvious to a child, or perhaps an idiot, "Thief wanted (or adventurer, if you prefer)." Here the dragon seemed almost to smile, although I cannot say it was a particularly friendly smile. "Usual pay and benefits (riches beyond the dreams of avarice). Survival *not* guaranteed." The dragon paused briefly. "The sign I believe is well known on your world, or it was the last time I visited. I believe it featured prominently in some book or other from your last century."

As I had never heard of a dragon visiting our world (and surely a dragon of this size, or of any size for that matter, would be a thing people would notice if it came visiting), except perhaps in fairy stories and the like, I assumed it had been some other world the dragon had visited. Or perhaps dragons live an unusually long time and the stories of their last visits were what had become our fairy stories. Who can say? In any case I had enough to worry about with the dragon lying in front of me without wondering whether he might have visited earth some time in the remote past.

"I'm afraid there's been some mistake," I began. "I didn't understand your message, or advertisement if that's what it was, and I'm certainly not a thief or an adventurer. And I didn't even mean to come here—wherever here is." I looked around the dark clearing and added, "where are we anyway?"

The dragon laughed—a deep rumbling sound that made me think uncomfortably of bones crunching in the dark. "You have a map," he pointed out.

I looked down. The book I had found in the basement was still lying open in my lap. I peered at it for a moment. There, roughly where my house had been on the old map, was an oval shape marked "Fire Pit." I looked back up at the dragon. It seemed as if a glint of malicious amusement lay somewhere deep within the green slits of his eyes.

"Of course," he went on, "if you're not a thief or an adventurer, you needn't accept the position. There are always . . ." He paused and licked his teeth. "Other alternatives. For instance, I could eat you."

"If that's a joke," I said, "I think it's in very poor taste. You'll pardon the expression."

The dragon laughed again. It was really not a pleasant sound. "Dragons never joke," he said, "and as to the taste, well, we could find out, or rather I could, though I'm afraid it would all be the same to you, however you taste."

I started to stand up. The dragon raised one of his front feet threateningly, loosing a small shower of coals, and I realized that I had no hope of running fast enough to get away from those enormous claws. I swallowed hard and sat back down quickly.

"What is it that you want me to do?" I asked, hesitantly.

"That's better," said the dragon. "Now we can talk sensibly."

"So what do you want?" I asked again.

"What do I want?" the dragon repeated, slowly. "A mere trifle, a bauble, nothing too difficult for a master burglar such as yourself." And again, I had the impression that the dragon was laughing at me behind those cold green eyes. Although since I had never, in fact, seen a dragon before I could not be certain. Perhaps dragons always looked like that.

"What does it look like?" I asked.

The dragon seemed to hesitate a moment, as if reluctant to say too much. "It is a small green stone, about the size of your head," he continued, and again his tongue slid languorously over his teeth as if he were tasting something invisible, but whether it was some scent emanating from my body or from this mysterious stone or from some other unknowable thing that the dragon tasted, I could not say.

"It is round," the dragon continued, "and smooth and polished like glass, with great depths inside if you look into it. But I would avoid that if I were you." And there was again a hint of laughter in his voice.

I started to ask why, but then thought better of it. Whatever peril there was in looking into the dragon's stone, I had no need to find out. Instead, I asked, "And where would I find this 'bauble,' as you call it?"

Two great jets of flame shot up out of the dragon's nostrils and he raked his claws over one of the stones surrounding the fire pit, scoring the rock deeply and I shuddered to think what those claws might do to me. This particular stone's location was, it seemed, a matter of considerable annoyance to the dragon, and I had no desire to annoy the dragon further if I could help it.

"It is not far from here," the dragon said after a pause. "In the Tower of the White Wizards. I will mark the way on your map."

And before I could ask who or what the White Wizards were, the dragon brought one of his huge front feet down upon the book, which still lay open upon my lap. So swift was the dragon's movement that I had no time to cry out, let alone run, before his claws descended, and yet so dexterous that I felt no more than a slight pressure on my lap as he ran one single claw over the open page. Where the dragon's claw had touched the map, there now appeared a wandering red line running from the place marked "Fire Pit" to the other large rock formation, which I remembered simply as East Rock from what all at once felt like my previous life, and which now on the new map indeed bore the legend "Tower of the White Wizards."

"I could, of course," said the dragon, "go myself to fetch it. But I am afraid I am a bit conspicuous, and wizards are very crafty in hiding what they do not want found. So even if I leveled their pitiful castle"—and here the dragon gave a snort of contempt, but whether he could indeed level their castle or was merely boasting, I had no way of knowing—"I would still lack the stone." The dragon paused. "I have tried sending my servants," he went on, "but my mark gives them away too easily."

I was puzzled at this until I glanced up again at the men who silently tended the fire. I noticed now that they were all completely naked despite the dampness and the chill of the night, and what is more, they seemed completely unaware of their state or indeed of anything except their appointed tasks. Their eyes stared vacantly as they moved, carrying armloads of wood to feed the great fire. As they moved silently in the firelight, I noticed that upon each man's chest was a huge mark, a brand, it appeared, outlining the imprint of an enormous, clawed foot with three great talons spread over the breast and the fourth stretching down over the belly. It was indeed a most conspicuous mark.

"So," said the dragon. "I require a new sort of servant. One who serves me"—he paused to let the smoke rise slowly out of his nostrils, and looked for a moment rather like a man smoking a pipe—"willingly. So do you accept? Or shall we consider the alternatives?" Here the dragon opened wide his mouth, displaying a fearsome array of teeth, and lifted his head so that his chin rose up high over the rock wall of the fire pit, leaving little doubt as to the alternative in question.

"Um, under the circumstances," I said quickly, "I should be glad to accept your offer."

"Excellent choice," said the dragon. "Though I do wonder what you would have tasted like. No matter, there are other fish in the sea, as they say. Of course, being human, you will lie and try to cheat me once you believe that you are safely out of my reach. However, I will point out, if it has not already occurred to you, that without that book, you have no way of returning to your own world. So I shall hold onto it for the time being." And so saying, the dragon snatched the book of maps from my lap with one swift swipe of a single claw. "When you retrieve the green stone for me, I shall return the book to you."

I almost cried out at the theft of the book but quickly thought better of it. In this negotiation, if you wanted to call it that, the dragon clearly held all the cards. And now he held my book as well. I wondered briefly whether the dragon had some sort of pocket that he would tuck the book into, but he merely held the book up before his eyes. Then there was a flash of blinding light, the same color as the lightning I had seen before, and the book was gone, and with it my chances of returning to my home and family. My heart sank. If I were to return home I would have to fulfill the dragon's quest.

Damn all dragons, I thought uselessly. However, as my heartbeat started to return to something resembling normal, I remembered something else the dragon had said. If I were forced to carry out my Faustian bargain with the creature, perhaps it would at least be a lucrative one.

"What about the, um, 'riches beyond the dreams of avarice'?" I ventured to ask, somewhat timidly.

"Ah, you remembered that, did you?" said the dragon. "We shall see. After you bring me the stone. Do you remember the way I showed you to get to the White Wizard's Tower?"

"I think so. Perhaps if you could let me have another quick look at the book I could..."

"Enough. Do not try my patience with your trickery, little human. Do you think to steal the book back from me, so you can flee back into it?"

"No. No, of course not. We have a bargain and I will fulfill my end of it," cursing inwardly since, of course, that had been exactly my thought.

"Good. Do not forget it. It does not do to cross a dragon."

"No, no of course not," I agreed hastily.

"Good, then I suggest you begin your search at once."

"At once? But it's the middle of the night."

"It will be well past dawn by the time you reach the Tower of the White Wizards."

"Yes, but how am I to find the stone once I get there? Won't the wizards have hidden it? And even if they haven't, they're hardly likely to let me just walk out of there with it, are they?" I protested.

"That, burglar, is your problem," said the dragon. "And now, I must hunt."

And having said that, the dragon rose to his full height, which was a very great height indeed, spun suddenly halfway around, and sprang out the other end of the fire pit. The dragon's servants leaped to the sides or flung themselves on the ground to avoid being trampled, but the dragon took no notice. There were loud crashing sounds as he disappeared into the woods surrounding the small hill where we had been sitting, only to reappear, a few short moments later, far in the distance, rapidly scaling the walls of the cliffs that bore his name on the now vanished book of maps, his size reduced by distance to that of a lizard climbing a wall. I blinked and he was gone, leaving me to wonder if I had perhaps imagined the entire conversation. Had I really just been hired by a dragon? I pinched myself to see if perhaps I could snap myself out of this bizarre dream I was having. The pinch hurt.

Chapter Three

Across the River

After the dragon's departure, his servants picked themselves up off the ground and resumed tending to the fire. However, they continued to ignore me, as before, neither coming over to speak to me nor attempting to drive me away from the fire pit. As I watched them, I wondered again at their nakedness. Enthralled, as they seemed to be, by the dragon they would have, perhaps, no need for clothes as vanity, but working in such close proximity to the fire, it seemed they would need something to protect them from sparks and flames at a minimum. Even their feet were bare of shoes or sandals. Perhaps the same magic that enslaved them to the dragon's will also protected them from the flames? Or perhaps the dragon was simply indifferent to their fate and ate those of his servants who were burned or injured and thus no longer useful. I had no way of knowing.

I sat for a moment peering out into the dark forest that the dragon had disappeared into. I distrusted these silent servants of the dragon, with their blank faces and his claw marks somehow stamped upon their bodies, yet I was even more fearful of what I might meet stumbling around blindly in the forest at night. It was a strange new world that I had suddenly found myself thrust into against my will, and I had no idea what other monsters might be lurking in the woods beyond this clearing. I leaned up against one of the rocks surrounding the fire pit for warmth and stared out into the night, longing for home, family and a soft bed with a pillow instead of a rock to lay my head on. I thought of Elizabeth and our children, separated from me by the thickness of a page on the magic map, but yet more distant than the ocean's farthest shore. I hoped that they were safe and the storm that had surrounded our house had moved on, leaving them unscathed. I wondered when or if I might ever see them again. I stared uneasily at the dragon's servants, wondering if at some moment their behavior might suddenly change and become hostile, but they continued to ignore me and eventually, weariness overcame me and I slept.

I awoke in the morning to find that all of the dragon's servants were gone. Dawn crept silently over the horizon, filling the sky with blue and pink clouds and a scarlet sunrise that rivaled the brightness of the dragon's blazing hearth. The last embers of the fire still burned within the great fire pit, but of the dragon and his servants there was no sign. Were it not for the ache in my back from sleeping against the hard rocks, I might almost have thought last night's events to have been a dream. But home and bed were far away, and the dragon's fire pit was a poor substitute for either.

I wondered briefly whether I could or should trust the dragon to uphold his end of the bargain. If I found this "bauble," as he had called it, would he return the book to me (with or without "riches beyond the dreams of avarice") and enable me to return home, or would it just be "one small step for man," and one tasty dinner for the dragon? On the other hand, if I did not do as the dragon had commanded, then I had no way of returning home, so there was really no choice. I thought again of Elizabeth and the children who would wake this morning and have no idea of what had happened to me. What would they think? That I had been kidnapped or simply disappeared? I had no way to even tell them where I had gone. *Damn all dragons*, I thought again, and set out in search of the dragon's bauble.

As I walked around the fire pit I came across the dragon's footprints leading away from it, down the side of the hill and toward the Cliffs of the Black Dragon. I followed the dragon's tracks into the woods until I came to the foot of the small hill and then turned away to head east, following my memory of the red line that the dragon had traced with his claw upon the map, toward the Tower of the White Wizards—or so I hoped.

The going was slow through the forest as there was no clearly marked trail to follow, but instead only a series of small clearings and what might have been deer paths that blended one into another in no particular pattern. I walked all day through the woods. The brambles tore at my clothes and caught in my hair, and swarms of mosquitoes and some sort of tiny biting flies appeared to take advantage of the sudden feast I offered them. I could hear birds singing in the thickets several times, but rarely glimpsed the singers. By the time I came to the next clearing the birds would be silent, watching warily from their thorny hiding places. Once, I thought I saw deer with their white tails flashing before disappearing into the woods ahead of me, but I saw no other human beings, only here and there the ruins or burnt-out remains of some cottage or small hut. I went into one of these hoping to find some clue as to what had ravaged the countryside. I saw scorched walls and the splintered remains of furniture but no trace of the people who had lived there. If this was the dragon's work, he had been thorough in his destruction. I shuddered to think of what had happened to the people who had once lived in this little valley and more so to think that the same fate might befall me if I failed to fulfill my bargain with the dragon.

It was late afternoon by the time I reached the foot of the second set of cliffs, the ones that had been marked Tower of the White Wizard on the mysterious map, and though I had gone only a short distance as the crow flies, I was footsore and extremely hungry. Thief or adventurer for hire, consultant to the Black Dragon, might sound like an exotic job title, but the working conditions certainly left something to be desired.

At the foot of these cliffs there wound a river, not a great river certainly, as rivers go, but I had no way to judge its depth and no desire to swim it if I could avoid doing so. I walked along it a ways, looking for a bridge. At length, I came to what at first I thought was a low bridge, but as I came closer I saw that there was only a rope, crossing the river scant inches above the water from a stake tied on my side of the river to a similar stake tied on the opposite bank. Seated beside the stake on the near side was a figure in a robe that might once have been white but was now grey with much wear and many washings. I hesitated and then approached the seated figure. As I approached, the robed figure rose and turned to face me.

"Who goes there?" the figure cried, challenging me. The voice was soft and yet deep, and whether a man's or a woman's, I could not say. The features, too, gave me little clue, for the robe was hooded and hid the wearer's face almost entirely. Nonetheless, I could see two piercingly bright blue eyes looking out at me from beneath that hood. "State your name," the voice commanded.

"Diogenes," I answered, lying impulsively.

"Indeed? And what brings you, Diogenes, wandering into the realm of the White Wizards?" the figure asked.

A dragon, I almost blurted out, but something told me that anyone who came on a dragon's business would not be welcome here, so instead I answered, "I would speak with the White Wizards."

"Would you indeed?" said the hooded figure, regarding me oddly. "Then you must cross the river."

I looked again at the rope that stretched from one bank of the river to the other but saw no way across.

"I see no bridge," I said simply.

"There is none," said the figure, "for the wizards have decreed that none shall enter into their realm save by passing through the river. The water is not deep, however, scarcely above your chest at the deepest point, nor the current too strong. If you hold onto the rope firmly, you can make it across."

I looked uneasily at the rope stretching across the river and thought without great enthusiasm about the prospect of wading through chest-deep water to cross it. But I was here, and had no place else to go, save back to the dragon's fire pit. And given the choice between fording the river and going back empty-handed to the dragon, the former seemed by far the better choice. Reluctantly, I stepped down toward the bank. But the guardian of the river crossing—as I had by now begun to think of him, or her—stopped me, pointing the end of a long wooden staff at my chest.

"Before you enter the water, I must see your skin," said the person.

"My skin?" I repeated, puzzled, and looked down at the skin of my hands and forearms, which could be seen easily enough.

"All of it," said the figure, "to be sure there is no mark of evil anywhere upon you."

I remembered the great-clawed foot marked upon the dragon's servants like a brand and understanding dawned upon me. This was how the wizards kept the dragon's servants from coming to prowl within their domain. Simple, yet effective, I supposed. *Until now*, I thought guiltily.

I was not sure how much of a threat the wooden staff posed to me. Was this in fact a servant or a guard threatening me with a simple, if potentially lethal weapon made of wood, or was this one of the wizards themselves, with a staff of magical power brandished at my chest? I had no way of knowing, but one thing was clear. If I wanted to go on I would have to put up with the inspection. I took off my shirt and stood before the maybe-wizard to show that there was no mark upon my chest. The figure regarded me coldly.

"All of it," the figure repeated.

"All of what?" I asked bewildered.

"All of your skin."

I looked down at my clothes. I had been wearing a yellow ox-ford-collar shirt with blue pinstripes (now held loosely in my hands), tan khaki pants, a leather belt, brown socks (all of which could do with a wash, as I had been wearing them since the previous day), and a pair of plain brown leather shoes. Ordinary enough where I had come from, but perhaps odd enough to raise suspicions here. Did the figure expect me to strip naked in front of them? Apparently they did. I thought briefly of putting my shirt back on and going back the direction I had come from, but the thought of the dragon and the likely consequences of failure quickly put an end to that idea. So, as the robed figure watched, I proceeded to take off the rest of my clothes. In a few moments I stood, completely naked, holding my small bundle of clothes before me like a fig leaf.

"All of it," the figure repeated a third time. And, feeling a fierce blush burning on my cheeks, I dropped my hands to my sides.

"Raise your arms," the figure commanded.

"What?"

"I need to see that there is no mark beneath them."

"Uh, right," I said slowly and raised my arms above my head, still holding my clothes and shoes.

The river guardian peered briefly at each of my armpits.

"Now the soles of your feet."

"Okay," I said and lifted each of my feet in turn for the guardian's inspection.

"Stick out your tongue," the guardian commanded, and I stuck out my tongue for inspection. Dragons, it seemed, could be quite devious in how they marked their servants. Either that, or the guardian was simply enjoying my humiliation.

"Turn around," the figure commanded. Slowly, suddenly fearful that I might be attacked from behind, I turned and stood with my back turned to the river guardian for inspection, unsure if I would be allowed to pass or simply struck down from behind. After a long moment, the figure said, "You may cross."

Since I was already naked, I decided to keep my clothes dry if I could. I stuffed my socks and underwear into my shoes, tied them together, and draped them around my neck. The shirt, pants, and belt I wadded together and tied around my neck by my shirtsleeves. Then, with my clothes and shoes tied on as best I could, I grabbed on to the rope with both hands and stepped out into the river.

As promised, the water was no deeper than my chest and the current was no more than a gentle push against my skin, but the river was cold and inky black, and there were forms moving in the depths I could not quite make out. Fish perhaps, or turtles, and once I thought I saw a silver eel, perhaps three feet in length and moving swiftly through the water, but a moment later I looked again and it was gone.

As I reached the center of the river, the current grew stronger and seemed to surge suddenly, sweeping my feet out from under me. I held tightly to the rope, and tried to regain my footing, my earlier hopes of arriving at the far bank with dry clothing now superseded by the more urgent need to avoid being swept away in the current. The river that a moment ago had seemed placid, almost sluggish in its flow, now foamed above my shoulders, threatening to pluck me from the rope and carry me off downstream. The rushing water seemed to probe my skin much as the river guardian's eyes had while I stood on the bank a few moments earlier. I clung on and in a minute the sudden surge of the current subsided and I felt my feet settle on the river bottom once again.

When the unexpected surge in the current had passed, I made my way across as quickly as I could, feeling gingerly with my feet for sharp rocks or other unseen dangers on the bottom. I emerged on the other side and began to put on my now waterlogged clothes.

The robed figure who had been watching me as I crossed now lifted up the hem of his robe, revealing two bare feet, and with an astounding agility ran swiftly across the rope like a tightrope walker holding the staff like a balancing pole. I thought angrily of the humiliation I had just endured, being forced to strip and then nearly swept away in the surging water, while the hooded crossing keeper, if that's what the figure was, had not even had to get his—or perhaps her? —feet wet. But I said nothing of that and asked simply, "Which way do I go from here?"

"That is for you to decide," the figure answered and then turned and walked back across to his post on the other side of the river.

I scowled at the retreating back of the figure and looked around for some path to follow. And suddenly, there before me I saw a wide stone-paved path that seemed to lead upward toward the top of the cliffs. I started walking.

Chapter Four

The Road

NIGHT WAS FALLING AS I set out on the road that led, or so I hoped, toward the Tower of the White Wizards. Earlier that day, as I walked through the woods, I had sometimes been able to glimpse spires high atop the cliffs, but now, at the foot of those cliffs, I could see nothing of my destination. The road, however, was easy enough to follow, even in the gathering dark. The road was not paved, but it was wide enough for two cars to pass, side by side, had there been any cars, though I realized I had no idea if there even were cars in this world. Certainly before coming across this road I had seen no sign of anything that suggested wheeled traffic, or indeed any traffic at all, beyond the deer paths in the woods. The only humans I had seen had been the dragon's mute and strangely marked servants and the odd cloaked figure I had just left at the river. In the trees on either side of the road I could hear faint rustlings, but whether of birds, squirrels, or something else, I could not make out. I decided to stick with the road. I had perhaps, left the dragon safely on the other side of the river, but who knew what new threats lurked in the woods on this side.

After I had walked for perhaps twenty minutes, I came to a fork in the road. There was no signpost to indicate the way, and the road appeared equally wide in both directions. My first thought was that I would take whichever fork seemed to go upward, since that seemed the most likely to lead to the top but, as near as I could tell in the crepuscular light, both roads ascended at the same pitch while the road I had been walking on led back down to the river. Sighing, I chose the left-hand fork arbitrarily and, trusting to luck, continued on my way. After perhaps another twenty minutes I came to another similar fork in the road. Again there was no signpost and both roads appeared to continue up the hill. Once again I chose the left-hand fork, reasoning that if I always chose the left-hand fork, I could at least retrace my steps more easily if I needed to.

The night grew darker: it was true night now rather than twilight, and the first stars began to appear overhead. I felt hopeful at that, for though I know next to nothing about the constellations, I thought I could at least make out the Big Dipper and perhaps the North Star. Was it the handle of the Dipper that pointed to the North Star? I couldn't quite recall. But no matter, at least if there was a pattern overhead that I could use to orient myself, the task seemed less hopeless. I walked on, looking now at the road and now up toward the heavens, trying to ignore the rustlings in the trees on either side of me. Was there something following me? I looked into the woods, but could see nothing and decided to keep walking. Whatever it was, as long as it stayed in the woods, it was no concern of mine. Every twenty minutes or so I came to a new fork in the road and, following my plan, each time I chose the left side.

I had been walking uphill for perhaps two hours when I came to the sixth such fork. My legs ached from the unaccustomed effort of this long night-time stroll on top of my day-long walk through the woods. Although from their base the cliffs had seemed to be the face of no great mountain (I had felt sure an hour's walk would bring me easily to the top) I felt now that I was no nearer to the top than when I had started. The more I looked at this fork in the road, the more I felt it was the same one I had seen when I first started out on this road two or more hours ago. But I thought, if I had come round somehow in a great circle, then at least one branch of the fork ahead of me should lead back down towards the river. But once again, both forks appeared to lead up towards the top. Looking back down the road I had been following, I could see nothing, but I thought I could hear the faint gurgling of the river, as near now as it had been when I came to the very first fork in the road. Wearily, I sat down in the middle of the road and considered my options.

"Which one of these roads leads to the top?" I asked of no one in particular.

To my surprise, I was answered by a small voice from the woods beside the road.

"What makes you think any of these roads leads to the top?"

I looked around to see who had spoken but could see no one, only a small grey squirrel, creeping along the branch of a tree.

"Who said that?" I asked, still looking around.

The squirrel sat up and regarded me curiously, and then to my astonishment it spoke again. "What has eyes but cannot see? What has ears but cannot hear? What has a nose but cannot smell? And what has legs but cannot walk where it wants to go?" asked the squirrel.

"What do you mean?" I asked, puzzled.

"Exactly," said the squirrel. "A human who cannot think."

After a moment I realized that the squirrel's riddle had been intended merely to insult me. It was too much. After many hours of walking, first through the forest and now upon this accursed road, I was bone weary, hungry, thirsty, and in no mood to be insulted by anyone, least of all some talking rodent.

"In my world," I said sharply, "squirrels don't talk."

"Don't they?" said the squirrel in a surprised tone. "That would account for it then."

"Account for what?" I asked, in spite of myself.

"Your inability to engage in intelligent conversation," said the squirrel, smugly.

I thought briefly of trying to catch the squirrel and wring its impudent little neck, but of course the squirrel was up a tree, safely out of my reach, and in any case would probably race off if I made any kind of a threatening gesture. Instead, I grumbled, morosely, "Look, who asked you to come along and insult me anyway? Haven't you got anything better to do?"

"You asked a question," said the squirrel, "'Which one of these roads leads to the top?' I answered it."

"With another question," I snarled, "and an impudent one at that."

"Impudent or not," said the squirrel, "it is the one you should have asked in the first place. What makes you think any of these roads lead to the top?"

I thought about it for a moment. Much as I hated to admit it, the squirrel was right. I had no way of knowing which, if any, of these roads led up to the summit, and no reason for thinking that any of them did, save my own wish that one of them do so. I looked suspiciously at the squirrel. Who or what was he, and why had he suddenly appeared now to taunt me like this? Did the squirrel know something that I did not? Almost certainly, I decided, given that I at this point seemed to know nothing at all, or at least nothing that was of any use in my present predicament.

"Let me rephrase that, then," I said after a pause. "How do I get to the top?"

"Ah, there at last is a sensible question," said the squirrel, who still however did not answer me, but seemed instead to be waiting for me to answer my own question. I waited for the squirrel to say something useful, but there was nothing forthcoming. We stared at each other silently across the dark road for what was probably only a minute, but seemed much longer in cold and dark.

"So, what do you think the answer is?" the squirrel said at length.

I ground my teeth. Like the hooded figure I had met by the riverbank, this animal seemed intent on answering every question with a question. The thought occurred to me, perhaps somewhat belatedly, that this might be one of the wizards in disguise, perhaps even the same wizard I had met by the river, or perhaps the voice of one of the wizards speaking through the mouth of this woodland creature. The thought irritated me, since if that was the case, the squirrel could easily guide me to the wizards instead of keeping me here playing riddle games all night. I decided that this must be another test, like having to show all of my skin before I could cross the river, and that my answer might determine whether the squirrel would lead me to the tower or leave me to wander in circles all night along this treacherous road. Swallowing my irritation, I spoke as politely as I could.

"I think the answer is that you know the way to the top, or more precisely, that you know the way to the Tower of the White Wizards, whether it is at the top of these cliffs or somewhere else, and I do not. And so, if I wish to go to the Tower of the White Wizards, I must ask you to guide me." I hesitated a moment and then added, "Will you lead me to the Tower of the White Wizards, Sir Squirrel? Or Madam Squirrel, as the case may be, or whatever I should call you."

"Whether I am a Sir Squirrel or a Madam Squirrel is certainly none of your business," said the squirrel, brusquely. "As to what you should call me, perhaps Teacher would do, or better yet, Guide and Master, for if you wish to reach the Tower of the White Wizards you must certainly follow my guidance. Now if only you could climb trees, the going would be quite easy, but as you are clearly unsuited for such a civilized mode of travel, you will have to follow along as best you may. If you keep up, you may get there before morning. If not, I'm sure a night or two in the forest would do you some good."

With that, the squirrel leaped across the width of the road, landing on a branch of a tree between the two forks of the road and headed off into the forest. I left the road and cursing my luck, I pushed aside the twigs and branches that barred my way and plunged into the thick undergrowth, trying to keep up with my diminutive guide, who leaped nimbly from branch to branch in apparent unconcern as to my ability to keep up. As we went deeper into the forest, the squirrel was always up ahead, never quite out of sight, but never pausing to let me rest either, as I stumbled my way through the tangle of branches and thorns that seemed to come into being as soon as I let my attention wander for even a split second. I soon lost sight of the stars overhead and my face and hands were scored with a thousand tiny scratches, as I plowed my way up the hill. Whether it was an hour or twelve that we climbed to reach the top I could not have told you. As we climbed I heard more rustlings in the woods to either side of us, but I did not turn to look, but strove with all my might to keep putting one foot in front of the other and to not lose sight of the squirrel who seemed to float through the branches ahead of me. I was wearier than I had ever been in my life when we finally emerged in a clearing at the top of the cliffs. As I stepped into the clearing, a great stone wall loomed before me, topped with a turret at either end, with a vast wooden door set in an arched doorway in the center. The sun was rising in the distance, and the sky behind the castle glowed orange-pink giving the walls of the castle an opalescent sheen that was almost blinding. I had come to the Tower of the White Wizards.

CHAPTER FIVE

IN THE WIZARDS' TOWER

"I WILL LEAVE YOU here," said the squirrel, and without further ado, disappeared back into the woods from which we had just emerged. As the squirrel had suggested, there was no road leading up to the castle, or none that I could see, only a broad open grassy space in front of the castle walls. The great wooden door was shut, and I could see no sign of movement either in the field before me or within the castle. There were no archers on the walls, no guards at the doorway. No one to either greet or challenge me. I stood for a moment wondering what I should do next. Then, feeling somewhat self-conscious, I walked across the field and knocked on the great door in the archway. There was no answer, but after a moment, there was a scraping sound and a small peephole opened, not in the large door in the archway on which I had knocked, but in a small side door that I had not noticed before, set in a recessed doorway beside the turret to my left.

"Who is it?" asked a sleepy voice from behind the peephole in a somewhat surly manner, "and what do you want?"

I walked over to the small door to see who was speaking, but no light came from whatever room lay behind the closed door and I could see nothing of the speaker.

"I want to speak to the White Wizards," I said, feeling still more self-conscious.

"Oh, do you now?" said the voice sarcastically. "Any one in particular? Or shall I line 'em all up and let yer choose?"

"Whoever is available," I said impatiently.

"And what if none of 'em is 'available' right now?" asked the voice.

"Then I shall wait," I answered, wondering if this were another test.

"Might 'ave a long wait then," said the voice, nastily. "I hear some wizards can sleep for an 'undred years."

The peephole slammed shut. I stood for a moment staring blankly at the locked door before me, wondering whether I should knock again or wait to see if whoever was behind the door would decide to admit me. When nothing happened for a few minutes, I sat down in front of the small door and waited. Having walked all day and all night and not eaten since the previous day, I felt both exhausted and ravenously hungry. My stomach growled and my legs ached, and I longed to leave this castle and its surly gatekeeper far behind me, but in truth I had nowhere else to go, so I stayed sitting outside the door.

I shivered in my still damp clothes in the cold early-morning air, but after a while the sun came up and began to warm me. I do not know how long I sat there—I think I must have dozed off—when I heard the squeak of the peephole being pulled open again.

"Are you just gonna sit there all day?" the same voice as before asked, sounding petulant.

"If I must," I answered.

"*Harrumph.* An' I s'pose you'd like to be let in, would you?"

"Yes," I said simply.

"Well?" said the voice, expectantly.

"Well, what?" I replied, feeling exasperated.

"Why don't yer ask me to let you in?"

"Very well," I said, feeling I was once more being bullied for the sake of bullying by the wizards' servants. "Will you let me come in?"

"Certainly," said the voice. "You might have asked sooner and saved yourself sitting out on the grass all that while."

The small side door opened with a creak. I stood up feeling just as creaky as the door and staggered toward the doorway. As I entered, I looked down at the doorman, if that's who he was. He was short, coming barely up to my chest, and stooped as if with great age. He was dressed in a grey hooded cloak and leaned upon a wooden staff with a curved handle, like a cane. We were in a small dark room with three doors. The first, which I had just come through, led into the field outside the castle. The second, to my left, led to a flight of stairs going up into the turret. And the third, which was actually two half-doors, led out into a large courtyard. The top half of this door was open, and I could see out into the courtyard, but once again, I could see no people and there was no sign of movement. On the fourth wall there was a wide wooden bench with a small pillow upon which the doorman had apparently being sleeping before I began banging on the door. If I had wakened him with my banging that might account for the surly reception, I decided. Or perhaps this doorman was always surly, who could say?

"There's none of 'em about right now, wizards, that is," began the doorman—but I wondered whether this was true, or whether he himself might be one of the wizards, testing me in some way. If so, it was an odd sort of test. "I'll show you a room where you can wait in the meantime. An' I s'pose you'll be wantin' brekkist?"

I paused for a moment before I realized he meant *breakfast* and replied eagerly, "Yes, please. That would be wonderful."

The doorman snorted. *"Harrumph* . . . Thought so. . . 'Speak to the White Wizards,' he says . . . Lookin' fer 'andouts more like."

I stopped, torn between the annoyance I felt at this trickery, as it seemed to me, and my real desires, both for food and to accomplish my mission, so that I might have some hope of getting back to my own world. For the past day and a half I had been buffeted from one unbelievable situation to the next so often that it began to feel as if this were the normal course of things, and my memories of home, Elizabeth, John, Ruth and Helen were more fantastical than any dragons, wizards, or talking squirrels I had met here. How could I hope to get back if every step forward led merely to another obstacle?

"I do indeed want to speak to the White Wizards," I said, "and if I must forego breakfast to speak to them, I will gladly do so. However, if, as you say, they are not around at present, and if you have food to spare, I would take some gladly, for it has been more than a day since I have eaten and I am not used to such hardship."

"'Ardship is it?" grumbled the doorman. "I s'pose it could be for some. Though from the looks of you, you've been storin' it up for a while 'fore this fast." He glanced meaningfully at my midsection which, despite its current protests, did indeed belie any notion that I had been starved for a prolonged period of time.

I said nothing to this and after a while the doorman dropped his challenging gaze and turned to lead me out into the courtyard. "Come along then, and I'll see what I can find for yer."

He led me through the half-doors out into a large courtyard. There were no people about that I could see, but on one side there were stalls with horses poking their noses over the tops of their stall doors and a rooster pecking after insects in the grass that sprang up here and there through the courtyard's dirt floor. From here, he led me through another side door off the courtyard and along a narrow passage that made several twists and turns at inexplicable points and then down a short flight of stairs to another hallway. A short distance down this hallway, the doorman stopped and opened a wooden door. The room on the other side of the door was small, perhaps eight feet by six, and bare of furnishings except for a wooden bench similar to the one I had seen in the doorman's room and a small low table. There was an open, unglazed window set high in the wall opposite the door, but it must have faced away from the rising sun, for little light came through it at the moment.

"Wait here," said the doorman. "I'll be back in a bit."

I sat down at the wooden bench and waited. I had almost drifted off to sleep when the doorman returned with a round loaf of new-baked bread on a square wooden platter and a small clay pitcher. The smell of the bread wafted up enticingly and I found my mouth starting to water as I stood up to accept them.

"Water and bread," he said simply, ignoring my outstretched hands and putting both the platter with the bread and the pitcher down on the table. "That should hold off starvation for a bit. Wait here and someone will come and fetch you when the wizards are ready to see you. That is, if they decide they want to talk to you at all," he added.

"Thank you," I said to his retreating back, but the doorman was already closing the door behind him as I sat back down on the bench. When he had gone, I devoured the entire loaf of bread and emptied the pitcher of water in less than five minutes. The bread was delicious, but my hunger was so great I did not take the time to savor it. I licked the crumbs from my fingers and thought of Winnie the Pooh asking, "Is there any more?" There wasn't. I finished eating and sat back down on the wooden bench to wait, but within minutes my eyes closed of their own accord and I fell into a leaden sleep.

When I awoke, the orange light of the setting sun was coming in through the window, and I realized I had slept the entire day. While I slept, someone had cleared away the platter and the pitcher, but otherwise the room was as I remembered it. My bladder felt full to bursting, but there was no one around whom I could ask for directions to the nearest bathroom. The doorman, I supposed, had returned to his room by the front door. Seeing that the door to my room had been shut while I slept, I wondered suddenly if the little space were really a prison cell and I, myself now a prisoner of the White Wizards. What would they do, I wondered, if and when they discovered that I had been hired by the Black Dragon to steal this precious bauble that they were hiding from him? Panic swept over me for a brief moment, but when I tried the handle, I found to my relief that the door was unlocked.

Feeling chagrined, I opened the door and looked out into the hallway. To my right, I could see the short passage leading to the stairs I had come down that morning with the doorman. To my left, the hall continued out of sight, with doorways lining both walls at irregular intervals. I hesitated a moment and then, following some odd impulse to explore, I turned and started walking down the hall to the left. The floor seemed to slant downward and the hallway grew steadily darker, colder and more tunnel-like as I walked. At the end of the hall I came to an abrupt right turn, followed closely by a left. Then came a series of twists and turns that seemed to have no bearing on any possible arrangement of rooms, and after a while I ceased to pass any doorways at all. There were short flights of steps here and there, some leading up, some down, that connected the passage's various segments. The texture and size of the paving stones often changed as I went from one segment to the next, as if this hallway connected buildings of very different ages beneath the surface of the ground. I say beneath the surface, for I was now fairly certain that what I walked in was not simply a hallway but a network of underground tunnels connecting different parts of the castle.

I thought of going back to my cell and simply waiting, or of turning back and going in the other direction to look for the doorman who had let me in, but when I looked behind me, I realized that I had taken so many twists and turnings that I no longer knew how to get back. Logically, this made no sense. There had been no intersecting passages, no forks in the road to confuse my way. All I had to do to get back was to turn around and retrace my passage back the way I had come, and inevitably I would return to the room where I had slept. So logic told me. Yet somehow I knew that logic was wrong. My night in the forest that surrounded this castle had been enough to teach me that in this world, geometry did not always work in quite the same ways that I was used to.

There was no daylight in the passageway where I walked now, nor indeed any windows to admit light even if it were still day outside, and the halls were lit by torches placed at intervals in sconces along the walls. Near the torches it was bright enough, but in between them the way was dark, full of shadows and the sounds of tiny scuttling feet. I walked in darkness for a long time and began to think that these tunnels might continue forever without end and I would be trapped here under the castle until the end of time.

I turned a corner and suddenly the hallway, that a minute ago I had believed might go on forever, dead-ended abruptly at a wooden door in an arched doorway. I looked suspiciously at the doorway, wondering just what sort of ending I had come to. Was this the entrance to some secret dungeon or hidden laboratory or just another segment of the seemingly unending chain of subterranean passages? I stood before the door wondering what to do. I could turn around and go back the way I had come. Logic told me that I would eventually return to the place I had started from even if some part of me doubted the wisdom of that belief. But having come so far, I would feel foolish and perhaps a little cowardly if I returned without even trying to find out what was on the other side of the door. And there was still the rather pressing issue of my bladder. In all this way I had seen nothing like a bathroom or even an exit to the upper levels where I might at least hope to find an outhouse or something similar in the courtyards. Should I try the handle? Should I knock? Barging in might be seen as rude and if there was a coven of angry wizards on the other side, or even just one, who knew what they might do to me.

I knocked. There was no answer, but the door opened inward. Inside was a room that might once have been a library. A candle, burned three quarters of the way down, provided the only light. Everywhere I saw stacks of books and papers piled on tables, on chairs and spilling over onto the floor. It reminded me oddly of the spare room in my own house with its piles of hoarded books, but here the chaos and signs of neglect were even more rampant. Many of the piles were covered with a thick layer of dust, though others seemed as though they had been moved more recently. In the middle of this clutter of books and papers, seated in an old armchair near the table where the candle burned, slept a very old man in a white robe. The hood on his robe was thrown back from his face. He had long wispy hair that lay across his pate in no particular order and a beard that hung down over his chest, both whiter than his robe. In his lap was what at first I thought was a black cat, but when it lifted its head to peer at me, I saw that it was, in fact, a very large black rat. I recalled the scuttling noises I had heard as I was walking down the hallway and wondered if it had been the same rat I had heard or another one, or perhaps more than one. For all I knew it might be the rats who were the true owners of the castle and the doorman I had seen merely their servant. The rat peered at me with two tiny red eyes for a moment and then scuttled off his lap and disappeared into the shadows. The rat's sudden movement woke the old man.

"What is it, Matilda?" he asked in a sleepy voice.

Then, noticing me for the first time, he turned and said, "You're not Matilda, are you?" He looked at me for a long while as if trying to decide where I might have come from and then, after a moment, he answered his own question, saying, "No, of course not. You're the visitor, aren't you? 'Diogenes,' or some such nonsense, they said."

I remembered then that that was the name I had given the wizard (if it had been a wizard) by the river. The name, it seemed, had gotten here ahead of me, and I blushed as I recalled my namesake's search for one honest man. The old man seemed to drift off for a moment, then woke again with a start.

"Did I send for you?" asked the old wizard, blinking.

"No," I answered. "Or, not that I know of."

"How did you come here?" he asked.

"I got lost," I said. "I was looking for the toilets."

At this the wizard began to chuckle, and then the chuckle turned into laughter that went on and on until the old man was bent over double, holding his sides and practically gasping for breath at its force.

"Looking for the toilets . . ." he wheezed. "I have heard many strange things from visitors such as yourself over the years, but this is the first time I have heard anyone say he came into our world because he was looking for the toilets!"

"No, I thought you meant, how did I come here, to this room," I said, blushing, and realizing how absurd, insulting even, my words must have sounded.

"And who is to say," the old man answered, "that this room is not a world?"

He stopped and seemed to ponder his own words for a moment while he considered me. Again, his eyes seemed to fix somewhere in the middle distance before they came back to me.

"But, be that as it may, the toilets are not here, and so we must venture out of this world, or this room, if you prefer, and seek another. Come, let me help you find them, and then you and I can talk, and you will tell me why you have really come here."

And so saying, he picked up the candle, and taking my sleeve in the other hand, began to lead me back down the corridors through which I had just come. Behind us I heard a scurrying of small feet in the darkness. The rat, it seemed, was coming too.

We went up a short flight of stairs that I had somehow failed to notice when I walked by them in the dark and emerged into a small courtyard, different from the one that I had seen when I entered the wizards' castle.

"Through there," said the old man, indicating a wooden door on the far side of the courtyard. "I think you'll find what you're seeking."

It was an outhouse, tacked on to the side of a series of wooden outbuildings. Inside was a simple one-seat affair over an open pit. Apparently whatever magical powers these wizards possessed, indoor plumbing was not among them. When I emerged, the old man was still waiting in the courtyard.

"Better?" he asked. I nodded. "Good, then let us go up to dinner, and we can talk."

He led me through another door, not the one we had used in entering the courtyard, and then up a long spiral staircase. Although there were no further landings, I felt sure we had ascended several stories, and I was winded when we reached the top of the stairs. The old man, however, made no comment and merely led me along yet another hallway and into a small room at its end.

Inside was a small round table set for two, with covered dishes and heavy looking silverware that looked like real silver at each place. It seems I was expected, though until we stepped into the room I had no notion that I would be meeting with one of the wizards (for so I took the old man to be) tonight, much less that I would be dining with him at such an elegantly set table. The silver covers over the dishes were still warm, though of the servers, or whoever had set the table, there was no sign. Beyond the table was a tall stained glass window that looked out over the valley toward the distant Cliffs of the Black Dragon (as they had been marked on the map). Night had fallen and the moonlight shone in through the window.

The food was excellent. There was fresh fish, trout, I think, grilled, and small red potatoes and carrots and some other kind of root vegetable I could not identify. There was a sweet white wine that the old man kept pouring into our glasses and I found my tongue loosening as the meal went on. I recounted my adventure, beginning with my meeting with the dragon, and after a moment's hesitation decided to tell him what the dragon had commanded me to find. There was no hope, or so I told myself, that I would find the dragon's bauble for myself in the maze of tunnels beneath the castle and still less that, having found it I could make my way safely back to the fire pit. If indeed a dragon's resting place could ever truly be called "safe." Given the way he treated his other servants, it seemed all too likely that having accomplished my mission for the dragon I would end up enthralled like his other slaves, or simply eaten. The old man's eyes widened when I mentioned the dragon's stone, but he said nothing and let me go on until I came to the point where I had found him, sleeping in his book-filled room.

"Interesting, most interesting indeed," said the old man at length. "So you are in the employ, so to speak, of the Black Dragon. And still you managed to cross the river and find a guide to lead you through the woods. I would not have thought that was possible. And yet, here you are. I must say, you are rather different from the dragon's usual slaves."

I shuddered as I remembered the naked men toiling beside the fire pit with the black claw marks burned onto their flesh, but said nothing.

"And so, having come here at the dragon's behest to steal this jewel, you now tell me freely of your task. Does this mean you have renounced it?"

I hesitated, uncertain of whether I could trust a wizard any more than a dragon, and then spoke truthfully. "I don't know. As the dragon pointed out, without that book I have no way of returning to my own world. On the other hand, I have no real assurance, even if I do return this jewel to the dragon, that he would return the book to me. After all, he made it simply vanish. Perhaps it is gone for good."

"Ah," said the wizard. "So it is the book and not the jewel that you seek. Or rather, you want what the book might do for you. The one is merely a means to the other. And, as you point out, an uncertain means at that. Am I right?"

"Yes," I said even more slowly, wondering where this was leading.

"And did the dragon happen to mention the nature of this jewel that he is so desperately seeking?" asked the wizard.

"No," I said, suddenly curious.

"I will tell you," said the wizard. "It is the dragon's heart, the source of his magical power. Even without it, he has terrorized this entire valley. You will have noticed, walking through it, that there are no longer farms or houses to be seen anywhere in the valley. All were destroyed by the dragon. Most of the people who once lived there he devoured. Some few he has kept as slaves. Only by our power is he kept away from the settlements by the shore and the lands beyond. And this, mind you, is in his weakened state, with his wings clipped, so to speak. Were he to regain this stone, his power would be vastly greater, and even we could hold him back no longer. He would regain his wings and be free to soar over the earth wherever he pleased, sowing death and destruction across an ever-widening sphere. Worse, his old lusts would return to him and he would seek a mate, and soon we would have not one dragon but dozens, and the land would be blighted beyond any hope of restoration. I will not show you this thing of evil that the dragon has sent you to find, for I suspect that he has laid some kind of geas upon you to return it to him if you can. I tell you these things so that you will understand why you must not seek it further."

The wizard looked into my eyes as if trying to peer into the bottom of my soul to see whether I acted as a free agent or whether, even now, the dragon held sway over my thoughts and actions.

"Then I am trapped here forever," I said.

"Perhaps," said the old man. "Would that be so bad?"

"My family, my wife, Elizabeth and our children, John, Ruth and Helen, they are in my world," I said, feeling heartbroken as I said it. "The world where I belong."

"That is a consideration, certainly," said the wizard. "Then you might be willing to go to some length to return to them?" He paused and then answered his own question. "Yes, of course you would. After all, you're here, aren't you?"

"But the dragon has the book," I pointed out, "or I hope he still does, and unless I return the stone to him, he won't give the book back to me. And without the book I am stuck here."

"All important considerations, to be sure. And did the dragon actually promise to return the book to you if you procured the stone for him?" the old man asked, with evident interest. "Dragons will not lie, they say, but neither do they always tell the truth."

"Oh, yes," I said, "he was quite clear on that point: 'When you retrieve the green stone for me, I shall return the book to you.' I remember the words quite clearly."

"Indeed, that seems clear enough," said the wizard evenly. "We could try sending you back with a different green stone to see if his sworn words would still hold him to the bargain. But the contract states clearly, '*the* green stone,' not merely '*a* green stone,' so I'm afraid that won't do. Most likely the dragon would just eat you, but he might try some more drastic method of forcing you to look for the stone, so on the whole I think we're better off not sending you back just yet."

I shuddered at the old man's apparent indifference to the prospect of my being eaten, but he seemed to be merely considering the possibilities.

"What else did the dragon say?" he prompted.

I thought for a moment, "'Riches beyond the dreams of avarice,' I believe was the phrase he used."

The old man raised his eyebrows slightly at that. "Did he really?"

"Oh yes," I replied. "That and 'survival not guaranteed.'"

"Ah," said the wizard, seeming satisfied at last. "There you are then. 'Survival not guaranteed.' So the dragon can give you back the book, along with his treasure, as much of it as you care to ask for, and it doesn't matter, because he can eat you up and get it all back the next minute—'survival not guaranteed,' after all."

"So what should I do?" I asked.

"Do?" repeated the wizard. "Who said you should 'do' anything? For tonight I suggest you finish your dinner before it gets cold, and sleep a while. We will talk again in the morning."

And that was all he would say on the subject. Though earlier I had thought the food excellent, I now hardly tasted it for all the thoughts spinning around in my head. After dinner, the old man led me back to the room I had slept in earlier that day, along a much shorter route than the one I had taken to reach his study. The water pitcher had been replaced, I noticed, and there was now an old-fashioned chamber pot, which the wizard delighted in pointing out to me.

"So you won't have to go wandering through any more tunnels, or worlds, at least not tonight," he said before departing.

I sat down on the wooden bench and stared out the window at the night-darkened sky as the candle on the table burned itself out. I thought of home and family, both now impossibly far away. After a long time, I fell asleep.

CHAPTER SIX

A NEW REQUEST

THE NEXT MORNING, BEFORE the sun had risen high enough in the sky to make its way in through the little window in my cell, the old man returned and led me back up to the same room in the uppermost floor of the castle where we had dined the night before. I saw that breakfast was waiting for us. There was a basket of newly baked rolls, still warm from the oven, honey, in a clay pot with a carved wooden dipper, and tea in an elegant china pot. I looked more closely at the teapot and saw that it was painted with a woodland scene featuring a silver squirrel leaping through the branches of pine trees, which reminded me of my erstwhile guide. The rolls and the honey were excellent, but again there was no sign of whoever had prepared the meal, or indeed of any sign of human inhabitants in the castle, save ourselves. The rat that I had seen the night before sleeping in the old man's lap joined us too. He did not sit at the table, but would sit up at the old man's feet, on his back legs, and beg for scraps like a dog. It seemed unnatural to see a rat behaving that way or, for that matter, a human who would want to feed a rat from the table. But then, I supposed, a dog's behavior under the same circumstances is hardly natural either. After all, what is a dog but a tame wolf? And to have a tame wolf that one feeds from the table can hardly be called a natural state of affairs.

"I have been giving your problem some thought," announced the wizard after we had eaten most of the rolls and started on our second cups of tea.

"And have you come up with a solution?" I asked eagerly.

"Perhaps," he said. "Or at least, a new way of looking at things. It seems to me, in any case, that it is the book you should be focusing on, rather than the jewel. It was the book, after all, that brought you into this world and it is the book that perhaps affords the greatest chance of your being able to return whence you came." He paused and seemed to consider for a moment and then asked, "You had never seen it before that night, I believe you said?"

"That's right," I answered. "I'm sure I would have remembered a book like that if I had seen it before."

"Perhaps," said the old man again, "if it did not have some powerful charm of forgetting laid upon it, which I think would be likely for a book such as you describe. So, one cannot be certain, but the point is, it is the book that brought you here, so it is upon the book that we must focus our attention, if we are to help you return to your own world."

This seemed logical enough, though I noted that the wizard seemed rather intent on turning my attention away from the jewel that the dragon had sent me here to find. Perhaps there was more than one reason that he didn't want me to find it. "But if I don't return the jewel, then how can I hope to get the book back from the dragon?" I asked.

"You can't," said the wizard, "unless you are a much better burglar than you have shown signs of being thus far."

I decided to let the comment about my skills as a burglar go (no point in advertising my own incompetence, after all) and after a moment passed the wizard went on smoothly, "However, just because the dragon has that book of maps doesn't mean that we can't make another."

"Yes, but I don't need just any book of maps, I need a magic one that can take me back to my own world. Could you make one like that?" I asked, trying to keep the note of desperation from my voice.

"Perhaps," the old man repeated yet again, "if I had the right tools. This book of maps you described cannot have been made of paper and ink, not if it has power like that. No, the very pages, I guess, must have been made from the hide of some magical creature, and the ink made from its blood. The blood of dragons has powerful magical properties that we are just beginning to understand. Even the quill used to make it should be from some magical source, a phoenix feather would be best, I think. There are books in our library describing how those elements might be combined to create such an object, a book that is both a guide and the source of its own magical power—but such spells have not been worked in this castle in many years—longer than I can remember. It seems likely though, that the dragon's book—and you can be sure it was the dragon who sent that book to you—comes from this very castle. Or, if not, from wizards using the same spells. So I think it likely that, given the right ingredients, we should be able to duplicate the result."

I pondered this information for a while before I realized what he was implying.

"Are you saying I'll have to kill the dragon—or *a* dragon at any rate—to make another magic book?" I asked.

"That would be one solution," said the wizard. "And it has the elegance of solving two problems at one stroke, so to speak. However, it seems more likely that you would perish in the attempt, which would do neither of us any good. So I think we will need to come up with an alternative plan. Unicorn blood, for example, is just as magically endowed as dragon's blood. Indeed, for many applications it is preferred, its magic being of a purer form, even if somewhat less abundant. Yes, I think if you could procure a unicorn and a phoenix feather or two, we might give it a try."

"Oh, well that makes it easy then," I replied sarcastically, "and shall I throw in a few moonbeams and a star or two while I'm at it?"

The old man looked thoughtful, either unaware of or ignoring my sarcasm. "That should not be necessary," he said at last. "Now as to the unicorn, there are no local herds that I am aware of, owing to the dragon's influence perhaps, but the old maps show quite clearly a large island within sailing distance of our shores where there are said to be herds of unicorn. And, luckily for you, the last known phoenix sighting was on that same island a few hundred years ago, so you should be able to accomplish both your goals readily," he said as if this were the most natural thing in the world.

"*My* goals?" I laughed. "Since when was it my goal to sail halfway round the world looking for unicorns and some bird no one has seen for hundreds of years?"

"Not halfway," said the old man, unperturbed. "Not even a quarter the way round. It's in the Atlantic, before you reach the British Isles or the European continent. Here, I'll show you."

The old man got up from the table and exited the room. I stared after him, dumbfounded at this unexpected turn in the conversation. Apparently, since I was a failure as a burglar, it was somehow decided that I should go off in search of mythical beasts to slaughter for their magical properties. It seemed absurd. Besides, weren't unicorns only supposed to appear for virgins or something like that? As the father of three children, I was unlikely to qualify. I wondered if the wizard had gone to get a globe or an atlas such as the one the dragon had taken from me, but then quickly realized the absurdity of this notion. If the wizard had such an atlas, he would not need to send me on this quest, which led me to wonder whether there might be some other motivation behind the wizard's desire to send me out in search of unicorns and phoenix feathers.

When the wizard eventually returned, what he brought back was not an atlas, but a single map, drawn on parchment, which, when unrolled, showed both Europe and the eastern coast of North America. There was also a large continent south of Europe, which was undoubtedly Africa, though the outline of the continent and its proportions were different from those I was familiar with. The west coast of North America was not shown on the map, but drifted off into ambiguous shadings. Perhaps in this world, explorers had not yet reached the far side of America, or perhaps he had other maps that extended beyond what was shown here.

Like the dragon's atlas, this map had at its four corners the whale, unicorn, gryphon, and dragon. I wondered if there were some particular significance to this constellation of mythical animals. Or at least creatures that were mythical in my world. And although once I might have shrugged off the creatures as fanciful decorations indicating unknown lands, the dragon at least I now knew to be a real inhabitant of this world. And now it seemed that I was to go in search of the unicorn as well. I wondered if I would see whales and gryphons as well on this journey. Whales we had in my own world, and I'd even seen wild ones once or twice from the deck of a ship, but never any of these other creatures. Were they extinct in our world, I wondered, or merely occasional visitors from another world (such as I myself had become) who had somehow made it into myth and legend? Who could say?

"So, you see," said the wizard pointing at the map and pulling me out of my reverie, "it is not nearly so far as you feared. A few weeks' sail at most."

I realized he had been talking for some time and hoped I had not missed anything of significance. Following the direction of his pointing finger, I stared at the map, with dismay. It seemed a poor guide indeed for a trek across the ocean and my heart sank at the thought of "a few weeks sail," as well as the apparent hopelessness of the mission.

"But if no one's seen a phoenix for hundreds of years, what's the point?" I protested.

"Perhaps no one has looked hard enough," the wizard replied with equanimity.

"Or perhaps they all died trying," I said, glumly, "or just of old age before they found one. In any case, I can't see that I need to go sailing halfway around the world—or even a quarter of the way—" I added quickly before the wizard could interrupt me, "looking for unicorns and some mythical bird that probably doesn't exist anyway."

"Of course not," said the wizard, mildly. "So, what do you propose to do?"

I realized then that I did not have a lot of good alternatives. The dragon had the magical book that had brought me here, but he wouldn't give it to me unless I brought him this green stone that the wizard had called the "dragon's heart." The wizards had the green stone, but they weren't about to tell me where it was, much less allow me to take it. The wizards might be able to make me a new book, but only if I brought them a unicorn and a phoenix feather. I could forget the whole thing and try to find a town with normal human-type people and try my hand at making a living in this world in an ordinary way (if there were such a thing here), but then I would have no way of getting back to my own world, much less my family, who by now must be calling the police to report me as a missing person. Any way I looked at it, my situation looked bleak.

"All right," I said at last. "I'll see if I can get you a unicorn and a phoenix feather, if you will promise to try to help me to get back to my own world once I've done it."

"Excellent choice," said the wizard, and in that moment, he sounded remarkably like the dragon. "I'll arrange for transportation," he said. "There are a number of whaling ships in the harbor now, and even some vessels that have sailed from the great ports of Europe. We ought to be able to find someone who will agree to take you to the Unicorn Isles. Perhaps a companion as well? Yes, I think for a journey as long and risky as this one, it would be well to send someone from our order with you. A magical guide, so to speak. And I know just the wizard to send. 'Greytail' I shall call him, for reasons that you may appreciate. After all, it was he who led you to our doorstep. It seems only fitting that he should take responsibility for the consequences."

I was puzzled at this, and then it struck me that he must be referring to the talking squirrel that had led me through the forest. Was I to have a talking squirrel as my guide to the land of the unicorns? I was, I think, almost beyond astonishment at this point, and so said nothing.

"We shall need a name for you as well," said the wizard. "No more of this 'Diogenes' nonsense. What shall we call you?"

Apparently my lie had been rather transparent. "Bob," I said, simply.

"Bob?" he repeated. "Like a cork on the water? It seems fitting enough. Very well then, 'Bob' you shall be for this voyage."

Chapter Seven

Setting Out

AFTER BREAKFAST, THE OLD wizard led me back downstairs to the room where I had slept the night before. The sun was now fully up and light streamed in through the window above, however the cell remained as bare as it had been the entire time I had been there.

"Wait here for a bit, would you? No more wandering around in the tunnels, please. We wouldn't want you to get lost."

I was unsure whether there was more to his words than their plain meaning. A veiled warning, perhaps, not to go looking for the stone? I said nothing and sat down upon the little wooden bench to wait.

"Greytail will be along shortly," said the wizard by way of goodbye and headed off down the corridor we had come from.

There was little to distract me save my own thoughts and these in truth were little more than a confused jumble. Ever since I had arrived in this world I had been buffeted about in one direction or another by events beyond my control. And now it seemed I was fated to go off in search of unicorns. Unicorns? How did the wizards imagine I was going to catch a unicorn, much less kill it? And did I really want to kill a unicorn? Wasn't it supposed to be bad luck or something? Maybe that was why the wizards wanted me to be the one to kill the unicorn, so whatever spell or bad luck was attached to the killing would fall on me and not on them. But if that were the case, what could I do about it? If I refused to go on this quest I was free to leave. Or, at least the wizard had implied that I was free to leave although I hadn't asked him directly. If I tried to leave, might not the wizards decide to lock me up in some dungeon to make sure that I never found their treasure or brought it back to the Black Dragon as I had promised to do? And even if I were free to leave, where would I go? And how would I get home? My thoughts chased themselves uselessly in circles.

After a few moments I was saved from further ruminations by a knock at the door to my cell Before I could get up to answer it, the door opened and a gray-cloaked figure came into the room. The figure was clearly human, not a squirrel at all. I wasn't sure whether to be pleased or disappointed. The talking squirrel had been annoying, certainly, but he had in the end led me to the castle. And it wasn't every day that one was gifted with a talking squirrel as a guide. But a human guide would certainly be easier to talk to and perhaps less conspicuous if we were going anywhere that we might encounter other people. Although in this world who could say? Perhaps in this world talking squirrels were as commonplace as cellphones were on my world.

The hood of the cloak was thrown back, and I could see a shock of silvery hair that fell in wavy curls to the wearer's shoulders. The face was youthful, with piercing blue eyes, like those of the watchman who had challenged me on the river, and for that matter like those of the old wizard who had left me a moment before. A family resemblance, perhaps. The face, which was handsome enough, bore no trace of a beard and might have belonged to a young woman or a boy on the verge of manhood.

"Hello," he said, his voice proclaiming him a young man.

"Hello," I said, a bit uncertainly.

"Have you recovered yet from your midnight stroll?" he asked.

"Well enough," I answered. We stood for a moment looking at each other, and he seemed to be waiting for me to say something.

"Should I know you?" I asked.

He laughed, and his laughter was like the clear, sparkling sound of a fine bell.

"Should you know me?" he repeated. "Now there is a question indeed. If you ask my advice, then I must answer that you should. For, if not, then how would you know whether to trust my advice? But is it wise to know me? Only time will tell, so I cannot."

Oh no, I thought, another riddling wizard.

"I meant," I said slowly, "have I seen you before?"

"Again a difficult question, for the friend you see today may become an enemy tomorrow, or vice versa, and since a friend is not an enemy, could you ever say, seeing your friend tomorrow, whether you had in fact seen him truly before? Since what we see is only what we see, and never the whole of what is. Indeed, since I cannot look through your eyes, who am I to say whether you have ever truly seen *anything* at all?"

And in the youth's mocking tones I indeed recognized those of the squirrel who had greeted me so rudely as I trudged along the enchanted road. "Are you really the squirrel?" I asked, wondering if perhaps he was a wizard who could transform himself into a squirrel, or perhaps take control of a real squirrel—seeing the world through its eyes and speaking through its mouth.

"Do I look like a squirrel?" he asked, mockingly.

"'Always answer a question with a question' would seem to be the rule here," I said. "No, you do not look like a squirrel, you look like a young man. But the old wizard had led me to believe that he would be sending a squirrel named Greytail with me as a guide on a journey I am to undertake to the Isle of the Unicorns."

"Did he?" asked the youth, raising one eyebrow. "Now that's very interesting, for just now he asked me if I might show you the way down to the harbor, and help you find a certain ship. The *Siren's Song*, I believe it was. So, perhaps I am the guide he spoke of, at least as far as the ship."

I tried not to let my disappointment show. First, that he was apparently not the talking squirrel of the previous night somehow magically transformed and, second, that it now seemed that I was to be going on this voyage alone, without the promised companion. And then I realized that he had never, actually, answered my question. So perhaps he was the squirrel after all.

"Are you Greytail?" I asked.

"You may call me that if you like," said the youth, who still did not directly answer the question of whether he was, or was not, a squirrel.

"Very well then," I said. "If you are Greytail, and you are to lead me, at least as far as the ship, then let us go."

"Hasty, aren't you?" said the youth.

"What do you mean?" I asked.

"Well, for one thing, there's the matter of your clothes," he said.

"What about them?" I asked. They were the same clothes I had worn since I had come into this world, for the simple reason that I had no others.

The youth wrinkled his nose. "Well, aside from their outlandish appearance, they seem unlikely to offer much protection against the elements. And if you mean to cross the ocean, it might be advisable to have something waterproof, and a bit warmer as well."

"What would you suggest?" I asked. "And where would I get it?"

"Just a moment," he replied. "I'll see what I can do."

Greytail, if that was indeed his name, went off leaving me once again to stare at the bare walls of my cell, and pondering the sanity of wizards which seemed doubtful, but perhaps no more so than my own. After a few minutes he returned with a long gray hooded cloak like the one he was wearing and handed it to me. I put it on over my clothes and admired the effect. As he had suggested, it was considerably warmer than what I had been wearing, and it looked as though it might be somewhat water repellent as well. The fabric, whatever it was, was finely woven but had a suppleness to it like fine leather. There was no mirror to admire myself in, but all in all I considered it a great improvement. The youth, Greytail, however, was grinning broadly at me, with more than a hint of laughter in his eyes.

"Do you mean to go on wearing those rags of yours under the cloak?" he asked, sounding almost shocked.

The question puzzled me. "Why? What do you wear?" I asked.

"The cloak," he said simply.

"I see that. And under it?"

"Under it?" he repeated.

"Yes, what do you wear under it?"

"The questions you ask. Why should you suppose that there is anything under this cloak but me?"

I was uncertain whether he was truly unfamiliar with the concept of underclothes, flirting with me, or simply mocking my naiveté. I recalled the guardian at the edge of the river, who had forced me to strip before I was allowed to cross. Was there something exotic about my otherworldly flesh that made all these wizards want to gawp at me? In any case, I had no time for it.

"In my world, it would be customary," I said, simply.

He wrinkled his nose again (rather like a squirrel, I thought) and said, "Evidently. Suit yourself then. I must see to our provisions. Can you be ready in an hour?"

I looked around at the bare room. It held the same bench and small table that it had since my arrival the previous morning, but I had nothing to pack.

"I don't see why not," I said.

Greytail left and I sat back down once again to wait. He returned within the hour carrying two small packs made of the same fine-woven material as the cloaks. Inside the one he gave me were what seemed to be leather water bottles, some sort of flat, dry bread like pita, a length of rope, a folding knife, two shallow pans and other cooking utensils, a folded piece of cloth that I supposed might serve as a ground cloth or a small tent, and a few apples.

"Does it meet with your approval?" he asked, after I had inspected the contents of the pack. I tried to remember camping trips I had been on as a child to see if there were anything else I could think of that one might want to bring on a journey that, from the looks of it, seemed to involve at least the possibility of being out in the weather. How long would it take to get to the harbor and the ship that Greytail had mentioned? The *Siren's Song*, I think he had said. Or perhaps the items in the pack were meant to be used on the unicorn hunting expedition, once we arrived at our destination. I had no idea. I had never camped for more than a weekend before and usually we could bring our supplies with us in a car. This, it seemed, was to be an entirely different sort of expedition.

"Could do with a few extra pairs of socks," I said, "and a flashlight and some matches might not hurt either, if we're going to be camping out."

"Flashlight? Matches?" he asked. Apparently, these were unknown to him.

"A flashlight is a thing that makes light when you push a button. About so big," I said, indicating the size with my hands. "You hold it in your hands. Matches are little things you use to start a fire."

"I have a tinderbox in my pack," he said. "As to the magical light you speak of, on this world we do not carry such things openly or reveal them, save at need."

"Oh," I said. I had never thought of a flashlight as being anything special, but I supposed there were all different kinds of magic. I had not seen any signs of electricity in the castle, so perhaps here all things electrical might seem like magic. Come to think of it, they were pretty magical in our world, too.

"As to 'socks,'" he went on, "if you mean the short stockings you have on under your shoes, I'm afraid there isn't time to have any

knitted for you before we leave, so you'll have to make do with the
ones you have. You might consider washing them, however," he said,
wrinkling his nose again.

I looked down to see what the young wizard wore on his own feet,
but since the robe he wore came down to the floor, I could not tell. I
wondered if, like those of the guardian at the river, his feet were bare,
or if he wore some type of boots or sandals. I started to ask, and then
decided that, perhaps, it was none of my concern.

"If we're leaving right away, I'll wait on washing them," I said. "I'd
like them to be dry when I put them on again."

"Then you're ready?" he asked.

"As ready as I'm going to be," I answered.

"Then let us go."

We left the castle by a different gate from the one I had entered
the previous morning, and although I had seen horses stabled in the
castle yards when I arrived the previous day, we left on foot. The
horses, it seemed, were for more important missions than the one I
was going on. Or perhaps it was merely that we would be going to
sea and there was nowhere in the harbor to stable them, or no money
to pay for the stabling. In any case, we walked. There was no road on
this side of the castle either, but a break in the foliage between two
trees turned out to be the start of a footpath that led gradually down
from the top of the hill where the castle stood. Greytail had thrown
back the hood of his cloak and, as we walked, he would cock his head
first to one side and then to the other, listening for sounds I could not
hear. About halfway down the hill, we came across a wide road, paved
with stone, like the one I had tried to follow to the wizards' castle,
and I wondered if this one would take us to the harbor.

"Ignore it," said Greytail, noticing the direction of my gaze. "It
leads nowhere."

"What is the point of a road," I asked, "that leads nowhere?"

"You would be surprised," he said, "at the number of people going
nowhere, every day. This road is for them."

I shrugged and followed Greytail back into the woods on the far side of the road. Evidently, in this world, following the roads did not always get you where you wanted to go. The same, I realized, might be said of my own world.

After a short walk through the woods, we came to the river at the bottom of the hill—the same small river I had crossed two days before (naked, I recalled with embarrassment) after the wizards' sentry had demanded that I strip before crossing over into their territory. I wondered if I would have to do the same to get out.

Seeing the look on my face, Greytail laughed. "Don't worry, you won't have to go for another swim."

The comment led me to wonder if it had been he who had forced me to submit to that humiliating interrogation. Was he the squirrel or the guardian? Or had they been one and the same? I had no way of knowing and my guide volunteered no information on the subject, so I decided to say nothing.

Stepping close to the bank of the river, Greytail put his fingers to his mouth and made a noise that was something between a whistle and the call of a bird, then lifted up his staff and brought the end of it suddenly down onto the ground. It may have been my imagination, but it seemed that the ground trembled slightly when he did so. I looked around. There was no answer to his call that I could see or hear, but shortly a boat came drifting down the river with the tide. His whistle, perhaps, had been a signal to some unseen person to loose the boat from its moorings, or perhaps it was the boat itself he summoned with his call. In any case, the boat came drifting slowly toward the spot where we stood waiting and settled with its bow against the bank. It was a small wooden rowboat, with two planks for seats and two oars lying in the bottom. We got in. I seated myself on the plank in the middle of the boat and reached down for the oars.

"Shall I row?" I asked.

"No need, at present," he answered.

With his left hand, he stroked the gunwale, almost as one might pat a large dog or a horse. Then he whispered something I could not make out, and the boat began to drift, as if of its own accord, out into the middle of the river, and we began to float downstream.

Chapter Eight

In the Harbor

WE DRIFTED LAZILY DOWNSTREAM for most of the afternoon. On either bank I could see dense foliage and many great trees, but no signs of human habitation. Was this the dragon's doing, I wondered, or the wizards' or was this area, which in my world had been a bustling city, so newly settled in the wizards' world that human inhabitants were still sparse? I saw a variety of birds flying overhead as we drifted downstream and amused myself by trying to identify them. Ducks, geese, seagulls and even a blue heron were all birds I recognized from my own world, but there were others with bright, almost metallic colors that I could not name. I tried to ask Greytail, but before I could point them out they had disappeared into the high reeds along the left-hand bank of the river. From that side of the river there was a cacophony of bird sounds, but on the right bank, in the land claimed by the Black Dragon, the birds were quiet.

Before nightfall we had come to the harbor. The little river we had been traveling along after leaving the castle joined another larger river just before both emptied into a larger body of water that from the map I knew to be the Sound. When we reached the harbor, I felt that suddenly we were thrust back into the world of men. Where previously we had been in a world where humans seemed all but absent, now, almost without transition, we were in the midst of the hustle and bustle of what appeared to be a thriving port city.

In the port there were a great many boats and ships of all sizes. Some had a single mast, some two, and some even three. The prows of most of them were of plain wood, but some had carved and painted figureheads resembling women or men or beasts as well as strange creatures combining characteristics of all of these.

When we reached the harbor, Greytail picked up the oars and began to row. The oars moved easily in his hands, as if he were well used to such work, and we glided smoothly over the water. It was late afternoon and the sun was going down behind the hills that overlooked the harbor. Looking back the way we had come, I could see the Tower of the White Wizards high atop the hill we had descended. Farther off I could glimpse the Cliffs of the Black Dragon, as they were known here, and in between the dense woods of the Old Forest. Of the city I remembered from my own world, there was no trace.

The buildings I could see near the harbor seemed mostly to be made of stone. They were low, one or two stories at most, with flat roofs and extraordinarily heavy-looking shutters on the windows. Whether this was to protect them from storms off the sea or from the ravages of dragons I could not say, but at least here the streets seemed full of people going about their business and the docks bustled with the loading and unloading of the great ships. After the desolation I had seen in the lands around the dragon's fire pit and the stillness and almost sepulchral quiet of the wizards' castle, it was uplifting to hear the sounds and commotion of ordinary people going about their lives again.

"The ship we are looking for," Greytail reminded me, "is called the *Siren's Song*. She has a figurehead like that one," he said, pointing to a ship whose prow sported the figure of a red-haired, rather buxom woman (the paint they had used for her coiffure was what I would call "fire-engine red," and the effect was a bit jarring to my eye). "The one we want has green hair and scales on the lower half of her body. Keep an eye out," he said.

Green hair, I mused. Perhaps the people of this town were not quite as ordinary as I had thought. Or perhaps their taste in hair coloring anticipated that of some of the "goth" youth from my own world.

A moment later, we rounded the stern of the ship we had been rowing alongside, and the ship beyond it came into view. It was a two-masted vessel with raised sections fore and aft. I know nothing of sailing ships, so I cannot say what type of vessel it—or perhaps I should say *she*—was. Ships are commonly referred to as *she* of course, and this one certainly merited the feminine pronoun. Like the ship Greytail had pointed out a moment before, she bore a curved figurehead of a woman at her prow. But while the other had been crudely carved and garishly painted, the figurehead on this ship seemed almost alive. Looking closer, I saw that it was not exactly a woman, but a mermaid. The hair, as Greytail had said, was green, but it did not have the appearance of human hair. Whoever had carved it had given it a frond-like appearance, as if strands of seaweed grew from her head, yet the effect was oddly natural. The painting, too, had a delicate, lifelike quality. The hair was painted in muted shades of grey and green that seemed almost translucent in the late afternoon light and the scales on the lower half of her body were rendered not in a uniform color but in myriad hues: blues, greens, white, and even red, all shot through with silver, like the scales of a newly caught fish reflecting the light of the sun. I stared at her for a moment before realizing that Greytail, who was still rowing, had his back to the prow of our little boat and could not see her.

"Just ahead. I see, uh, *her*," I said.

Greytail looked over his shoulder, saw the ship, and nodded.

"Good. We'll tie up alongside her and see if the captain's aboard. But first, I'll need a name for this trip. Can't have you calling me 'Greytail' when I haven't got one, or people will wonder. What do you propose?"

This constant shifting of names seemed odd to me, but *'When in Rome . . .'*

"How about Nutkin?" I suggested.

He raised one eyebrow.

"It's a squirrel from a story, back home," I said.

"Very well then. Nutkin it is," he said.

Greytail shipped the oars as we pulled up alongside the larger vessel. *Nutkin*, I reminded myself, *his name is Nutkin*.

"Ahoy, the *Siren's Song*!" he shouted.

After a moment, a grizzled face topped with a knitted cap peered down over the rails at us.

"Ahoy, yerself," the sailor answered. "What do you want?"

"Is your captain aboard?" Greytail—Nutkin—asked.

"No!" the man shouted down, but volunteered no further information.

"Can you tell us where to find him?"

"Couldn't say. But he'll most likely end up at the Pickled Parrot sometime tonight if he's true to form. Or you c'n wait here if you've a mind, but it may be tomorrer afore he's back, and I can't let you aboard wi'out cap'n's orders."

"We'll try the Pickled Parrot then. Much obliged."

Greytail rowed a bit farther along the dock and we found a place to tie up. A short climb up a ladder to the dock and we were on solid ground again, or at least the relatively solid planks of the pier where *The Siren's Song* was moored. I looked back at *The Siren's Song*, moored a few yards away, and noticed that the way the figurehead had been painted made the eyes seem to look at you no matter where you stood. The effect was unnerving and added to the impression that the ship herself was alive.

"Come along," said Greytail, and we headed into town.

Chapter Nine

The Pickled Parrot

WE MADE OUR WAY along the narrow cobblestone streets that ran up from the harbor into the town proper. By the shore, there were great warehouses lining the docks where I could see crated goods being unloaded from some of the ships while others were being loaded with different goods bound, presumably, for other ports. I recalled the old wizard in the castle telling me that there were ships in the harbor bound for some of the great ports of Europe and wondered which ones they were. Even this late in the afternoon, there was still some activity: longshoremen in rough cotton shirts and trousers pushing carts laden with goods back and forth along the docks between the ships and the warehouses. An open-air market could be seen not far away, but almost all the stalls were closed for the day.

The houses here were low stone buildings with few windows, and as I had noticed while we were in the harbor, the windows were all closed with heavy wooden shutters. As evening fell, a fog rolled in to mingle with the chimney smoke, and a gray pall began to form over the rooftops and in the alleys. The streets were narrow, most barely wide enough for a cart to pass and some were small enough that you could almost reach from one side to the other just by spreading your arms. Noises of tiny scuttling feet, like those I had heard in the wizards' castle, could be heard coming from the mouths of the alleys and as we walked by one of them, I had the impression of tiny red eyes watching us intently. I looked again, but the eyes had disappeared. Greytail, however, seemed unperturbed and we walked on, gray cloaks blending with the nighttime fog.

We found the Pickled Parrot a few blocks from the waterfront. There was a wooden sign hung outside with a picture of its namesake, a green parrot lying on its side with X's for eyes and an empty bottle clutched in its claws. It did not seem the most auspicious of omens.

We went in. It took a few moments for my eyes to adjust to the dim light. When they did, I saw a long wooden table where a group of men, sailors perhaps, were drinking and talking noisily among themselves. There were pewter tankards set at each place and I noticed that they seemed to be chained to the table. To keep people from stealing them, perhaps? A barmaid passed along one side of the table and then back along the other filling the tankards as she went from a large tin pitcher. I tried to catch her eye, but had no luck. Farther back was a group of smaller tables clustered around a great open fireplace, and in the fireplace the carcass of some animal, a pig I think, was being turned on a spit. I saw Greytail wrinkling his nose at the smell of the roasting flesh, but it smelled good to me. Along the wall to our left, opposite the fireplace, was a long wooden bar with a half dozen stools in front of it. Behind it was a stout man with an apron tied around his middle and a red handkerchief covering his hair, assuming he had any. When the barmaid came back, he took the empty pitcher from her and filled it from a large keg with a wooden stopper and handed it back to her. He filled a second pitcher and took it himself over to the group of smaller tables nearer the fireplace.

We walked over to the bar and waited. It took more than a minute to catch the barman's eye, busy as he was with the crowd of sailors, but after a moment we did, and he walked back over to where we were waiting.

"What'll you have?" he asked after looking us over carefully.

"A pint of your braggot for each of us," answered Greytail. "And if you could tell us where we might find the captain of the *Siren's Song*, I'd be much obliged."

The barman nodded and went behind the bar to fill two tankards with some kind of dark brown ale and placed them on the table in front of us.

"Here you are, gentlemen," he said politely, though I noticed that he kept ahold of the handles of both mugs while he looked enquiringly at Greytail. With a smile, Greytail took out a silver coin from somewhere inside his robe and laid it on the table. I was grateful, for while I still had the wallet that had been in my pocket when I left my own world, I doubted that my money would be good here, and my credit cards and ATM debit card even less. The barman picked up the coin and answered casually, as if he had not been waiting to see if we paid our tab before answering Greytail's question.

"That's him in the back there. Bright red jacket at the table nearest the fire."

Sure enough, at the center table sat a middle-aged man in a bright red jacket with brass buttons, trimmed with gold brocade. His hair was black shot through with strands of silver. He had a neatly trimmed beard and a mustache, and he was smoking a long ivory-handled pipe. The smoke curling from his lips and nostrils reminded me uneasily of the dragon. Greytail thanked the barman for the information and we headed over to the captain's table.

"Are you the captain of the *Siren's Song*?" asked Greytail as we walked up to the table.

The captain looked up from his drink and nodded. "I am. Captain Fleischman, at your service. And who might you be?"

"I am Nutkin and this is Cork," said Greytail, with a small bow. I raised my eyebrows at the new appellation I had just been given, but said nothing as Greytail continued. "Two travelers in search of passage."

"And where might you be bound?" the captain asked.

"The Unicorn Isles," said Greytail.

The captain looked us over more closely, as if wondering if this was some sort of a joke. "Unicorn hunters, are you then? You don't look it, I must say," he said.

"I said travelers, not hunters," answered Greytail. "I understood you had been sent a message from our order and that this had all been arranged?"

The captain frowned. "Aye, we got the message from the demon-bird, or devil-bird as some call 'em. Your ravens are not well loved aboard ships, I can tell you that. Nor those they consort with, for that matter. There's no luck in meddling in the affairs of wizards, they say."

"Nor in turning one from your door. Much less two," Greytail continued. I was startled at this, for I had certainly never considered myself a wizard, but I supposed that, dressed as I was in the cloak from the wizards' castle, I might pass for one—at least until someone asked me to perform a spell. He spoke with an even tone, but the threat was unmistakable.

"Threats, is it then?" asked the captain, bristling.

"No threats, captain, just some friendly advice. Our gold, I assure you, is as real as any, and there may come a time when you'll be glad enough to have a wizard standing on your decks if a storm rises."

"Can you work the weather, then?" asked the captain, doubtfully.

"If need be," answered Greytail. "But first let us see what sails and honest wind can do for us without wizardry."

"Fair enough," said the captain. "I'll take your gold then, and see you to the Unicorn Isles, if that's what you want. And after that, you and the unicorns can have at one another to your heart's delight."

Greytail reached once more into his robes and pulled out a small cloth purse, which closed with a drawstring. He opened it and spilled six gold coins out onto his open palm. Three of these he handed over to the captain.

"Half now," he said, putting the other three coins away, "and half when we land."

"Fair enough," the captain answered again, putting the coins into his own purse.

"Ye've bought yer own drinks, I see," he said, nodding toward our tankards, and seeming happier now that the gold was in his purse. "Now how about a drop for a poor seafarin' man?"

"If I see a poor seafarin' man, I'll buy him one," Greytail answered.

The captain laughed. "I like that," he said. "Very well then, we'll drink to a safe voyage, and to poor seafarin' men, wherever they may be."

The captain raised his tankard, which was filled with a dark amber liquid, and we raised ours too, and we drank. Braggot turned out to be a special ale, flavored with honey. It was thick and sweet and filled my mouth and nose with a rich mix of flavors quite unlike the ordinary beers I was used to at home.

"You'll join me for dinner?" the captain asked.

I glanced at Greytail, unsure how to answer, since I had no coin of my own, at least none that would be good on this world. Greytail wrinkled his nose at the smell of the pig roasting on the spit over the great fireplace a few feet away from us. After a slight hesitation, he nodded and said, "We will."

The captain waved an arm at a serving boy, who came hurrying over at his gesture.

"Dinner for my two friends here, and myself," he said grandly. "A cut off that fine beast you've got roasting there, new potatoes, carrots, and fresh bread if you've got it. And you can fill our glasses all around."

The serving boy nodded.

"Anything else, gentlemen?" asked the captain.

"Do you have any greens?" Greytail asked the serving boy.

"We've some turnip greens," the boy answered, "but they're a bit past their prime, I'm afraid."

"Well, it's more than we're likely to find aboard ship. Bring 'em out."

"Very good, sirs, and captain," the boy said with a nod to Greytail and myself, and a half bow to the captain, before running back to the kitchen to fill our orders.

"You're well known here," Greytail commented.

"I should be, after all the coin that's left my purse here," the captain answered. "Sometimes I think I put to sea solely for the benefit of tavern owners and innkeepers."

"And innkeeper's daughters . . ." Greytail answered.

The captain raised his eyebrows and looked at Greytail. "And what do you imply by that?"

"Captain Fleischman is the half-owner of the Pickled Parrot," Greytail said for my benefit. "His daughter, Alicia, owns the other half and runs the business while he's at sea."

"You seem to know a lot about my business," scowled the captain.

"I like to know who I'm dealing with," said Greytail.

"I could say the same to you, Masters Nutkin and Cork—if you can recall which of you had which name when you walked in here."

Greytail and I exchanged glances. He smiled. "Ah, but that's easy. Cork floats. So when we are halfway to the Unicorn Isles, simply throw us both overboard and whichever of us floats shall be your 'Cork.'"

The captain laughed. "Oh no, Master Nutkin, that will never do, for then I would be bereft of your excellent company for the remainder of the voyage. And besides, it is you who are carrying the gold to pay your fares."

"There is that," Greytail admitted. "But as you are now paid in half for two fares, if but one arrives, then you are paid in full."

"Well, you are a devil-may-care sort of fellow," said the captain, "to talk so gaily of being flung to the fishes, though I fancy you might talk differently were you at sea. And you, Master Cork, seem awfully silent."

"I float," I said, "upon the waves of your conversation, waiting to see which way the wind will blow."

"Well said, if but little answered," said the captain. "Very well, you know who I am, it seems. And I do not need to know your full intent and purposes to take you to your destination. We will sail tomorrow at first light. Will you sleep aboard, or have you rooms for the night?"

"Aboard, if it please the captain," answered Greytail. "For having paid for our berths, we would not want to risk missing our departure by oversleeping if we can help it."

"Nor are you overanxious to part with coin for your night's lodgings. It seems to me you wizards are a tightfisted lot."

"Do you think so?" asked Greytail. "Then hold out your hand, and I shall fill it with gold a second time."

The captain looked suspicious but held out his hand. Leaning forward, Greytail reached a hand to the captain's ear and seemed to pluck out a gold coin, which he laid in the captain's palm.

"Grab it quick now," he said, "before it gets away."

The captain looked at the coin and closed his fist. "What means this?" he asked.

"Do you have it?" asked Greytail.

The captain looked down at his closed fist. "Of course I have it, what do you mean?"

"Are you sure?" asked Greytail. "Let me see."

The captain opened his hand. The gold coin was gone, and in his palm instead rested a small gray pebble.

"You call *me* tightfisted," said Greytail, laughing, "but never have I squeezed gold so hard that it turned to stone."

The captain scowled, and then a new thought seemed to occur to him, and he reached into his purse to check the first three coins Greytail had given him. Greytail laughed again.

"No, those are real enough," Greytail assured him. "They were given in honest exchange and will remain true—at least as long as you do."

The captain scowled again and said, "Do you doubt my word then?"

"No more than you doubt my gold," said Greytail, smiling.

The captain frowned and put the coins back into his purse.

They stared at each other for a moment, and then Greytail flared his nostrils and drew a great breath.

"The food is coming, I perceive. Of that, at least, there is no doubt."

And so it proved.

The food was excellent, and the innkeeper herself, the captain's daughter if what Greytail had said was true, served it to us. She was a comely young woman, with golden hair and gray eyes that seemed oddly familiar, although I was quite certain that I had never met her before. I pondered this through dinner and could come up with no explanation for this odd feeling that I had seen her somewhere before.

It was not until after dinner—which the captain, to my great surprise, gave us on the house—when we had made our way back to the *Siren's Song* through the fog-filled streets, each of us carrying a torch that the captain's daughter had been kind enough to provide, that I realized where I had seen that face before. The captain's daughter, our erstwhile hostess, Alicia, had the same face as the ship's figurehead. Or perhaps it would be more correct to say that the figurehead had her face, for I supposed that she had served as the model for the sculptor who carved the figurehead, though the idea of putting my daughter's face on a bare-breasted mermaid on the prow of a ship was not one that would have occurred to me.

We went aboard with the captain, and he showed us to our cabin before leaving to talk with the mate in preparation for the morning's departure. The cabin was one of only two aboard the ship, the other, larger one being the captain's own. The mate, it seemed, had a bunk in the hold, though it is possible that this was the mate's cabin when there were no passengers aboard, while the crew slept in turns on the deck, or huddled on the floor of the hold if the weather was bad. She had seemed a great ship to me when I looked up at her from our tiny rowboat, but now as I contemplated crossing the ocean aboard her, she seemed a very tiny vessel indeed.

A thought occurred to me. "Will you just leave the rowboat tied up here till we get back?" I asked.

"Not to worry," Greytail answered, "Once I was sure we had our places aboard the *Siren's Song*, I sent her home. She'd be lonely just hanging around a great port like this with nothing to do."

He laughed—I was not sure whether at his own jest or at the look on my face. Come to think of it, I was not sure he had spoken in jest. I recalled the way the little boat had seemed to come when he whistled and floated along the river to the harbor, never once veering into the banks or needing to be steered around obstacles. Perhaps she could find her way home, although it seemed to me that the sight of an unmanned boat floating upstream would surely cause some comment as it passed. At least it would in my world, but perhaps here such things were as common as horseless carriages and other such wonders had become at home. The thought of home put me in a wistful state, wondering how long it would be before I would see Elizabeth and the children, or if I ever would.

"I thought you were only guiding me as far as the ship," I said, recalling my conversation with Greytail that morning when we had set out from the wizards' castle.

"That is true," he replied. "I have guided you as far as the ship. Now it is Captain Fleischman who must guide us, or perhaps *steer* us would be more accurate, to the Unicorn Isles."

I wondered if this had been his plan all along or if something about this evening's conversation with the captain had caused a change in plans, but Greytail, typically, volunteered no information on this subject. I shrugged.

"Did you notice," I asked, "that the ship's figurehead has the same face as the captain's daughter? Do you find that odd?"

"I did notice," he said, "but I do not find it odd. What could be more natural, after all, than that a mother and daughter should resemble each other?"

"What do you mean?" I asked.

"The ship's figurehead is carved in the likeness of Alicia's mother. So, naturally Alicia resembles her."

"Do you mean that Alicia's mother was a mermaid?" I asked.

"Not a mermaid, a siren. And still is, so far as I know. And so would Alicia herself be, I suppose, were it not for the tragedy of her deformity."

"What deformity?" I asked, shocked. She had seemed a perfectly well formed woman to me, at least as far as I could tell with her clothes on.

"She was born with her father's deformity: legs. And so her mother was forced to abandon her, and she was brought up by her father, mostly aboard this ship, I believe. And then, when she was old enough to be left alone ashore, he bought the Pickled Parrot for her."

"But why didn't she stay and help her father aboard the ship?" I asked. "Surely someone who is half-mermaid, or half-siren, or whatever she is, would belong at sea at least as much as on land?"

"Exactly," said Greytail. "And the sea calls to her, but unlike her mother, were she to leap overboard out at sea, she would drown. And so it is safer for her to stay on land, where she is not tempted so deeply by the sea's call."

"And how do you know so much about all this?" I asked.

"Wizards hear many things," he answered. "Some of them might even be true."

CHAPTER TEN

AT SEA

WE WEIGHED ANCHOR AND set sail the next morning shortly after sunrise. The sky was clear and blue and the rising sun turned the few clouds in the sky to that delightful hue of sky-blue-pink that you get only at sunrise and sunset. What cargo the *Siren's Song* carried beside ourselves I did not know as she had been loaded before we came aboard last night. That was the captain's business and not mine, but it was clear that the first business of the *Siren's Song* was her cargo. Passengers were an afterthought, and while I knew next to nothing about how money worked in this world, it seemed unlikely that the six pieces of gold that Greytail had offered for our passage would have been enough to pay for outfitting even such a small ship as the *Siren's Song*. Onboard, besides Captain Fleischman and ourselves, there was the cook, the surly old fellow who had shouted down to us when we first came alongside *The Siren's Song* in our rowboat; the first mate, a sandy-haired man with two days' stubble on his chin, who might have been anywhere from twenty-five to fifty; and four crewmen. The cook's name was Hans, and the first mate's was Peter. I did not learn the names of the crew that morning, but resolved to do so as soon as I could. It was tight enough on board that it felt foolish to behave as strangers, although they were all busy at their work while Greytail and I sat idly watching the buildings onshore and the ships in the harbor grow steadily smaller as the shore slipped away behind us. A flock of seagulls followed us for a while, hoping perhaps for a handout, but when nothing was forthcoming they turned and headed back towards the fishing boats closer to shore.

There was a large island about twenty miles offshore. This acted as a natural breakwater, so the harbor was sheltered from the worst of the sea's storms. We made for the north end of this island, which in my world had been called Long Island, as I surmised, and which in that world was tied by a ribbon of concrete to another cluster of islands and harbors called New York City. I did not know if there was a city in the same location in this world, but it seemed unlikely that if there were it would be called New York. Thinking of New York, of course, got me thinking of my own world and Elizabeth and the children. What were they doing I wondered and what explanation, if any, had they come up with to account for my sudden disappearance? I watched the waves and felt both homesick and slightly seasick. Watching the horizon seemed to help with both of these, so I stared out at it and tried not to get lost in my own sea of melancholy.

As we approached I saw the trees on the island grow from a faint green line on the horizon to reveal their true forms. I saw no houses, but perhaps these would be invisible from the shore. In a few hours, we reached the north end of the island, rounded it, and headed out onto the open ocean. For a few hours more we watched the island dwindling slowly in the distance, then it, too, was gone and we were truly at sea.

It was a new, and very strange, sensation to be surrounded entirely by water. Water, stretching away in every direction as far as the eye could see, a vast circular horizon of sea meeting sky with nothing to indicate direction save the occasional cloud, and the up-and-down motion of the ship herself over the waves. At night, of course, there were the stars, and we watched them on every clear night. Greytail would point them out to me, though the names were not ones I was familiar with, and the shapes he tried to point out to me were very different from the maps of constellations I had seen back home. The stars, however, were I believe the same. At any rate, I could pick out the Big Dipper, and from there the North Star, or so I thought. And if that was not enough for the captain to sail by, at least it gave me a sense that we were headed in some definite direction and not just drifting endlessly over the waves.

We had been at sea for just over a week. My seasickness had subsided in that time and I had learned to loathe the taste of hard tack and fish stew, though I marveled to see how much of our provisions came from the sea itself. I had learned too that the tall, red-haired lad with freckles was Duncan; the shorter, dark-haired one was Séamas. Both were young men who had sailed with Captain Fleischman since they were boys, and neither knew or wanted any other master. The other two crewmen were older, the captain's age or perhaps more, and had sailed on many ships and served under many captains, but both said they meant to stay with Captain Fleischman as long as he would have them. One of them, Kostas, was a Greek who had worked on fishing boats in the Mediterranean before deciding that he wanted to see the new world. The last, Odo, was a grey-haired man with coal-black skin who had been born a slave on an island in the Caribbean, escaped, and stowed away on a ship that turned out to be a privateer's. So, it was join the pirates or be fed to the fishes for him, and he had been a pirate for many years and under many captains before giving up pirating to join Captain Fleischman's crew. At least that is the story he told me; whether there was any truth to it, I could not say.

Greytail made friends easily with the crew. He had repeated his joke about throwing us both overboard to see which one was Cork, and they laughed and now repeated it endlessly to me. I grew tired of it, but at least it helped me to remember what my name was supposed to be, which might, I admitted to myself, have been Greytail's reason for telling it to the crew in the first place.

I countered that since he, Nutkin, should be kin to a nut, we should bury him once we got to land to see what sort of a tree he would grow, but the others did not seem to find this as funny as his jest.

After a week of sailing under fair skies, I scarcely noted the rocking of the ship with the waves and had begun to feel, if not a competent sailor, then at least something less of a landlubber than I had been when I stepped onboard the ship. The days had been clear and bright and the wind as steady as you could ask for. It took me by surprise then when the horizon began to darken with the approach of a coming storm. I knew nothing of storms at sea, but noted how the crew watched, apprehensively, as the storm drew nearer. From the reaction of the crew, it seemed this was no ordinary storm. We were a week from land, or so the captain said, with no shelter in sight, with the storm front racing toward us at a speed we could not hope to outrun, so there was nothing to do but prepare to meet her. Captain Fleischman called Greytail and me over to where he stood at the helm.

"Well, Master Wizards," he began, including us both, although apart from my borrowed cloak, I had nothing that remotely resembled wizardry at my command. "As you can see, there is a storm approaching, and it looks to be a hard blow. Is there aught you can do to calm her?"

"There may be," answered Greytail, "though I am loath to speak spells of wind calming while we are this far from shore. For if we force the winds to be still here and now, we shall go nowhere. And, as the force of the winds must go somewhere, we will create a great tension in the force fields around us, and once I loose the spell, that might bring the winds crashing back upon us with greater force than before. So, at least for now, I will not seek to calm these winds. Rather, let us see what a small bit of magic, and your good seafaring skills, can do to bring us safe through the storm, for that, after all, is what matters."

"Well," said the captain, "whatever it is you mean to do, I would suggest you do it quickly. Unless my eyes are much deceived, the storm will be upon us in a matter of minutes."

"Let me go up and take a look," said Greytail, excusing himself with a bow. Then he turned and ran up the ship's rigging as nimbly as any squirrel (not surprisingly, I thought).

For perhaps five minutes he stayed up there, surveying the sky in every direction while he hung from a small basket at the top of the mast before scrambling back down to the deck where I stood with Captain Fleischman. Greytail's voice when he returned was calm and businesslike, not betraying the least hint of his recent exertion, much less the sheer terror I would have felt clambering up the ship's rigging (even supposing I could do so) in the face of an oncoming storm.

"It is as I feared," he said. "This is no ordinary storm which approaches."

"How so, Master Nutkin?" asked the captain.

"See how it closes in on us from three sides?" said Greytail. "And how the storm clouds do not gather in the sky but rather seem to form a wall rising from the surface of the water?"

And sure enough, looking into the distance, we could see that it was as he had said: a black wall of clouds or mist seemed to boil up out of the water, blotting out the horizon, and now it was as if the horizon itself were rushing in toward us in a most unnatural way.

"But can you calm it? Or is there aught else you can do to save us?" the captain asked again.

"There is no calming this storm," said Greytail. "There is too much powerful magic in it. But, if it is a storm they want, then a storm they shall have, and we shall see whose storm proves the stronger."

"What do you mean?" the captain asked, with more than a touch of anxiety in his voice.

"I mean," said Greytail, "that since I cannot calm this storm, I will call up one of my own, and stand ready to send it upon the head of whoever has sent this storm our way."

"And how will that help us?" cried the captain. "If their storm does not send us to the bottom, then yours shall finish the job, Master Wizard. Is this wisdom or folly?"

"Both perhaps," said Greytail. "But it is either that or stand here and do nothing but wait for the storm to fall upon our heads. You are the captain. What would you have me do?"

The captain frowned, indecision plain upon his face. Clearly the prospect of calling up one storm to fight another while he and his crew were caught in the middle did not appeal to him. Yet, he was also a man of action, and whenever pirates had attacked his ship, he had given back as good as he had gotten or better, whatever the odds—or so said his crew. And what was this storm but some new kind of magical pirate, come to rob him and his crew of their treasure, and of their very lives too?

"If you think you can fight this storm, Master Wizard, then fight it. Tell me what my men and I should do."

"Reef your sails and batten down, as you would for any storm. Leave the rest to me."

And so, while the crew worked frantically to reef the sails and make sure that everything aboard ship was tied down as securely as it could be, Greytail stood alone on the foredeck, gripping the ship's rail with one hand, and his staff with the other, watching the approaching storm. Once, he raised his staff into the air and gave a loud whistle, or something like it. Almost, I thought, like the cry of an eagle heard from far off. But there was no answer that I could hear or see. The sky grew darker as the storm approached and the sea grew rougher. Whereas earlier, in the calm weather of the morning, we had seemed to slice through the waves, surging forward with the wind filling our sails, now the ship rode the waves like a great roller coaster, rising up ten, twelve, fourteen feet into the air on the crest of a wave and then plunging down twice that height into the trough below. Still,

Greytail stayed on the foredeck, saying nothing, watching the storm closing in. Slowly clouds began to form overhead as well as in front of us, and I thought I saw the hint of a smile beneath the determined look on his face.

Rain began to fall. I say *fall*, for that is what one usually says of rain, but in truth it blew at us in sheets out of the wall of clouds that had now closed in around us on three sides. Greytail raised his staff again and whistled, and this time it was as if an eagle stood right behind me on the deck. A flash of lightning shot out of the clouds above us and into the cloudbank in front of us, and in the same instant came the sound of thunder, like an explosion, booming directly over the ship. A second later there came a second flash, this time lancing out to the port side, and a second peal of thunder, and then a third to starboard, and a fourth toward the stern. The crew had gone below to huddle together in the hold, but the captain, out of bravery, foolishness, or simply not knowing what else to do, stayed at the helm, though in truth there was now no way he could steer the ship, even if he could see which way to steer her.

Burst after burst of lightning Greytail sent out in all directions, probing through the wall of clouds that now surrounded us on all sides for some enemy he could strike at, and our ears roared with the sound of thunder overhead, a furious chain of explosions like the finale of a fireworks display but so close and so loud that I feared it would shake the ship to pieces. The only answer that came was the rain. At first it had seemed to blow in toward us from the front of the storm before us, but now that the storm encircled us, it blew in upon us from every direction, and I felt myself to be in the very center of a maelstrom. Greytail's hood had fallen back from his face and his silver hair streamed back behind him like a banner, blown now this way, now that by the contrary winds, despite being drenched with rain. His cloak, too, streamed back like wings, and I found myself thinking of the statue of the Winged Victory I had seen once in a museum in Paris. Indeed, I now thought that I perceived, in the rain-lashed silhouette on the foredeck, the unexpected contours of a woman's form beneath the young wizard's cloak. But while the Winged Victory soared triumphant, Greytail, it seemed to me, was fighting for his life—or for *her* life perhaps, if the startlingly female form I had seen beneath Greytail's cloak were the true one. But, however hard she struck at it with lightning, the opposing storm closed in on us, inexorably, like a slowly tightening noose.

The captain, I had said, had stayed on deck to man the helm, and whether this was bravery or foolishness I cannot say, but for my own part, to stay on deck was surely folly, for I added nothing either to the manning of the ship or to Greytail's attempted defense of us from the attacking storm. But stay I did, clinging with both hands to the rail while the rain poured in upon us from every direction. By this time, the encircling clouds formed a solid ring around the ship, rising vertically up from the surface of the water hundreds of feet on every side. At the base of this ring, I noticed a dark shape moving beneath the surface of the water, creating a ripple behind it like the wake of a ship. As I watched, it began to circle us, winding around and around in a tightening gyre. A spray of water shot up from this dark shape, and after a moment, I recognized the dark shape as a whale, its great size made seemingly small by the distance and the immensity of the wall of clouds surrounding us both. It seemed to me that we and the whale were trapped alike within a huge cylindrical storm, the walls of which were slowly closing in on us both so that soon the whale would be forced to the center of the cylinder, where it would collide with the ship.

Then an even stranger thing began to happen. The surface of the water itself began to spiral, following the whale's motion around the great cloud cylinder. Slowly at first, and then more rapidly, the ship began to turn like a top on the surface of the water. Greytail raised her staff and called out to the storm above us. A flash of light came down from the clouds above us. Not jagged like lightning but straight like the beam of a flashlight. This beam of light struck the end of her staff, which blazed like a mirror in the sun, and then like a lens, it refracted the beam of light, sending it out along a new path toward

the whale, which continued to circle us. The whale was illuminated
for a brief, blinding moment with a halo of light that rose up from
the waves, shimmering with all the colors of the rainbow. In the next
moment, the halo of light was gone, and the whale swam on, circling
faster than ever. It seemed to me then that the surface of the water
began to fall, and we were being sucked downward to the bottom of an
enormous vortex. Above us, I could see the whale still circling at the
lip of the vortex, while the ship, pitched onto her side, rode the wall
of that vortex as if in a dizzying nightmarish centrifuge. From the
hold, I heard the voices of the crew screaming, while Greytail, on the
foredeck, clung to the ship's rail with one hand, trying desperately
to keep us from being pulled down into the bottom of the great
whirlpool, and the captain clung for his life to the helm. Then a great
wall of water poured down upon us all from the lip of the vortex high
above and swept us from the deck of the ship. I felt myself plunged
into icy, swirling salt water. The water's taste was harsh in my mouth.
I wanted to spit it out, but no longer had any idea which way led back
to the surface and the sweet taste of air. After that, I knew no more.

Chapter Eleven

The Halls of the Sea King

I AWOKE—IF YOU COULD call it waking, for I emerged into a realm even more dreamlike than any of the strange places I had been in since turning that fateful page and entering this world—and found myself floating weightlessly in an odd sort of a chamber. I say *chamber*, for I do not know what else to call it. There were floors, which were paved with minute, colored tiles forming elaborate mosaics depicting various sea creatures: a bewildering variety of fish, most of which I do not think I had ever seen before, as well as squid, octopi, crustaceans of all varieties, and seahorses. Some of these were like the tiny seahorses I knew from my own world, with curled tails and fins instead of legs, others had forelimbs like those of a land horse, though what use these would be underwater I could not imagine. Some of the seahorses in the mosaics had riders, too, and I noticed that the riders, like their mounts, had forelimbs like those of creatures on land, in this case, men, but also tails like those of fish or dolphins.

The floors, as I said, were tiled with these mosaics, and there were pillars rising from them to a vaulted ceiling high overhead, but no walls that I could see, or at least not ones shaped by human hands, although I suppose given my surroundings that was hardly surprising. Instead, there were what looked like the rock walls of a cave, which were pocked with a variety of different sized openings and decorated, if that is the word, with a variety of different colored fronds and coral as well as sea stars and urchins that moved gently with the motion of the water around us. Some of the openings had little fish darting in and out of them, and in one of the bigger ones I thought I saw the head of an eel disappearing as I turned to look at it. I breathed in, and wondered as I did so, that I was able to breathe at all. But although I was, as far as I could tell, still underwater—indeed I was probably deeper underwater than I had ever been—I did not choke, breathing in, any more than I would have had I been standing on dry land breathing air as I had done all my life. I breathed out and looked up to see the stream of tiny bubbles escape from my nostrils float upwards to be lost in the vaulted recesses of the ceiling. I wondered, vaguely, whether there were holes at the top to let the bubbles out, or whether the carbon dioxide I breathed out would somehow dissolve back into the water and be carried away by the ebb and flow of the tide. My thoughts, too, seemed to be dissolving into the enveloping sea and I felt an unnatural calm seeping into me, despite the strangeness of my surroundings.

I felt the tide pulling at me. Just as on land we seem to feel the wind outside on a stormy day even when we are safely indoors, so here, even though there was no real current, the ever-present force of the tides could be felt, vibrating faintly, or perhaps sensed more than truly felt in the water all around us. I looked around. A green-golden light filled the room, though I could see no obvious light source, no lamp or window to account for the strange luminosity. Floating above the tiled floors, I could see the bodies of two of my erstwhile shipmates,

Captain Fleischman and Greytail. They lay still, but the tide tugged at their clothes, rocking them gently from side to side, and from time to time I could see a tiny stream of bubbles escaping from their open mouths and drifting slowly upward. By that I knew that they too lived by whatever strange magic it was that allowed us to breathe here beneath the waves. I waited for them to rouse. Of the rest of the crew, I saw no trace. Whether they lived or had all perished when the ship went down I could not say. The thought filled me with dread. It occurred to me then that I, too, might have died and this strange underwater existence that I now experienced might be some odd kind of aquatic afterlife. It was a strange thought. Could I have died and not noticed? How would I know?

Before I could come up with an answer to this question Greytail awoke. She thrashed about, shaking her head and trying to cough. But if water came out of her mouth when she coughed, just as much went back in when she drew breath, since we were all underwater. She opened her eyes wide and looked around in panic. She reached for her staff, but it was gone. She saw me and pulled her robes more tightly around her, but the fabric of the cloak was sodden and heavy and moved sluggishly in the water, and a momentary glimpse told me that what she had said in the wizard's castle was true: there was nothing under her cloak but her own definitely female form. I glanced hurriedly away.

"Where are we?" she asked, coming to something that resembled an upright position, though in the near weightlessness of our watery surroundings it was hard to maintain anything that resembled a normal posture on land. Hearing her speak, I marveled that I was able to understand her words. As a child, like all children I think, I had played the game of trying to speak to someone underwater in a pool, and on those occasions was scarcely able to understand my own words, much less those of anyone else who tried to speak to me. But here, perhaps through the same magic that allowed us to breathe, I found that I could hear almost normally, with only the hint of an echo as the sounds bounced off the chamber's rock walls.

"I don't know," I said. "Underwater, it seems, but breathing some-how, and talking too. Perhaps we've become fish. Do fish talk?"

"I don't know," she said, echoing my words. "I've never spoken to one."

I laughed at the absurdity of her answer, and then stopped when I realized I didn't know if she was joking. Some questions, it seems, can only be answered in the affirmative. If a fish talks to you, then you can say with certainty that fish talk, or at least that *that* one does, but if you have never talked to a fish, does that mean that fish never talk? Or merely that they have never talked to *you*?

She looked around and saw the floating form of Captain Fleis-chman.

"Is he . . . ?" she asked, leaving the question unfinished.

"Alive," I answered, "or so I infer from the bubbles coming from his nostrils."

"So I see," she said, after she had looked more closely. "And the others?"

"I don't know," I said again. "I awoke myself but a few moments ago, and so far, you two are all of our company that I have seen. The crew may have stayed aboard the ship when we were washed overboard, but whether they live or not I cannot say."

"And the ship?" she asked.

"Your guess is as good as mine. Better, perhaps, if you have some understanding of what befell us. It seemed to me that the bottom had fallen out of the sea itself, and the ship sailed, not on the surface of the ocean, but on the sides of an enormous whirlpool."

"So it seemed to me, too. And the vortex, or whirlpool as you call it, was called forth by some power much greater than my own meager magic. Did you see a black whale?"

"I did, and it seemed to circle the rim of the wall of cloud we were trapped in."

"Yes, and I struck at it with lightning, but it remained unscathed. The whale is sometimes an avatar of the Sea King, so it may be that we are now in the Halls of the Sea King. Or in his dungeon perhaps."

"His dungeon?" I asked, looking around. There were no bars that I could see.

"Yes, that is where one usually puts prisoners, is it not? Since he has captured us so neatly—and gone to the trouble of taking my staff, I see—then I assume that we are in his dungeons. Although if this is a dungeon, it is a strange one, since he does not seem to have gone to the bother of posting guards, at least none I can see. Indeed, there do not even seem to be walls to keep us in."

I looked around and saw that she was right. For though there was a ceiling above us, and pillars reaching up to the ceiling in various places, the rock walls I had noted earlier did not form a closed room around us. They seemed more like a natural landscape—or undersea-scape: the walls of a canyon, turning this way and that, branching in unexpected places, with spurs of stone sticking out from the main wall or folding in to form three-sided rooms or pockets, such as the one we were in, here and there along the wall.

"It's like a maze," I said.

"So it is," she answered. "And maybe that is why they do not need to bother with guards."

"So perhaps it is no prison at all, but simply a place we happen to be in," I said.

"It is certainly the place we happen to be in. But I do not forget that we didn't come here of our own accord."

"Does one ever?" said the captain, joining in unexpectedly to the conversation.

I started, for I had not seen him awake. I looked over and saw that he, too, floated in a semi-upright position. Oddly, the natural buoyancy that should have brought us all back up towards the surface did not seem to be affecting any of us. Perhaps, I thought, because our lungs were all now filled with water. The thought was disturbing, but did not fill me with terror as it might have a few weeks ago.

"What do you mean?" I asked.

"I mean," he replied in a calm tone, as if we were discussing some abstract question over dinner, "that since none of us choose to come into this world, and much of what happens to us is beyond our control, then wherever we happen to be is seldom entirely a matter of our own choosing."

Greytail regarded him oddly, as if she were wondering whether the captain recalled any of what had happened to us before we awoke here.

"You are very philosophical for a man who has been washed overboard and wakes to find himself breathing and talking beneath the sea," she said.

"And what should such an experience make a man, if not philosophical?" he asked. "Besides, I have been in such a place before."

We waited for him to explain.

"You are familiar, I believe, with the story of my daughter's birth?" he asked. We nodded. "I thought as much. There were too many questions, you see, that you did not ask—questions one would normally ask out of curiosity or politeness, but which, knowing or guessing the answers, you did not. In any case, I have been in such a place before, these castles of the Seafolk. Castles or caverns, if you will, for that is what they are, great caverns beneath the sea that have been carved and tiled to resemble the palaces of men."

"Are you sure?" I asked.

"What do you mean?" asked the captain.

"Are you sure that it is the Seafolk's caverns that have been carved to resemble the palaces of men, and not men's palaces which have been made to resemble these caverns?"

"Who can say?" he replied. "My point was merely that I have been in such a place before. When I was a young sailor, my ship was drawn onto the rocks by the call of the sirens. We knew it was our death we went to, but we went willingly. Not like a soldier marching into battle with brave determination, but eagerly, lustily, with every fiber of our beings willing our sweet obliteration, so taken were we by the magic of the sirens' singing. They are the black widows of the sea, calling to lure their mates into their rocky webs, and full willingly we answered their call.

"Our ship was smashed on the rocks, as of course the sirens intended, and I and my fellow sailors sank into the waves. Some, like myself, may have fathered new sirens before they died. But, unlike all my shipmates—*all*—I did not die. I don't know why. It may be that the siren who chose me was in some way defective, somehow too human to be fully the siren she should have been. Perhaps that is why our daughter—

"But I am getting ahead of myself. In any case, she did not kill me, but instead used that magic, which all sirens have, to let me breathe the salt water. Normally, as she told me later, the sirens use such magic for just a few brief moments, to keep their human mates alive long enough to fulfill our function, and then, that purpose served, they leave the humans to drown. But, as I said, she did not let me drown but instead took me away into a place not unlike this, and there we spent many days beneath the water.

"Each day I awoke, thinking that everything that had happened before had been but a dream. But each time I woke, I found myself still dreaming the same dream. And when she told me what had become of my shipmates, I feared that sooner or later this would be my fate too. Indeed, I believe that at first, she herself thought this. She was a siren, after all, and I had answered her call, and so, of course, I should die. But in the end, she decided that she could neither kill me nor keep me with her. Had her sisters discovered that she had kept me alive, it would have meant both our lives. So she swam with me to a remote island, far from the shores her sisters normally inhabited. And there we lived for some months, she in the water, and I on the land, except when we would meet in a secret grotto. It was there, some months later, that she gave birth to our daughter and there we raised her for the first few years of her life. But eventually, we decided that if our daughter were to live fully as a human, she would need to have human company other than my own. And so I became a sailor again, this time aboard my own vessel, the same which we sailed coming here, and my daughter sailed with me until she was old enough to live alone on land."

We were silent a time after this speech, although my head was filled with a thousand questions.

At length I ventured to ask, "Is that what happened to us then? Have we been captured by sirens?"

"Did you hear the sirens' call?" he asked, by way of answer.

"No," I replied. "I don't think so. Though perhaps being from another world, I am deaf to the sound."

The captain raised his eyebrows in surprise. "From another world, you say? Perhaps there is more than one strange tale to be told this night."

I realized then what I had said and kicked myself mentally for my stupidity, but there was nothing to be done about it now.

"Be that as it may," the captain continued. "As you seem to hear my voice plainly enough, I am sure you could hear the sirens did they call. As for me, I can hear them now, even if I am a thousand leagues distant. If I am sleeping and they call on the far side of the ocean, I wake with a start. But I did not hear them when our ship went down this time. And the sirens have no need for magic whales or walls of clouds to bring ships to them. No, whatever power brought us to this place, it is not the sirens'."

"I agree," said Greytail. "It was no siren's call that brought us to these depths. The leviathan, they say, is the avatar of the Sea King himself, and certainly that was no ordinary whale circling the vortex. It might even be that leviathan brought the vortex into being by his circling. In any case, I think it likely that we are now in the Halls of the Sea King, and whatever his purpose is in bringing us here, he will reveal it to us when it suits his purposes."

"And what would a wizard know of the Halls of the Sea King?" asked a new voice.

We turned to look, and there floating before us was a creature I could only assume was the Sea King himself. The upper half of his body was shaped like a man's, but he was more massive than any man I had ever seen on land. His head alone must have been three feet across. He had a great gaping, red mouth and hair and a beard that looked like the pelt of a black bear. Each of his arms was as long and as thick as my entire body, and his body was proportioned along the same lines. Its lower half was shaped like a tail—not sleek and scaly like the painted form of the siren on the ship's prow, but broad and covered with thick, brown fur and ending in two great flippers like a whale's. He wore a crown of braided gold wire set with pearls the size of my fist, though on him they looked almost dainty, and in his right hand he held the fabled trident, perhaps twelve feet in length, or nearly as tall as the King himself.

Greytail turned to face him and bowed, which looked slightly comical, as her feet did not quite touch the floor, yet I believe she intended her reverence in all seriousness. "Your majesty," she said, "we thank you for the gifts you have bestowed upon us, of life and breath beneath these waters."

The Sea King snorted, making a sound like a seal barking but deeper, and a cloud of bubbles floated up through his bushy mustache. "Spoken like a true wizard," he said, "long on flattery and short on substance. So, you claim you do not know these halls?"

"Your majesty," she said again, "we would all be pleased to know of your halls, whatever you wish to show us of them."

"Another wizard's answer," said the King. "Well, I know better than to spend all day trying to get a straight answer out of a wizard. Your tongues are like eels that slip away whenever you try to grasp their meaning too firmly. But come, follow me, and you shall see something of my halls—those of you who have not seen them before." And here, he turned to look again at Greytail, but what the meaning was behind that look I could not guess. "And then we can eat, and talk some more, and ponder what is to be done."

And so saying, he turned and with a quick flip of his tail propelled himself from the room, or grotto as it may have been, in which we had awakened. We followed. Lacking tails, we struggled to keep up, sometimes swimming, sometimes pushing off the walls or floor with our feet, or using the outcroppings from the rough stone walls to thrust ourselves forward. Of the three of us, Greytail, seemed to move the most easily underwater. Pushing from outcropping to outcropping was perhaps not so different from leaping from branch to branch as a squirrel, as similar perhaps as the flight of penguins beneath the water to the flight of other birds in the sky above. But she was careful, I saw, not to get too far ahead of the captain and myself as we struggled to keep up with our royal guide. After a short time, the Sea King seemed to grow impatient with our slow progress, so he stopped and made a kind of chirping noise, like the call of a dolphin, and instantly, or so it seemed to me, there appeared two mermen, such as I had seen in the images in the mosaic floor tiles. From the waist up, they appeared as men, but from the waist down they had the tails of dolphins. They were mounted on seahorses that were almost as large as their counterparts on land. The Sea King spoke to the mermen in the same high-pitched chirping language he had used to call them, and they answered him in the same way. Then, they bowed and rode off on their mounts.

"I had forgotten how clumsy you humans are in the water," he said. "We shall have mounts brought."

And, sure enough, a few moments later the mermen returned leading three other seahorses fitted with saddles. The seahorses were perhaps eight feet tall from the tops of their heads to the tips of their tails. The seahorses I had seen in the mosaics had been of two varieties at least. Some had forefeet and some only fins. These were of the finned variety. Each was a different color: one was a bright coral pink, one the color of orange sherbet, and the third a vivid lime green. All had a luminescent, almost translucent quality to their skin, as if their colors came not from any reflected light source, but from unseen fires that burned within them. The saddles were oddly shaped, more like a pack carrier for an infant than a horse's saddle. There was a curving seat that curled back like the bottom of the letter J and, higher up, two short rods that were evidently meant to serve as handles. There were no reins or stirrups.

"As you can see," said the Sea King, "these saddles have been fashioned specially for our occasional two-legged visitors. Though,

I must say, we do not have occasion to use them very often. You may mount your steeds, but do not attempt to guide or steer them. They will take you where you need to go more easily if you leave them to it. Now, up you go."

Somewhat hesitantly, we climbed up into the odd saddles the sea-horses wore. As we did they twitched nervously, like a horse being mounted by an unfamiliar rider, but they did not buck or try to bite us. Then, at a chirped command from the Sea King, we headed off again, now at a much more rapid pace than we would ever have been able to achieve on our own.

As we sped through the Halls of the Sea King, I began to realize they were far larger than I had imagined. Mile after mile we raced along among twisting canyon-like passages. Much of the palace—if that was the right term for these caverns—had tiled floors like those in the room where we had awoken, with tall pillars that twisted like the horn of a narwhal going up toward vaulted ceilings, but in other places we seemed to swim through vast kelp forests, and I would think we were out in the open ocean until suddenly we would ride past a row of columns, and looking up, I could see the vaulted ceiling high above us. Here and there were window-like apertures with thick glass panes, curved like the lens of a magnifying glass, set into the rocky walls and, peering through as we rode past, I saw an array of vast sea creatures: great whales, giant squid, and strange monstrous fish with glowing lights that dangled from tentacles projecting from their bodies and made even larger by the lenses of the windows, but whether these windows looked out into the open sea, or into some vast aquatic zoo, I could not say. At length we came to a vast marble staircase, built on a scale that only giants would have used, had there been giants with legs beneath the sea to use them, but our mounts, like the Sea King himself, had flippers, not legs, and we fairly flew up over the steps into the chamber beyond.

The chamber we now entered was more ornate than anything we had seen previously. There were vines of gold shaped like ivy twined round the pillars, and the ceiling was painted with scenes like those

I had seen on the mosaics on the floor, but on a much larger scale. There was a long table that must have been at least ten feet wide anchored to the floor in the center of the room, and at one end of it, a huge chair like a king's throne, but constructed on such a scale that no human could ever use it. The Sea King, however, seated himself comfortably into it and indicated that we should dismount. We did so, and floated awkwardly at one side of the great table. The table was tall enough that if we had held on to the edge with both hands above our heads, our feet would have just reached down to the floor, but of course, if we did that, then we could not reach anything on top. Aside from the King's throne-like chair at the head of the table, there were no other seats. With a wave of his hand, the Sea King dismissed the three seahorses. They bowed, turned, and sped from the room, leaving us alone with our gigantic host. Dwarfed by the size of the table, the room, and of course our host himself, and feeling insignificant, as no doubt the Sea King had intended, we bobbed up and down, clutching at the side of the table, and waited to see what would happen next. I glanced at my two companions hoping for some clue as to how to proceed, but they seemed as adrift here beneath the sea as I was myself.

Chapter Twelve

Of Pearls and Oysters

"Welcome, friends—for so we shall be, at least for the moment—to my feasting hall," said the Sea King and I wondered what sort of a greeting this might be.

He waved one of his great arms towards the table which was covered with a number of golden bowls of varying sizes. The smallest bowls were the size of a dinner plate, and the largest perhaps six or even eight feet across. I noticed that most of the larger bowls were clustered around the end of the table nearest the Sea King. Over each bowl was a net, weighted at each corner with a stone, which kept the contents of the bowl from floating away, or in some cases swimming away, for I noticed that several of the bowls at the Sea King's end of the table were thrashing, as whatever was inside struggled to break free of the nets.

"We will not stand on ceremony," said the King with a flourish of his hand. "I pray you, begin."

And with that he removed the net from the bowl nearest him. A small school of mackerel swam out, perhaps half a dozen fish, but before they had time to scatter, he seized them with a rapid swipe of his hand and stuffed the lot of them into his mouth.

The next bowl he uncovered held a fully-grown octopus that tried to shoot away, leaving a cloud of black ink. But this, too, the Sea King grabbed and stuffed, tentacles still wriggling, into his cavernous mouth. He chewed the tentacles with obvious relish as the cloud of ink floated up above his head like a murky halo.

"But, my friends," he said, laughing through the cloud of black ink that still floated around his head, "you are not eating. Can it be that you have lost your appetites? The fish is not fresh enough, perhaps?" He laughed again. "Fear not, I know that you land dwellers are too slow and clumsy to catch your dinner even if it is put in a net before you. I will have my daughters prepare it for you."

He spoke again in what I assumed was his own language, and the sound was now like the clicking and chirping of dolphins, with now and again a deep bark like a seal's. A minute later, the Sea King's daughters entered the chamber. They were seven in number. Like the Sea King they had tails, not unlike a walrus's, but from the waist up they were human in form if not in size. Their skin was pale where it was not covered in brown fur and had a greenish tint to it. Their massive breasts would have looked ridiculous on any woman on land, but here beneath the waves, they seemed almost graceful as they swayed with the ebb and flow of the tides. Each wore a circlet of silver on her head, set with pearls larger than any I had ever seen, save those on the Sea King's own crown, and each carried a knife with a blade as long as my forearm, a short sword I might have said, save that in their hands the blades had the appearance of ordinary cutlery.

"My daughters," said the King, "serve our guests."

Three of the merwomen swam over to assist us.

"I am Tigris," said the one nearest me. "May I serve you?"

I nodded, unable to speak, as she swam over, her giant breasts almost colliding with my face.

She lifted the net from the bowl nearest me and a fish, a small tuna perhaps, darted out. She seized it with one hand and filleted it with the other in a matter of seconds, liberating a small cloud of blood that drifted up through her open fingers, and started handing chunks of raw fish to me, still warm. I looked from the fish, neatly splayed out in her oversized palm, to the small piece, still pink with blood that she was offering me with her right hand.

Well, I thought, *I've eaten sashimi. This can't be so different.*

I grabbed the piece of fish as it floated from her hand and put it in my mouth. It was delicious, and yet quite disturbing to eat something that had been alive a minute before. I tried to concentrate on the food and not goggle overmuch at my hostess as she floated above the table beside me.

The captain, I noticed, seemed to be enjoying himself immensely, trying everything that was offered to him and drinking, if that is the word, from a leafy sac that floated by his head. There were no goblets, naturally, since any liquid in them would have simply mixed with the enveloping seawater and dissipated into nothingness. But I watched as the captain seized the sac-like flask, put it to his lips, and squeezed. A thin jet of amber liquid, denser than the surrounding seawater, shot into his mouth and disappeared. I noticed a similar flask floating near me and followed his example. The amber liquid burned in my throat like strong brandy, but it tasted pleasant enough, and soon a feeling of warmth and lightness began to fill my body, and I yearned to throw off my heavy, water-laden clothes and swim freely. Greytail, I saw, had not touched her brandy sac but was picking at some kind of seaweed in one of the bowls in front of her. Her face looked drawn and tense.

"Now you, Master Seaman," said the Sea King, addressing Captain Fleischman, "I know of. The stealer of sirens and their babes."

"The siren belongs to herself, as she ever has, and the babe is mine, and not the sea's," said the captain, "though, as you know if you are familiar with my tale, it has been many years since she was a babe."

"We shall see," the Sea King answered. "We shall see. The sea may yet reclaim what was taken from her."

"Is that a threat?" the captain asked.

"No threats tonight when you are my guests. And indeed, I have no need to threaten. What belongs to the sea shall come back to the sea in due time, will it not?"

And turning to Greytail, he said, "And you, Master Wizard, I know also, though you claim not to know me."

"All know of your glory, Your Majesty," Greytail replied carefully, but the Sea King dismissed this with a wave of his hand before turning to me.

"But you, sir, I do not know. What manner of creature are you, and how do you come to be on a ship with such as these?"

It may be that the drink in the floating sac had loosened my tongue, or it may have been simply the force of his presence and his command, but I found myself recounting to him everything that had happened to me from the moment I had first opened the magic book up to the present. I could see Greytail's eyes growing wider, wordlessly telling me to guard my tongue and our secrets, but I could not stop myself. It was as if the cork had been pulled from a bottle and all the wine poured out. Everything that was in my head flowed out of my mouth whether I willed it or no. When I had finished, the Sea King regarded me curiously.

"So," he began, "dragons do not lie, but neither do they always tell the truth, they told you. The same might well be said of wizards."

"Yes," he repeated, "the same might well be said of wizards. And now, at the wizards' urging, you have given up looking for the green jewel, the dragon's heart as the wizards named it, and come instead to hunt for unicorns and phoenix feathers, is that it?"

"Yes," I answered, simply, wondering what he was getting at.

"And did the wizards tell you what they would do with such powerful magical trophies?" the Sea King asked.

"They would make a book," I said, "to return me to my own world."

"How very noble of them. And your plight has moved them so much that they have sent one of their own to accompany you on this venture. How touching. And did you consider why they might be going to such lengths to help you? Or what they might do with the blood and body of the unicorn and the feathers of the phoenix after they had returned you to your world?"

"No," I said.

"Well, let us consider then. What might they do? If the body of a unicorn and the feathers of a phoenix could be used to make one magic book, might they suffice to make a second book?" asked the Sea King.

"I suppose so," I said.

"I also suppose so," said the Sea King. "Indeed, they might make many books. After all, that's what wizards do, isn't it? Make books and put spells in them. But these spells, being formed of the body and blood of a powerful magical creature and being set down with a quill itself possessed of a powerful magic, would be stronger than ordinary spells. So strong, in fact, that they might bind the whole of a world's magical forces to their command. Did they tell you this?"

"No," I said again.

"And that magic stone, the dragon's heart, did they say why they would not return it to the dragon?"

"Because if they did, the dragon would become even more powerful than he is now and be able to wreak even greater destruction than he already does," I answered.

"That may be. It may also be that so long as they have the stone, the wizards are able to use its powers for their own ends. That lightning you saw, that your companion here used against my storm—I am almost certain that its power came from the dragon's heart. Do you deny this?" he asked, turning toward Greytail.

"I do not," said Greytail. "But it is one thing to use the stone's power to defend myself and my shipmates from harm and quite another to use it to lay waste to the countryside, as the dragon would. And we do no such thing."

"*Hmmmm* . . . and I suppose that it was to protect yourself and your fellows that you stole the pearl?" asked the Sea King quietly.

"Pearl?" asked Greytail, as if unsure what the Sea King was referring to.

"A pearl. One that belongs to me. You know what pearls are, I suppose?" the Sea King asked mockingly. "Or are you going to tell me that you know nothing of that?"

"I know something of pearls, Your Majesty," said Greytail smoothly, "and those that adorn Your Majesty's crown are certainly magnificent. Do you mean to say that one of them has been stolen?"

The Sea King's face darkened with a terrible scowl, and his eyes glowed in a way that reminded me all too vividly of the Black Dragon. If the thin stream of bubbles that floated up from his nostrils had been wisps of smoke, I might have said that they were twins.

"Do not lie to me, little wizard. You know perfectly well of what I speak. And do not deceive yourself that your puny powers can avail you in any way against me here in my own halls," he said fiercely.

"I would not presume to doubt Your Majesty's power when every breath I draw here beneath the waves is proof of it," said Greytail.

"So you do not doubt my power. Only my intelligence, apparently. Do you deny that someone from your order stole my pearl?" he asked.

"Forgive me, Your Majesty," Greytail pleaded. "I am by no means the most elevated of our order, and there are many secrets that are not known to me. Thus, I cannot deny with certainty that what you say may be true, but neither can I affirm that it *is* true."

"You quibble," said the King. "And you, Master Mariner," he said to the captain, "what can you tell me of my stolen pearl?"

"My lord, forgive me," said the captain, "I am as ignorant as my passenger, if not more so. Until tonight—if this is night—I had no idea that any pearls had been stolen from you, much less that a wizard might be the thief."

"A wizard, perhaps—or a sea captain. One who knows the secret of breathing beneath the sea? You told your fellows you had been in a place such as this before."

"If you, or your guards, overheard me telling that story, then Your Majesty will know of the circumstances by which I came to be in that place and how I left. I did not steal your pearl."

"And you, wanderer from another world?" asked the King, turning toward me. "What do you know of this pearl?"

"Very little, I confess. There are stories on my world about a Sea King and realms beneath the waves, but before tonight I would have said they were mere legends."

"And are legends, in your world, so devoid of substance that none believe them?"

"People in my world believe many things," I answered, "but I do not see how all of them can be true. But whether some are true and others false, or all false alike, I cannot say. It may even be that all are true in some way I cannot understand."

"And of my stolen pearl?" he asked.

"Nothing, my lord. Tonight is the first time I have learned of it."

"So you, too, like your fellows, claim ignorance of its theft. All three of you deny any knowledge of the theft of my pearl." He looked at each of us in turn before going on. "And yet, for all of that, the pearl is missing, and here are the three of you. Mighty spells I wove about that pearl to bind its magic to my own. And today I have pulled in the strands of that magic like a net, so that whoever stole it should be brought within my grasp. And here are you three before me, all saying you know nothing of my pearl or its theft. Which of you is lying, I wonder, or all three?" He paused. "Perhaps it will jog your memories if I show you where it was taken from. Yes, that might prove very useful indeed."

He spoke again in the kind of barking and clicking language he had used to summon his daughters, and two mermen appeared.

They listened to his orders and sped off again to fulfill whatever unknowable command the Sea King had just given them and we sat, anxiously wondering what our fate would be. As none of us spoke their language, or at least not that I knew of, none of us could guess the Sea King's intent. Had he just ordered our executions? Imprisonment or some more subtle torture? In a few minutes the mermen returned. Between them, they were pushing the largest shell I had ever seen, an oyster shell more than six feet across, which they set on the floor in front of the Sea King. The King barked again and, at his command, the shell began to open. Inside was a gelatinous pink mass that wriggled like a tongue in an enormous mouth.

"My treasure box," said the King. "And now, thief, thieves, or innocents, it is time to prove the worth of your words. You first, I think, Captain. Step into the shell."

"What?" cried the captain, a look of horror on his face.

"Step into the shell. It will not harm you. Not even if you are guilty. I swear it. But when you step out we will know whether the words you have spoken are truth or lies."

The captain shuddered and would have backed away, I think, if two of the Sea King's daughters had not seized him by the arms and brought him forward to face the enormous oyster. When he stood before it, they released his arms, but stood behind him ready to grab him again if he should try to flee. The captain looked back over his shoulder at the Sea King, who said nothing, but stood impatiently grasping his trident, waiting for the captain to step forward into the giant oyster. Then slowly the captain turned to look first at Greytail and then at me. I, too, said nothing as there was literally nothing I could think of to do or say at that moment, except to watch to see what happened.

"Well, if it's truth you're after," said the captain, "you will find that I spoke nothing less, assuming that what I myself believe to be truth is true. And if not . . ." He paused. "Well, it has been an interesting life anyway. I can't deny that, though I might wish it were just a trifle less interesting at the moment."

He stepped into the satiny pink mass that lined the shell of the giant oyster. His feet sunk into the oyster's flesh and it seemed to grab onto his ankles. The captain started but did not cry out.

"So, Master Mariner," said the Sea King, "I ask again. Did you steal my pearl?"

"I did not," said the captain.

He stood there a moment with the oyster's flesh grabbing onto his ankles, waiting to see what would happen, and then slowly, the oyster began to loose its hold of him.

"So, you spoke the truth," the Sea King said, sounding surprised. "At least about the pearl. Very well, you may step out."

The oyster released its hold on Captain Fleischman's ankles and he stepped, shakily, out of the giant shell.

The Sea King turned to me.

"You next, other-worlder," he said, gesturing with his trident.

I did not wait to be dragged, but stepped forward, bowing to the inevitable. And having seen the captain survive the ordeal, my own fear was somewhat lessened, although I cannot say I felt no trepidation as I stepped into the giant shell. The flesh of the oyster when I stepped onto it was rubbery and yielding, like stepping into a pool filled with jello. My feet sank into it until I felt the hard inner surface of the oyster's shell beneath my feet. I tried to turn to see what was happening behind me but found that my ankles were held fast by the oyster's rubbery flesh. The Sea King swam over into view.

"So, other-worlder, I ask you again. Where is my pearl?" the Sea King thundered.

"I don't know," I answered, as before.

"Did you take it?" he asked.

"I did not."

"Do you know who took it?"

"I do not."

The Sea King said nothing, but continued to peer intently at me, and it began to seem as if the shell of the oyster were closing upon me like a great pair of jaws. But after a moment, that feeling passed, and I wondered if the shell had moved at all.

"You may step out," the Sea King said to me, just as he had said to the captain, and I did so quickly, eager to be out of that terrifying space.

"So, wizard," said the Sea King, "now we come to you. The captain and the other-worlder have proven the truth of their words. It is time for you to do the same."

"I have never lied," said Greytail, bravely. "And if I do not speak the full truth to you, that is because it is not mine to give, even if you could stand to hear it. The truth, after all, is larger than any one of us, and one can speak but his or her own portion. Cork," she said, turning to me, "if you manage to float yourself back to the surface, I beg you, return to our order and tell them what has happened. They will know what must be done."

"Brave words from a lying wizard," said the Sea King. "Stop wasting my time. Will you swim or be dragged?"

A look of fury crossed Greytail's face and her eyes blazed like blue fire. For a moment I thought she might actually be going to attack the Sea King in his own hall, so fierce did she seem, but she merely stood, pushed off the floor, and swam into the giant oyster's mouth. Planting both feet on the giant oyster's rubbery flesh, she said defiantly, "I do not have your pearl, and I do not know where it is. And so, your worst unto me if I lie."

Nothing happened for a moment, and I thought perhaps that she would go free as we had, but the Sea King turned to her and asked, "Did you or one of your order take the pearl?"

She did not answer but stared defiantly back at him without speaking.

"That is answer enough," said the Sea King, and raised his trident. There was a flash of blue light that shot out of the tips of the trident and enveloped Greytail like a liquid lightning bolt. She stood, trapped in the radiant blue glow with her feet planted in the oyster's mouth, and the shell began to close. I rushed forward, unthinkingly, to try and pull her out, but our erstwhile hostesses, the Sea King's daughters, now became our jailors, and I found myself pinioned by two sets of burly arms and watched helplessly as Greytail was swallowed up by the shell of the giant oyster. The captain's arms were similarly restrained though he had made no move towards the giant shell that now imprisoned Greytail.

"She will come to no harm," the Sea King assured the captain and me. "My magic will enable her to breathe as surely as you are breathing now. I merely wish to keep her 'safe' for a while. How long a while that may be is up to you and the other wizards. I would bid you follow the little wizard's advice. Return to the surface and go to the wizards' castle and tell them what has befallen her. Tell them, also, that when my pearl is returned, I will release the little wizard. Until then, she will stay here for . . . *safekeeping*."

How long I stood there staring dumbly at the ridiculous oversized oyster shell I cannot say. I had never before thought of oysters as particularly sinister, but at that moment the giant shell seemed the most hideously ugly thing I had ever seen. There was no sound of struggle from within it, and I was not sure whether to feel relieved or terrified at that thought. The captain, too, looked ashen-faced and badly shaken. Up till now, it seemed, this had all been some sort of grand adventure to him, or a daydream without consequences, but with Greytail gone, the jest had soured.

"What, gentlemen, lost your appetites? A wizard on the half-shell is not the sort of delicacy you see every day, I'll admit, but there's no reason for such glum faces. I assure you that your friend's absence is merely temporary. As soon as you return the pearl to me, she will be released unharmed. But perhaps, if you've finished your dinners, you will want to get back to your ship, so you can begin looking for it right away," concluded the Sea King with a jovial smile that seemed, nonetheless, vaguely, or perhaps not so vaguely, threatening. "Unless, of course, you'd rather stay . . ." he added with a casual wave of his arm toward the shell where Greytail was imprisoned.

"Thank you, no," said the captain, recovering his tongue at last. "We would not wish to overstay our welcome."

"I will convey your message to the wizards," I said, "and I hope they will look more kindly upon the messenger than on the message, or else who knows what sort of creature I may find myself turned into."

"Have no fear for your person, other-worlder. The message you carry is mine, and while you bear it, you shall be under my protection. If the wizards give you any trouble on account of the message you bear, blow this." And here he handed me a great conch shell, with scenes such as those I had seen depicted on the mosaics carved into its spiraling sides. "When you blow it, wherever you are, I shall hear it, and answer your call, so do not use it lightly."

"A kingly gift," I said, admiring the delicate carvings on the shell, "but I would rather have my friend back."

"And so you shall," said the Sea King, "just as soon as my pearl is returned to me. Bear my message to the wizards."

Apparently that was to be his last word on the subject, for having said it, he rose up from the table, hovered for a moment to add, "My daughters shall convey you to the surface when you are ready," and with one mighty swish of his tail, sailed from the room.

I went toward the giant oyster shell with the vague idea of trying to pry it open somehow but was blocked by two of the mermen with long pikes, which they crossed in front of me. I thought briefly of trying to wrestle my way past them but concluded I would only end up getting myself speared like a fish. I turned back to the captain.

"Any suggestions?" I asked.

"None, save the obvious one of doing as the King bids us. We will be of more use to our friend alive than dead in any case."

"Then let us go."

"You are ready?" asked the mermaid who had introduced herself to me as Tigris.

"As ready as we can be under the circumstances," I answered.

"Then come," she said.

She and one of her sisters, the same I think who had stopped me earlier when I had tried to go to Greytail's defense, each took me by an arm, while two other mermaids took the captain in a similar manner and began to swim with us in tow through the arched doorway and then up through the many levels of the palace. I had little time to marvel at the architecture and less inclination after what had just happened to Greytail, but I noticed as we ascended that the planes and right angles that would have defined any building made by men were far less common here and many rooms seemed to be built as a series of interconnecting caves of varying dimensions with only here or there the plane of a floor or the right angle of column to mark it as something built rather than carved out of the surrounding stone. We emerged after a few minutes through the palace roof and continued to swim upwards.

Soon the opening in the roof where we had emerged was just a distant square of light far below us, and then it vanished entirely, swallowed up by distance and the blackness of the seafloor. The light grew stronger as we approached the surface. I had heard that when deep-sea diving, you cannot rise too quickly because of the danger of getting "the bends," something to do with nitrogen dissolved in the blood, I think. Apparently whatever magic the Sea King had used to let us breathe beneath the waves would prevent this from happening too. Or perhaps "the bends" was something that only afflicted mere humans, and the mermaids, unaware of this possibility, were rushing us up toward our deaths. There was nothing I could do about it in any case, but hold on and hope for the best as the mermaids towed us rapidly up through the water to the surface.

We did not die, but no sooner had my head emerged from the water than I was filled with a terrifying sensation. There was no air in my lungs and they were full of water! Having seconds ago been able to breathe comfortably and easily beneath the water, I was now suddenly choking, drowning, unable to draw breath now that my head was out of the water. The mermaid who held me, placed one great hand on my chest and pressed hard on my back with the flat of the other, forcing the water out of my lungs. I drew in a great gasping breath, but before I could do or say anything, she lifted me up out of the water and flung me through the air like a rag doll to her sister. I landed with my face pressed up against those enormous breasts, and then the sister picked me up and did the same—first holding me in her hand and striking me on the back to force water out of my lungs, and then flinging me back to her sister like a toy. This went on for some time, with the sisters laughing and tossing me back and forth between them like a sodden doll, but with each pass, I felt more of the water forced out of me and soon I was yelling at the top of my lungs, "Stop! Please, you're killing me! Just put me back in the boat, please!"

For I saw now that we had emerged alongside our ship, the *Siren's Song*, and the crew stood at the railings, watching open-mouthed as the mermaid sisters played their odd game of catch with the captain and me—and he, I could see, was getting just as rough treatment as I. The sisters laughed and continued tossing us back and forth between them.

"Doesn't want to play?" laughed one of the mermaids. "Silly little boy to come down into the water if he doesn't want to play with mermaids. We know lots of lovely games, don't we, sisters?" she said, laughing, and then threw me back to her companion.

"Oh, yes," said the one who had caught me, with a smile that showed rows of tiny spiked teeth, like a dolphin's, "lots of lovely games. Come down to the bottom again, and we will show you!" And she flung me back again.

"No, please!" I begged. "Just put me back."

"Spoilsport," she said, laughing. "If you want the boat so much, then swim for it."

And here, she flung me high into the air. Thirty feet or more above the surface of the water I rose and then came down with an enormous splash. The mermaids did not catch me that time, but floated there, watching, contemptuously it seemed to me, as I swam tiredly over to the side of the ship.

When I got there, the crew were hauling up the captain with a rope. I waited, treading water as best I could, while the captain was pulled to safety. After the captain had been hauled aboard the rope was lowered down a second time, and it was my turn. I hung onto the rope with both arms, far too tired to climb, while the crew hauled me up and pulled me onboard the *Siren's Song*. I collapsed onto the deck, still coughing up water. By the time I felt strong enough to turn back and look, the mermaids had vanished beneath the waves.

Chapter Thirteen

The Siren's Song

WHEN WE LEFT THE Sea King's palace, I had assumed that once we were back aboard the *Siren's Song* we would leave immediately to take the news of Greytail's imprisonment and the Sea King's demanded ransom back to the other White Wizards. However, despite our eagerness to return to the wizards' castle, we were becalmed for three days and could go nowhere. During that time, the captain and I recounted endlessly to the crew our adventures beneath the waves in the Sea King's palace. The tale took some time in the telling, both because the crew would interrupt constantly with questions, and because, once we had coughed all of the water out of our lungs, both the captain and I found ourselves easily fatigued and we became short of breath after even a few minutes of normal conversation.

On the fourth day, there was a change in the air. At first I did not recognize it for what it was, but from the crew's excitement I knew that something had changed. There was wind, a slight wind perhaps, but enough to fill the sails. The captain emerged from his cabin with a spring in his step for the first time since he had returned from beneath the waves. "It's time to sail," he said as he ran up to the poop deck. "She is calling."

"What do you mean?" I asked.

"My wife, she is calling. It is she who sends the wind to us, that we may answer her call."

"But I thought we were going back to the wizards' castle?" I protested.

"Your wizards have sent us no wind," he replied, evenly.

"How can you be so callous?" I shouted. "Just four days ago you saw our friend, Nutkin, being swallowed up inside that giant oyster. We promised we would go back to the wizards' castle to fetch the Sea King's pearl, so he'll release Nutkin. Have you forgotten?"

"I have not forgotten," he answered, "but returning to the wizards' castle would do us no good. The pearl is not there."

"How do you know?" I asked, "You told the Sea King you knew nothing about any stolen pearls."

"Not exactly," he replied. "I said that I did not steal the pearl, which is true enough, and that before that night I had no idea that any pearls had been stolen from the Sea King himself, and that is also true, though in hindsight it seems clear I should have suspected whence it came. But I know very well who stole it. It was the wizard whom you have been calling Nutkin. And it was my wife who gave her the spell to breathe underwater so she could get it. So, if we want answers, it is to her we must turn. You'll excuse me, Master Cork, I must speak to my crew."

He left me standing open-mouthed on the upper deck trying to make sense of this strange new twist in the tale. Greytail had stolen the pearl. To what end? And the captain's wife, a siren, had helped her do it. How, and why? And if he knew all this, why had the captain chosen to remain silent when the Sea King questioned him? I could make no sense of any of this. I scratched my head in bewilderment while the crew set sail and we got underway.

I had no sense of direction on the open ocean, and after the hours we had spent underwater, could not say from which direction we had come, nor in which we were now heading. But the captain seemed to know, and the ship's compass showed us to be heading northeast, while the port from which we had sailed was presumably somewhere far behind us to the west.

The wind grew stronger as we sailed and we picked up speed over the course of the day so that by evening we fairly flew over the waves, almost skipping from one wave crest to the next and the spray from the waves splashed up onto the deck with each one that we crested.

"Shall we reef the sails?" the mate, Peter, asked the captain.

"No time for that," the captain answered. "We will be nearing the shore soon, and you must stop up your ears and bind me before she begins to call again, or we will end up on the rocks.

"Aye-aye, sir," the mate replied gravely. He gave a quick nod to the captain and hurried away quickly below decks.

"What are they doing?" I asked the captain.

"Stopping their ears with wax so my wife's song will not drive them to madness."

As I watched, I saw that they were doing just that. The first mate, Peter, brought out a small pot filled with soft wax and went from one crew member to the next, plugging their ears with the gummy substance.

"And you?" I asked the captain.

"Her song is for me," the captain answered. "The crew must have their ears stopped so they can sail us in close to the shore without breaking the ship on the rocks. But I myself will be bound to the mast and take what madness she sends me. The crew know they must disregard any orders I give when I am bound, and in any case, their ears will be stopped."

"You must have done this before, then, to have it all worked out so neatly. Surely you must."

"Every year," he confirmed. "Each year at midsummer I return to her. But enough of talk. See to your ears."

The ship's mate, Peter, passed me the small pot filled with sticky wax, which he instructed me, by gesture, to place into my ears. His own ears, it seemed, being already plugged with the same stuff, he no longer even thought of speaking, but communicated through mime, both with me and the rest of the crew, who now set about binding their captain to one of the masts. I had thought that some sound at least would make its way through the wax, some hint of the siren's song, but the wax was stickier by far than beeswax and seemed to fill the very pores of my skin and so wrapped me in a shroud of cottony silence that made me think there must have been at least a hint of magic in the stuff..

The captain, now bound fast to the mast, listened with his head cocked to one side. He smiled oddly, and then, a wild, almost rabid look came into his eyes, and I could tell that the song had begun. Sweat poured down his face, and I could see him laughing and shouting and straining against his bonds, though I heard no sound. As the mist cleared, I could make out a rocky shore in the distance, toward which we were rapidly approaching. Calmly, methodically, the sailors brought us to within a few feet of one of the largest rocks, against which, had they heeded their maddened captain's urgings, we would surely have been smashed. The crew lowered the sails and set anchor, and then they did what seemed to me a most foolhardy thing. They began to untie their captain. No sooner had they loosed his bonds than he ran straight for the ship's rails and leaped over them with a mighty bound and disappeared beneath the waves. I ran over to the rail to see where he might have gone, but there was no trace of him. I turned back to the crew to see if they would attempt to rescue him, but they did nothing, but went about their duties as if nothing had happened. I wondered that they did nothing to try and save their captain. Were they, too, enchanted? True, none of them was trying to leap over the side of the ship, but their very calmness seemed as strange to me as the captain's sudden dive into the sea.

As I watched, the ship's mate went into the captain's cabin and brought out an hourglass, which he set on the deck. I waited, puzzled, wondering what was happening as the crew waited for the sand to run out of the hourglass. When the hour had run out, the mate beckoned to one of the crew, Kostas, the Greek, a big barrel-chested man, who came and wrapped his arms around the mate's waist. Slowly, cautiously, the mate reached up and began to pull the wax from one of his own ears while the rest of the crew looked on anxiously. When he had got one ear unstoppered, he shook his head as if to clear it of water, listened for a moment, and then nodded to the crew, who began to unstopper their own ears, and I did likewise.

When we could talk again, I asked Peter, "Why did you untie the captain?"

"Because he ordered us to," he said. "I am the ship's mate and I follow the captain's orders."

"But the captain was mad," I said. "You knew that. That's why you all stoppered your ears, so you would not become mad yourselves, isn't that true? And besides, if your ears were stoppered, how could you hear him?"

Peter laughed at my confusion. "Nay, this was before. These orders were given long before he heard the song again this time. Though I wonder sometimes if perhaps he hears it in his sleep, even when he's ashore. But this is the way we've always done it, and he's always come back before."

"But where is he?" I asked.

"Below," he said, nodding toward the water, "with her."

Her, presumably being his siren wife. I wondered again at the crew's calm acceptance of this bizarre situation, although compared to what I myself had been through just a few days ago, I suppose this seemed almost normal.

"So what do we do now?" I asked, staring at the waves lapping against the side of the ship.

"We wait," he said, simply, like one who had spent many hours in his life doing just that and saw no problem continuing to wait as long as necessary if that was what his captain had ordered. My own impatience to learn more about this stolen pearl and to try to find a way to ransom Greytail did nothing to change the situation, so I tried to emulate Peter's stoic attitude and practice waiting patiently. I cannot say that I felt truly patient while I waited, but I did manage to keep from throwing myself overboard in search of the captain, so I guess I was at least partly successful.

Chapter Fourteen

The Captain's Wife

AFTER THREE DAYS, THE captain reemerged from beneath the waves. The mate, Peter, was the first to notice. We had been standing by the ship's rail, talking of nothing in particular, as we had been doing for most of the past three days, when suddenly he started and called for a rope to be brought to him, and quickly. I wondered what he had seen that had caused him to react like that, then looked out over the rail and saw, perhaps ten yards from the side of the ship, the captain's head bobbing above the waves, and then an arm waving.

"Never mind about the rope!" the captain called. "I'm not ready to come aboard yet. Not by half. But send Master Cork down to me. It's time to see if he floats."

"What?" Peter shouted back.

"Master Cork, there beside you at the rail. Pray send him overboard to join me. Don't bother with the dinghy, he'll do as he is."

I had but a moment to ponder whether this was an invitation or a death sentence he had just ordered for me when two of the crew grabbed me by the arms.

"Wait, what are you doing?" I asked, shocked.

One of them said to me, not unkindly, "You heard the captain, Master Cork. Over the rail you go, then." And with no more ceremony than that, they lifted me up bodily and flung me from the deck into the sea.

I landed with a splash and began to tread water, finding that my cloak dragged heavily in the waves, while the captain began to swim over to me.

"Well, Master Cork, it seems you float well enough," he said by way of greeting. "But we'll be going below for a bit, so I suggest you pop this in your mouth and give it a chew before we go down, for the air's a bit thin below the water, if you catch my drift." And so saying, he handed me what looked like a piece of greenish-grey seaweed.

You would think that having just recently had the unusual experience of being in the Sea King's palace and being able to breathe underwater might have cured me forever of any fear of drowning, but in fact just the reverse was true. I knew now just how deep the ocean's floor was, and how it felt to come up and find that your lungs were full of water, leaving no room for air.

"You mean you want me to go back under the water again, like in the Sea King's palace?"

"Just so, lad. Although I'm afraid my Lady's accommodations are not so grand as the Sea King's"

"That's all right. You can go on without me. I'm happy enough staying aboard the *Siren's Song* while you visit with your wife."

He laughed. "So you'll stay aboard with the crew and miss the chance of seeing she for whom the *Siren's Song* is named? I thought you had more spirit of adventure than that."

"Adventures are fine things when they're told around the fireplace in the evening, but under the water with no place to stand and no way to breathe is another thing altogether."

"Ah, but that's what the seaweed's for. So you don't have to worry about breathing underwater. And, as I recall, you were the one who was all fired up to find out what had happened to the Sea King's pearl. If you want answers, my wife is the one who has them, and if you want to talk to her you must go below."

Hesitantly, I took the greenish-grey piece of seaweed, put it in my mouth and began to chew. After a moment, a choking, burning sensation began to fill the back of my throat. I gagged and started to spit out the seaweed.

"Nay, lad," said the captain. "Don't be spittin' that out, just yet. Not if you want to be able to catch your breath below. Take a mouthful of water to ease your throat."

I cupped a mouthful of the briny seawater with my hands and splashed it into my mouth, then spluttered as it went down the wrong way. To my surprise, the water did not choke me as it entered my lungs but filled me like a breath of fresh air.

"That's good enough then," said the captain and, grabbing me by the wrist, dove beneath the waves.

I held my breath as long as I could—despite the captain's hints that the seaweed, or whatever it was he had given me, would let me breathe beneath the waves as we had in the Halls of the Sea King. My time above the waves since we had left those halls had served to reawaken my instinctual fear of drowning that had somehow been held in abeyance before by the Sea King's powers. But when my lungs could hold out no longer, I opened my mouth and sucked in the water, both longing for and dreading its cold rush into my body. The seaweed's magic worked, seemingly as well as the Sea King's, and I breathed the salt water as easily and comfortably as the air above.

"Stop holding your breath then and swim," the captain commanded and down we went. Down and farther down still we dove, until the light of the sun on the surface above was just a memory and dark shadows among the forest of kelp fronds were all that I could see.

At last we reached the bottom and we walked along the murky ocean floor, with the impossibly tall strands of kelp towering above our heads like the trees of a forest. After a time, we came to a cave-like opening in the seafloor that reminded me of the mouth of some enormous creature. To my surprise, rather than going around this mysterious opening, the captain dove down into it. Suppressing my fear, I followed the captain down into this chthonic orifice. Ahead of us, the cave extended to form a tunnel, lined with rocky outcroppings, which after a hundred feet or so leveled off, turned, and began to climb back up towards the surface. There was no light in the tunnel, so I had no sense of where we might be going, except up, nor what dangers might be lurking in the crevices of its rock walls, but I could feel the waves from the captain's feet ahead of me as I struggled, blindly, to keep up.

Gradually the tunnel grew lighter, and soon I could see the surface of the water above me. As it reached the surface, the tunnel widened into a large pool, and we emerged beside a small beach in a dark grotto, from which I could see no exit, although light came in from small openings in the rock walls above us, so I knew we had arrived above the surface of the water and not just entered into some strange subterranean bubble. On a rock, in the center of the pool, sat she who I instantly felt certain must be the captain's wife.

Her resemblances to both their daughter and to her own carved image on the prow of the Siren's Song were as striking as the differences were jarring, as when something seen a thousand times in counterfeit, copies of a famous painting or images of some iconic building perhaps, is glimpsed for the first time, real and immediate. And just as the carved figureheads on the other ships in port had seemed dead wooden blocks beside the intricately carved and painted figure on the prow of the Siren's Song, so now did that carved image seem dull and lifeless when I beheld its original.

She was taller by far than the captain himself, though not of the same gargantuan proportions as the Sea King and his daughters. And where their tails had been covered in soft brown fur, like a seal's, hers glittered with thousands of iridescent scales. From the waist up, she was human in form, except for her hair, which was a mass of silver-grey fronds that fell over her shoulders. She was clothed in nothing but her own aura of power, but so great was that aura that, had the captain not been standing beside me at that moment, I would scarcely have dared approach her.

"Come hither, traveler," she bade me gently, and I approached. "So you are the visitor from another world my husband speaks of, who dined with him in the Halls of the Sea King, and saw a wizard eaten by an oyster. Is that your tale?"

"That is some portion of my tale, my lady," I answered. "Though for my part, I hope that what the Sea King said is true and that the wizard you speak of is not eaten, but merely held captive until we can ransom her with the Sea King's pearl, which pearl, your husband tells me, was stolen from the Sea King himself by that same wizard who he now holds captive. And that you yourself aided the wizard in this theft."

She raised her brows at this, and I saw that the brows of her eyes, too, were made of silvery fronds.

"My husband speaks very freely if he told you this much," the siren answered. "And I marvel that the Sea King did not close you up in a shell, husband, if you said so much within his halls, for surely you would be a better gage for my good conduct, as he would see it, than that poor wizard."

"Nay, wife, I said not so much," the captain said, "and certainly not so much within His Majesty's halls. Indeed, I told him, truthfully, that I only learned that night that any pearls had been stolen *from him*, and that much is true, for you never told me whence came the giant pearl."

"And the wizard?" I asked. "You told the Sea King that before that night you had no idea that Nutkin could be the thief. But once we were back on board the Siren's Song, you told me that you were *sure* Nutkin was the thief."

"But of course. Since I did not know before that night that the pearl had been stolen, I could have no idea of the thief's identity. And before I heard your tale of a talking squirrel, whom you named as the wizard Greytail when you told the tale to the Sea King, or Nutkin as she introduced herself to me, I had no reason to connect that wizard's name with another mysterious visitor who came to these shores many years ago, when my daughter was but a babe."

"And who was that mysterious visitor?" I asked.

"A sea otter," he said. "But no ordinary one. Although in appearance it was perfectly like its counterparts, it had such a lively aspect of keen intelligence that I felt sure its mind was the equal, if not the superior, of any man's. Moreover, my wife spent many long hours closeted with this beast—so much so that I began to wonder if sirens were some species of sea witch, and this otter her new familiar. Then it went away for a period of three days, and when it returned, it carried in its paws a pearl of such size and beauty that I have never seen its equal. Thus, when I heard the Sea King's story and your own, putting two and two together, I deduced that the oddly behaving otter and your shape-changing wizard might be—must be—one and the same. Am I right, wife?"

The siren hesitated before answering. "You speak very freely in front of this visitor from another world, husband," she said at length, "and of things whose full import you little understand."

"And whose is the fault for that, wife?" the captain replied. "If you had told me in full of these things before I would not have to guess at their import."

"True enough," she said after another long pause. "And your guess may be true as well, as far as I know. It was indeed a wizard who stole the pearl from the Sea King, though I never saw him in any form but the otter's."

"What was his name?" I asked.

"A wizard's name means little," she replied. "They change them oftener than they change their cloaks. For my part, I knew him only as Otter, but 'twas plain enough that he was a wizard, whatever his shape."

"You say 'he,' I notice," I said, persisting. "But the wizard Greytail who was with us in the Halls of the Sea King was female. I am certain of that."

"Are you?" the siren said, archly. "Then perhaps she was. And so, perhaps the wizard I knew as Otter was a different one. Although as I look back I cannot recall if I ever looked closely enough to tell if Otter was male or female, though I thought of him as 'he.' For that matter, it seems to me that a wizard who can change from human to squirrel, or human to otter, and back again, could surely manage so small a change as from male to female or vice versa."

I considered that. It seemed logical enough, although for some reason I found it more disturbing to contemplate a creature who drifted in and out of sexes than one who shifted species at will. I recalled my brief glimpse of Greytail's definitely female form when we awoke in the Halls of the Sea King and felt jolted to think that this form might be no more "real" than the squirrel's or the otter's. Did wizards have a "true" form at all and, if so, what was it? Or was each form "true" only in the moment it existed, just as being a baby and a man might each be true, though very different, forms of being the same human person? My head swam as I struggled to bring myself back to the concrete realities of our current peculiar situation.

"In any case," I said at last, "the pearl is here, so we can ransom Greytail."

"You are presumptuous, visitor from another world," the siren said. "In the first place, the pearl is not here. And in the second place, and perhaps more importantly, the pearl is not yours to give, even were it here."

I stood, momentarily tongue-tied by this, staring up at the siren with her iridescent grey-blue eyes that glared back at me, inscrutable, from atop her rock.

"I beg your pardon," I said at last, biting back the flood of anger I felt ready to overwhelm my deliberately patient words. "I presumed that were the pearl in your possession, you would be as willing as I to use it to ransom a friend's life. For, whatever her form, Greytail was a friend to me and to your husband, or so it seemed to me. But, as you say, I am presumptuous."

She laughed. "Presumptuous indeed, if you would lecture a siren on politeness in her own cave. These are not the Halls of the Sea King, I grant you," she said, waving her hand airily to indicate the watery cavern in which we stood, "Nor I so great a monarch as he, perhaps. But at the sound of my song, you would dash your brains out willingly against these rocks. Do you doubt it?" she demanded.

"I do not," I said, boldly enough I thought, though my eyes were drawn against my will from her face to the side of the boulder on which she sat, picturing what it would feel like to hurl myself against it.

"And yet," she continued, "You would lecture me still?"

"It is as you have said," I persisted. "I am presumptuous. I thought of my friend's life, never doubting that you would be as eager to ransom it as I, and gave no thought to my own peril."

She snorted. And it may have been only self-deception on my part, but I fancied that she seemed impressed in spite of herself by my reply.

"In any case," I continued, "if, as you say, the pearl is not here, it will us do little good to discuss what we ought to do with it—unless you know where else I should seek it?"

Again she gave a snort in reply.

"As to where it is," she said, "I have some idea, but no sure knowledge. But as to whether you should seek it, that is another matter. And I would say that you should not."

"But why should I not seek it?" I asked, "if you have at least some idea of where it may be, and if, by finding it, I can ransom my friend's life?"

Again, she seemed to hesitate before replying. "You may, perhaps, be able to ransom your friend's life with this pearl if you return it to the Sea King. But, if you do so, you will doom my sisters and me to cruel subjugation and perhaps even death at the hands of the Sea King and his mermen. For although he claims it as his own, and rails that it has been stolen from him, the pearl you speak of was stolen by the Sea King himself from the diadem of the Siren Queen. From my mother he stole it, and with it, our power over those creatures that move in the depths of the sea. With it, he and his mermen overwhelmed my mother's armies, scattering my sisters, like me, to the rocky shores of the far corners of the seven seas. As it was my mother's, so it is mine by right of birth, and what I could not take by force of arms, I took by stealth, enlisting the wizard, who I knew as Otter, to help me."

"But I thought you said you did not have the pearl."

"I don't," the siren replied. "Even though I regained the pearl, and thus a measure of relief, if not true independence from the Sea King's domination, I still do not dare to wear it openly with our forces weak and scattered as they are."

"And your mother, the Siren Queen, what of her?" I asked. "For did you not tell me that the pearl was hers?"

"She is dead, or else held captive by the Sea King in some dark dungeon, for I have had no word of her since our disastrous defeat, though my spies have searched everywhere beneath the waves these past twenty years."

"So where is the pearl?" I asked.

Again, the siren hesitated before replying. But having said so much, it seemed she could not stop herself from telling all. "As I told you," she said, "I do not know, though I have my guesses. In any case, the last I saw of it was when I entrusted it to that same wizard, Otter, of whom I told you."

"What?" the captain shouted. "The chiefest treasure of your realm, a prize over which whole armies of mermen and sirens contend, and you gave it to the wizards?"

"Not gave, entrusted," she replied.

"A small enough difference where wizards are concerned," her husband countered. "Have you not noticed how they seek to gather every treasure or object of power unto themselves?"

"That may be," she said. "But I had no means to ensure its safety here, this close to the Sea King's realms. And likewise, they had no means to safeguard their greatest treasure, a great green gemstone, reputed to be the very heartstone of a cruel dragon, who to this day still wreaks devastation on the countryside surrounding the wizards' tower, seeking to discover its whereabouts. So we agreed that each of us would keep guard over the other's treasure, even as they have kept guard over our daughter during the times you were at sea."

"If that is what they call guarding, then they are fickle guardians indeed," the captain said.

"Has any harm befallen her?" asked the siren, who for the first time appeared worried.

"None that I know of," the captain reassured her, "but no thanks do I give to the wizards for that, for it is rare indeed that I ever saw a wizard anywhere near the Pickled Parrot. At least that had been true until Greytail and Master Cork here stepped into the alehouse."

"Then I count the job well done, if they can keep such watch that a woman as young as she can keep a tavern among a town full of bloodthirsty humans and come to no harm, and you none the wiser of the means they employ to safeguard her," the siren replied.

"If they've any means beyond hoping for good luck, I've seen no trace of them," the captain said, "but perhaps, as you say, they have means that are invisible to me. In any case, all this brings us no nearer the answer to our question: How shall we ransom Greytail? Unless you think the Sea King would accept a dragon's heart in lieu of the contested pearl?"

The siren looked startled at this suggestion but then shook her head, saying, "The stone is not mine to give, any more than the pearl belongs to the wizards. And I will not betray their trust in me, even to ransom one of their own, and even supposing that the Sea King would accept such a substitution. And we still have not agreed that ransoming Greytail is the right thing to do."

"Do you mean," I shouted, "that after all you have told me, you still propose to leave Greytail to rot inside that oversized oyster?"

"I did not say that," she replied. "I merely said that we have not agreed that ransoming Greytail is the best course of action. After all, I did not ransom my mother's pearl from the Sea King, but I was able to get it back all the same."

"By stealing it, you mean?" I asked. "Are you proposing then that we should steal Greytail back from the Sea King?"

"Is it stealing to take back what is rightfully yours?" the siren demanded. "I say no. And, yes, I am proposing that we, or rather you, Master Cork, though you may wish a new name for the present enterprise, should rescue—and *rescue*, I think, would be a far better term than *steal* under the circumstances—Master Greytail, or Mistress Greytail if you prefer, from the Sea King's clutches."

"And how do you suppose that I should do that?" I asked.

"Did you not tell the Sea King, or so my husband recounted to me, that the Black Dragon had hired you as a burglar? That being the case, I would think that you might have some ideas of your own, Master Burglar."

It was odd to hear her addressing me with words that were so like those of the Black Dragon, and doubly so since in my own world I had never stolen so much as a candy bar. Why, I wondered, did the people in this world insist on thinking that I was some sort of master thief? Her words reminded me, too, of my promise to the Black Dragon to find the green stone, which I had since learned was the dragon's heart, as well as of the wizards' warnings of the consequences that would befall me if I were to keep that promise. It occurred to me for one guilty moment that the stone was in all likelihood somewhere in this very cave, and could I but locate it, I could perhaps return to my own world and forget all about wizards, dragons, Sea Kings, sirens, and all their attendant troubles. There would be, of course, the minor difficulty of returning the stone to the dragon, who was now on the far side of the ocean from me, as well as that annoying clause in my "contract" with the dragon, if you could call it that, "survival not guaranteed." I decided I could worry about all that after I had rescued Greytail (so persuasive was the siren that it seemed as if I had already agreed to this). After all, the old wizard I had dined with that night had seemed sure that he could recreate the dragon's book (or make one that was close enough for my purposes) if only I could provide him with some unicorn blood and a few feathers from a phoenix. How hard could that be for someone who could rescue captured wizards from the Halls of the Sea King? Though that mission, too, seemed as if it should have a clause reading, "survival not guaranteed."

"You seem unsure of yourself, Master Burglar," the siren said. "Perhaps I will be able to offer you a few suggestions after we have dined."

I looked around the cave, the floor of which was covered almost entirely with water, save for the boulder where the siren sat and the small rocky beach behind her. Unlike in the Halls of the Sea King, here there were no servants waiting to bring out laden tables when she clapped her hands, or none that I could see at any rate, and I wondered what it was she proposed to dine upon.

The question was answered before I could ask it. With a bound, the siren dove from her rock and disappeared beneath the waves. The water's surface churned as she splashed about doing something I could not see. Then she reemerged, holding in one hand a crab whose body was nearly as large as my head with legs nearly two feet in length. With a sudden sharp blow, she cracked the crab's body against the boulder she had been sitting on, and then began to tear off the legs, handing the first one to me, and the second to her husband.

I looked at the enormous crab leg in my hand, uncertain of how to proceed, until I saw the captain pick up a rock, slightly smaller than his fist, and, using this as a hammer and the side of the boulder as an anvil, begin to crack open the hard shell and pick out the bits of soft meat hidden within. I copied him, though somewhat less expertly, and was surprised at how good the uncooked crab meat tasted. The siren herself had no need of such crude tableware as our rocks and simply ripped the crab to pieces with her hands. Her skin, I realized, must be tougher than leather, since the spines on the crab's shell did not seem to bother her in the least.

After we had eaten the crab, the siren disappeared once more beneath the water, coming up this time with a sea urchin, which she dispatched with similar ease. Sirens, like Sea Kings it seemed, liked their food not merely fresh, but raw. For dessert there were mussels, which the captain opened using a long knife that he wore at his belt, but his wife cracked hers like peanuts with her teeth, which must have been harder than any nutcracker. There was no water, at least none that was drinkable. The siren, I guessed, might have no need of fresh water, but I wondered what her husband, the captain, had drunk for the three days he had been absent from the ship. Perhaps the odd seaweed he had given me to chew, which allowed us to breathe underwater, overcame the need to drink as well—though for my part, I found myself becoming increasingly thirsty as we ate this odd meal.

"Is there water?" I asked at last, my tongue feeling thick with the taste of salt water and raw crab meat, "drinkable water I mean?"

"There is a spring on shore not far from here," the captain answered, surprising me. Though I had seen the rocky coast when we laid anchor a few days before, I had been so long either above or below the waves these past weeks, I had almost ceased to believe in life on land.

"Come, I'll show you," the captain said and led the way to the rocky beach at the back of the cave.

We picked our way towards the rear of the cave among the mass of slippery rocks and stalactites hanging down from the roof of the cave. At first I had taken these to form a solid wall, but following the captain, I saw there was a place where it was possible to squeeze between the rocks into a narrow twisty passageway that led up towards the roof of the cave. In the lower part of the passageway the floor was covered knee-deep in water, and we had to step carefully to avoid twisting an ankle among the sharp rocks. As we went farther back, the level of the water dropped, and only then did I realize we were ascending. Soon we emerged into a small dark cave which sat above the one where we had been dining with the captain's wife. The entrance to this smaller cave was blocked by a large boulder. However, there was a small opening at the top of the cave, a little wider than my shoulders and, scrambling up the sloping cave walls, we were able to reach out and grasp the lip of this opening and pull ourselves through.

When we emerged, we were on a flat outcropping of rock about halfway up a bank of cliffs that rose from the sea to meet a narrow strip of land that stretched from the mainland to a point some fifty yards above our heads. There was a kind of trail leading from the promontory where we stood up toward the top of the cliffs. In places it was level enough that we could walk easily along a ribbon-like path up the cliff face. In others, the path stopped abruptly and we had to climb to reach the start of the next segment of the path above us. I tried not to look down as we made these short ascents, as I had never been much of a climber, and the sea was a long way below. At length, we reached the top, and I looked down to see the *Siren's Song* below us, still floating at anchor in the little bay formed by the narrow strip of rock on whose pinnacle we now stood. Looking back toward the mainland, I saw that where the strip of rock joined the main wall of cliffs there was a further fearsome ascent to be made if one wished to reach the plateau above, and my heart sank at the thought of the steeper climb to come. However, when we reached the base of the cliff bank, I saw that there was a trickle of water seeping from a crack in the rock which emptied into a small pool somewhat larger than a bathtub. I tasted it and found that the water was sweet. We each drank our fill and then stripped to wash the salt grime from our bodies. Our clothes too we washed in the little pool of fresh water, and then spread them out on the rocks to dry in the sun. I lay in the sun with my eyes closed, feeling the ocean breeze blowing over my skin and, though I was now on dry land for the first time in weeks, it seemed I could still feel the pitch and yaw of the waves in the ground beneath me.

I thought back to when I had stood before the river guardian, Greytail as I now guessed, and been forced to strip before crossing the river into the territory of the White Wizards. Then, being naked in front of the demanding stranger had made me feel vulnerable, helpless even, which I suppose may have been the true intent as much as the inspection served to guard against intrusions by the servants of the Black Dragon. Here, I felt only calm, as I lay naked in the sunshine with my eyes closed.

"Careful there," said the captain, waking me from my reverie, "or you'll wake to find yourself feeding the fishes, if you wake at all. We're not at the top by a long shot, but it's still a fair ways down."

I looked and saw that he was right. The rock on which I had been lying was perhaps a yard in width, wide enough for me to stretch out easily. But, were I to roll off the edge of that rock, there was a hundred-yard drop onto jagged boulders at the water's edge below me. I wondered if these were the rocks onto which the sirens' songs lured their victims, or whether the captain's wife had chosen some new location to hide her human husband when she decided (if one can speak of deciding where the heart is concerned) to break with tradition and allow her mate to remain alive.

"I'm glad we don't have to climb all that way today," I said, pointing at the rocky cliffs above us.

"Not today, perhaps," the captain answered, "but soon enough."

"But why?" I asked, looking up at the cliffs with apprehension.

"These are the Unicorn Isles," the captain said. "And if I recall correctly from what you said in the Halls of the Sea King, it was unicorns that you and Master Greytail proposed to hunt when you hired passage on my ship."

"But what about rescuing Greytail from the Sea King?" I asked.

"To be sure," he said, "that will be a challenge. A challenge for which you will be far more fit once you have completed your hunt for the unicorn and the phoenix."

"Why is that?" I asked, puzzled.

"To rescue Greytail," he replied, "you will need to return to the Halls of the Sea King. And while my wife's magic would allow you to breathe beneath the waves, as you have seen, your present form is not particularly well suited to swimming, besides being altogether too well known to the Sea King and his guards. So, you will need a new form for this mission, I think."

"A new form?"

"Yes, a new form. An otter, perhaps, like your wizard friend, although since the last otter to visit the Sea King's halls made off with his magic pearl, perhaps an otter would not be the best choice. An octopus might be good, since they have so many arms, although I did notice that the Sea King seemed rather fond of octopus as a dinner entrée. We shall have to give the matter some thought."

"We can give the matter all the thought you like, but it will do no good," I said, exasperated. "For all my borrowed robes, I am no wizard, as I think you will have guessed."

"I would not be so sure, Master Cork," the captain replied. "Let us say, rather, that if you are a wizard, you have not yet learned how to use your powers."

"Which comes to much the same thing, under the present circumstances," I replied.

"Not at all," said the captain. "The first is a statement of impossibility. It says there are certain things you cannot do, now or ever. The second is a statement of possibility. It says that we do not yet know what you may do. Whole worlds and many lifetimes can lie between those two statements."

"Very philosophical for a sea captain," I said.

"And who should be more philosophical than a captain of the sea?" he answered.

"So you have said, but none of this tells me why hunting for mythical beasts should make me better prepared to rescue Greytail," I grumbled.

"It is precisely because they are mythical—or more precisely, because they are magical—that they will be useful to you. Did you not say that the Order of Wizards had sent you in search of unicorn's blood and the feathers of a phoenix?"

"Yes," I said, "but that was to make a book of magical maps, so I don't see how that will help me to rescue Greytail, unless you are suggesting that I could use the book to travel to the Halls of the Sea King?"

"An interesting thought," said the captain, "but that would require that you return to the wizards' tower and get them to make it for you, since I have no idea of how such a book could be made, even if I had the magical elements you mention. Shape-shifting, however, I do have some knowledge of, and my wife even more, being, as she is, a magical creature herself. And, as it happens, the two essential ingredients for the shape-shifting potion (at least the one I am familiar with) are unicorn's blood and phoenix feathers."

"What? You're sure?" I shouted.

"Quite sure," he said. "This is news to you, I take it. It makes me wonder if perhaps the wizards had more than mapmaking on their minds when they sent you on this quest."

"What do you mean?" I asked.

"Well, I do not know for certain what means the wizards employ to change their shapes. However, if the spell is the same one that I am familiar with, then they too would need to replenish their supplies of unicorn blood and phoenix feathers from time to time. It would be convenient, would it not, from their point of view, if in offering to help you return to your own world they arranged that at the same time you should be the one to replenish their larder?"

I considered this. Given what I had seen of the behavior of members of the Order of Wizards' so far, it seemed all too likely to be true. On the other hand, had they offered me this bargain explicitly, that in exchange for their help in returning to my world, I would provide them with the blood of a unicorn and the feathers of a phoenix, I would probably have agreed. After all, what choice did I really have if I wanted to return home? I could, of course, have gone back empty-handed to the Black Dragon, but that seemed likely to result in my being eaten, a possibility I was not eager to put to the test. On the other hand, I felt irked, to say the least, that the wizards had, apparently, not dealt openly with me and had instead tricked me into doing their bidding. It occurred to me only then that the captain and the siren might be doing likewise.

"And so, instead of the wizards' larder, it is now yours and your wife's that I will be filling should I succeed in this absurd quest?" I asked.

"As it happens, yes," the captain answered. "Though I will point out that it is you who are so eager to rush out and rescue Greytail. I seek merely to provide you with the means to do so. You may, of course, refuse to have anything to do with this proposal, or with me for that matter, but unless you plan to spend the rest of your brief life sitting on that rock, you must either climb up to the summit or climb back down—or fall down, if you are not careful — to the sea below. As it is rather a long swim from here to anywhere else in the world, I would suggest climbing up. What you do at that point about the unicorn blood and phoenix feathers is, of course, up to you."

Put that way it sounded almost reasonable. It was a strange thing, I noticed, that all of the people I had met on this world managed to sound reasonable while they got me to do whatever it was they wanted me to do, all while pretending that they were merely doing me a favor. So I suppose that at least in that way, this world was not so different from my own.

I looked out once more at the sea, and then down to where the *Siren's Song* lay at anchor in the bay. It seemed that if I were to return to my own world, a prospect that was seeming more hopeless with each passing day, I would first need to return to the now distant continent where I had met the Black Dragon. And for that I would need a ship, which meant, of course, making peace with Captain Fleischman.

"So . . ." I asked after a pause. "Just how does one go about hunting unicorns?"

Chapter Fifteen

The Unicorn Isles

WHEN OUR CLOTHES HAD finished drying in the sun, we dressed and returned to the siren's cave by the same tortuous route we had taken coming up to the spring. And while the brief climb we had made on the way up had been difficult, going down was ten times worse. For, of course, going up I could see each handhold or foothold before I placed my weight on it, but going down I had no such luxury. I think had it not been for Captain Fleischman, who went before me each time and told me where to place my feet as I descended, I would surely have fallen onto the rocks below. I wondered briefly why we had bothered washing our clothes in the spring, as we were soon knee-deep, and then waist-deep, in the salt water of the cave. But at least I had had the brief moment of feeling clean and dry.

The cave was empty when we returned to it, but the captain seemed unperturbed by his wife's absence. He explained to me that while this cave was her home, or one of them at any rate, she was not trapped in the cave and often ventured out of it to hunt for food or just for the joy of swimming in the open sea. Sharks and other predators of the deep held no terror for her. She could outswim all but the fastest of them and with her magic even the great toothed whales were no danger to her. It was only the Sea King and his minions that she feared and this far from the Sea King's palace she was unlikely to run into any of these.

She returned just before sunset and brought dinner with her. As perhaps I should have anticipated, we dined again on fresh-caught seafood, a giant octopus this time. I thanked her politely and swallowed the raw rubbery flesh but cannot say that I really enjoyed it. The captain and his wife, in contrast, ate theirs with evident relish, as well as two large crabs and some sort of pale green seaweed, which I found to be rubbery and tasteless except for the briny flavor of the seawater, but they evidently found it delicious. No accounting for taste, I suppose.

After we had eaten, we returned to the topic of hunting unicorns. The siren, whose name was as unpronounceable to me as the chirping of the dolphins, seconded her husband in urging me to go up to the high plateau at the top of the cliffs known as the Unicorn Plain and to hunt for one of these magical beasts. She, too, saw the use of a transformation potion as the surest way into the palace of the Sea King, and thus, my best hope for rescuing Greytail. I had my doubts about this as well as doubts about my ability to hunt and kill a unicorn but, absent any better plan, I kept those doubts to myself.

"I will give you this," the siren said, handing me a long spear tipped with a white horn with spiral markings. It reminded me of the pictures I had seen of unicorn horns in story books and in the tapestries at the Cloisters.

"Is the tip made of unicorn horn?" I asked, incredulous.

"Nothing so exotic, I'm afraid," she answered, laughing at my naiveté. "It's merely narwhal, though I suppose the resemblance might be close enough to fool someone with little experience of either."

"And how do I use it?" I asked, turning the spear uncertainly in my hands.

"That's up to you," she replied. "If you have a good arm and can get close enough, you can hurl it like a harpoon. Otherwise your best bet may be to find a place where you can lie in wait and lunge at the unicorn when it comes near. Finally, if you see one out in the open, it may charge you. If you stand your ground and brace the spear against the ground, you might be able to spear it before it gores you."

"And if not?" I asked.

"Do you believe in an afterlife?" she asked.

"I'm not sure."

"It might be a good time to decide," she said, "since if you fail to kill the unicorn, you could soon have the opportunity to find out."

I had always considered the question to be somewhat pointless, figuring that I would find out, or not, as the case might be, when the time came. The thought that that time might come sooner rather than later was, however, not particularly welcome.

"And the phoenix?" I asked, as if with those few words of hers I had somehow absorbed all the fine points there might be to the art of unicorn hunting.

"The phoenix will be found near the peaks of the mountains surrounding the Unicorn Plain. And I would suppose that the techniques for hunting them would be much the same as for the unicorns, with the addition, of course, that you must catch it on the ground if you are to make use of your spear. Unless, of course, you are extraordinarily gifted at spear throwing."

Having never thrown a spear in my life and having only the one spear with which to practice, it seemed highly doubtful that my first cast would be worthy of someone "extraordinarily gifted" with a spear. A pike then, and not a javelin, my weapon must be.

"Take these also," the captain said, handing me two large leather flasks. "The first you can fill with water at the spring, the second will be for the unicorn's blood, should you succeed."

"And the phoenix feathers?" I asked.

The captain laughed.

"So, you're feeling that sure of yourself, are you?"

"No," I replied, "I'm not feeling sure of myself at all, but I would feel foolish indeed if I somehow succeeded in my quest and then had nothing to carry the feathers back in."

"And have you no purse or hidden pocket under that fine wizard's cloak?" he asked

"None that I can find," I said, "save the small and rather soggy pockets in my pants, but I'm not sure how well the feathers would fare in those."

"Then take this," the captain said and handed me a large leather wallet, handsomely stitched with gold-colored thread. I looked inside, but it was empty. Whatever purse the captain kept his gold in, it was not this.

We slept that night on the damp, rocky shore of the siren's cave. Or rather, I slept. I do not know exactly when my hosts left me during the night, but when I awoke to the first pale rays of the sun coming through the small openings in the rock walls above me, they were gone. I walked around as much of the cave as I could negotiate while keeping my head above water, but there was no sign of them. Presumably they had gone out through the opening in the bottom of the cave, but with no more of the magic seaweed that the captain had given me yesterday at my disposal, I could not go out the way I had come in. Whether they were gone for a few moments or a few days I had no idea.

I considered my options. With my hosts gone, I was free to search the cavern for the mysterious green stone, which might lie even now within a few feet of where I was standing. On the other hand, even if I found the stone, I still had no way of getting back to the port we had set out from, and I shuddered to think what the captain's wife might do to me were she to return and find me with the green stone in my possession. The wizards, too, would no doubt take a dim view of my upsetting their arrangement with the siren by making off with the dragon's heart. And, of course, without the help of either the siren or the wizards I had no way to make the shape-shifting potion the captain had mentioned and thus, no way to rescue Greytail. Unicorn blood and phoenix feathers it must be then.

Before setting out, I paused to think about how I was going to be able to climb while carrying the various items I would need. The two flasks had leather straps that I looped crosswise over my shoulders. After some thought, I slid the spear behind me under the crossed straps from the flasks, then removed my belt and fastened it around the outside of the cloak over the spear. Finally, I tucked the leather wallet under my belt in front of me.

Feeling more than a little awkward with all of these things strapped, none too securely, to my body, I set out, back up through the tunnel I had taken the day before with the captain, then out through the hole at the top of the cave. When I came to the spring, I did as the captain had suggested and filled one of the two flasks with water. I looked around. There was no obvious path leading to the top. But as a certain squirrel had taught me, who says the road to the top, is always a road?

The day before, we had made a series of short ascents, moving from one segment of the path to the next. Today there was no path, and no sure-footed captain in front of me to point out the way. Instead, I climbed awkwardly, inching my way cautiously upward from one precarious handhold to the next. In some places, there were no handholds at all, but merely crevices in the rock face, an arm's span or less in width. In such places, I could ascend only by pressing my arms and legs out to the sides and "walking" up through the void like a spider. Had it been possible, I might have turned around and climbed back down but, having started my climb, down would be even more perilous than continuing up.

In one such place, as I stood suspended in midair, with my hands and feet pressed tight against the rock walls and only thin air beneath me, I caught sight of a great red-and-gold bird with two long tail feathers trailing behind it like the tail of a pheasant, but more brilliantly colored than any bird I had ever seen in my own world. I hung, wedged into the crevice in the rock wall, helplessly watching my prey soar up and away from me but could no more have brought it down than I could have taken wing myself and flown. I kept climbing, trying to move carefully, focusing only on the next hand or foothold in front of me, and not on the prize that might be waiting for me at the summit, but by the time I reached the top of the cliffs, the phoenix was long gone.

I made it up to the top of the cliffs, a feat I would have found unimaginable only a few short weeks before, and then lay a long time catching my breath before I turned and looked out at the sea. From here I could not even see the *Siren's Song* in the little bay that was now hidden by the great crags of rock I had just climbed. When I turned away from the sea, I could see a great grassy plain with a range of mountains rising up in the distance. This, then, was the Unicorn Plain the siren had spoken of, though how she knew of it I could only guess, since with her fishlike tail she could no more have scaled those cliffs than I could have flown. Perhaps it was her husband, the captain, who had told her of the plain, or perhaps she, like the wizards, could change shape at will, or with the aid of this potion the captain had spoken of, and had climbed, or even flown, up to the plain more easily than I. I looked out across the plain and was both disappointed and somewhat relieved to see that, though this might be named the Unicorn Plain, there were, at least at present, no unicorns to be seen. I recalled what the siren had said about the phoenix being found near the peaks of the mountains that surround the plain. I unfastened the spear from the various straps that held it to my back and put my belt back through the loops in my pants, with the leather wallet now hidden away under the cloak, and began walking toward the mountains.

The grass on the plateau was tall, nearly up to my shoulder in places, which made for slow going. I walked all day through the tall grass, but aside from a few flattened circles in the grass that might have been made by deer or any other large creature, I saw no sign of unicorns. By nightfall, I still had not come to the edge of the mountains and I was footsore and hungry. There was no real shelter I could see, but I came at length to a stand of trees on a small hillock. I made for these and, setting the spear where I could reach it easily, I settled in among the trees for the night.

Sometime later, my stomach began to rumble, reminding me that I had not eaten all day. I had brought no provisions other than the one leather flask that I had filled with water, but when I looked again in the leather wallet the captain had given me, I noticed some yellowish, bristly-looking seaweed that he must have put in before he left me during the night. Had I asked, I suppose I could have had fresh fish in abundance. However, transporting it up the cliffs would have been problematic and, in any case, it would not have lasted long in the hot sun. The water flask was more than half empty, and I found myself wishing I had filled both flasks with water, although the added weight would have made the climb up the rock face even more arduous. Hesitantly, I took out some of the seaweed from the wallet and put a little of it in my mouth. It had a bitter taste but was surprisingly filling. Since I had no idea how long I would be up on the Unicorn Plain and no idea of what, if any, kinds of food I could forage here, I tried to be as sparing as I could with the small supply of seaweed I had in the pouch. My hunger was lessened, but not truly sated, but I made myself put the rest of it away, and settled back to try and sleep.

Night fell, but sleep was a long time in coming. I lay awake watching the stars come out and listening to the sounds of the insects that chirruped in the dark and imagining unicorns and other fiercer, wilder beasts moving in the blackness, just beyond my sight. Eventually my exhaustion overcame my fears and I slept.

CHAPTER SIXTEEN

SNAKES AND BIRDS

IN THE MORNING, I awoke feeling cold, stiff, and ravenously hungry. Resolving to husband my scant provisions more carefully from here on, I contented myself with a mouthful of the yellowish seaweed and a swallow of water before resuming my march toward the mountains.

I walked all morning through the tall grass of the Unicorn Plains, but saw no sign of the fabled beasts. Whether this was because there were no unicorns there to be seen or because they were invisible to my aged mortal eyes, I could not say. Around midday I saw a rabbit. I hefted the spear, thinking that if I could hit it, it would provide a welcome change from seaweed to my diet. However, the rabbit scampered away into the bush before I could even try throwing the spear. It occurred to me that if unicorns were half as fast as the rabbit, I would have a time in bringing one down with the spear even if I did manage to find one. I thought briefly about turning around and heading back down the cliff, but down was likely to be worse than coming up, and then what? All of the plans we had discussed, whether it was rescuing Greytail or going back to the wizards and trying to convince them to make me a new book, somehow required me to catch both a unicorn and a phoenix, however unlikely either of those might seem at the moment. When you reach the place where going back is no longer an option, the only thing left to do is to keep going on. I kept walking.

The siren had told me that the phoenix nested near the peaks of the mountains surrounding the Unicorn Plain. I decided that if I saw no sign of unicorns, I would keep going up into the mountains and see if I could catch sight of the phoenix again. I was pretty sure that the bird I had seen while I was climbing up the rock wall from the siren's cave had been the phoenix, or at least a phoenix, although by the time I reached the top it had gone and I had no idea which direction it had gone. Nor was there any reason to suppose that the first mountain that I came to would be the one that harbored the phoenix's nest, but it at least had the advantage of being closer than the ones behind it. I set my eyes on the peak of the nearest mountain in the chain of mountains I could see up ahead of me at the far edge of the Unicorn Plain and kept walking

By evening, I was now well into the foothills though not yet into true mountain country. The tall grasses I had been walking through that morning were well behind me, replaced by what looked like juniper and sagebrush. The vegetation was sparser here, with many bare patches of rock amidst the sandy soil, and pines were beginning to edge out the leafy trees that grew below at the edge of the plain.

I stopped to camp that night near a small cluster of boulders. I walked slowly around with my spear held out in front of me, but saw no sign of large predators. Unfortunately, I also saw no sign of any smaller creatures that might have made a meal for me. Wearily, I set down my pack and settled back against one of the boulders to rest. The rocks did not provide any real shelter, but the feel of solid rock against my back when I sat down gave me at least the illusion of safety.

I fished through my pack and took out another small handful of the yellowish seaweed. Although my belly protested about the inadequate size of the meal, I contented myself with a single handful since I had no idea how long it would be before I could get anything else. Or for that matter, if I could find anything else to eat in this strange place. What would I do when it ran out? I wondered. Die of hunger, I supposed, if I couldn't come up with a better plan. My belly rumbled again, but I told it to be quiet and go to sleep, then tried to follow my own advice. I was about to close my eyes and let myself drift off when something moved suddenly among the rocks, scant feet from where I had been sitting. I jumped up and grabbed the spear. *What had it been?*

Suddenly, I was wide-awake with visions of a half-dozen kinds of predators, real and imaginary, racing through my mind. Cautiously, I stepped forward and began probing among the boulders with the tip of the spear. I jerked back when I felt something move in one of the crevices, and an enormous snake reared up between the boulders, hissing its displeasure from a wide mouth displaying venomous-looking fangs. Whether this was a cobra, a rattlesnake, or something unique to the Unicorn Isles I couldn't tell you, but whatever it was, it was not happy with me. It started moving closer to me, fangs still bared. One of us, it seemed, was going to be dead in the next few minutes, I didn't want it to be me. I thrust at it with the spear, but it danced nimbly aside. It coiled to strike and I jumped back out of reach. We stood staring at each other for a handful of seconds, each willing the other's death. The snake coiled to strike again and as it lunged towards me, almost without thinking, instead of jumping back I took the spear, leaned in towards the snake and thrust the tip of the spear through the snake's body just below the head, pinning it to the ground. The snake thrashed violently, biting at the haft of the spear with its fangs as it convulsed for a few moments and then shuddered and lay still.

I held the spear that pinned it to the ground for a minute or so, catching my breath in great gulps while I waited for my nerves to steady, watching to see if there were any signs of life in my foe, fearful that if I took the spear out before it was truly dead, it would manage to give one last bite with those poisonous looking fangs and we might both die here tonight. After a few minutes, when my breathing had returned to something like normal and I was sure the snake was truly dead, I pulled out the spear and wasted some of my precious water cleaning the spear tip and then drank some myself, before sitting back down again next to the dead snake.

My stomach growled, reminding me I had eaten nothing but a few mouthfuls of seaweed for the past two days. I looked at the dead snake and wished mightily for some means of making a fire so I could cook it. I had never eaten snake before, but they say that hunger is the best sauce and right now, even a dead snake looked like a better meal than anything I had had in the past couple of days.

I remembered talking to Greytail about matches before setting out on this trip, but I supposed that even if I had had some, with all the time I had spent underwater they would have been useless by now. Greytail had a tinderbox, whatever that was, and for all I knew could light a fire with some kind of magic spell, but I certainly could not and, as I could now attest, wishing is indeed a poor way to make a fire. I ate some more of the yellowish seaweed and looked with distaste at the dead snake, trying to decide if I was hungry enough to eat it raw. My stomach continued to growl, answering the question for me. I got up and began to hunt for a sharp rock. My Cro-Magnon forebears would, no doubt, have found just the right stone and with a few hours' delicate tapping crafted it into a finely honed blade. They could probably have found the means to make a fire as well for that matter. Unfortunately for me, my own education had been somewhat lacking in those essential skills, one of the hazards of a more "civilized" upbringing. So instead I settled for finding a rock with the semblance of a natural edge, which was easier said than done. I used the rock to sever the snake's head from its body and then made a long vertical cut down the animal's full length. Then

I proceeded to eat my snake in a proper "civilized" fashion: pulling hunks of raw flesh off the bones with my fingers.

I decided I needed to conserve the little water I had left, so I did not wash my hands after this messy meal, but settled for wiping them as best I could on a patch of grass. Feeling rather pleased with myself for having not only survived the snake's attack, but managing for the first time, to hunt and kill something to feed myself, I settled back down against the rocks and tried to close my eyes again. Noises, real or imagined, intruded on my thoughts. I could hear crickets chirping and birds calling to their mates in scrubland around the little mound of boulders. In the distance I heard what might have been an owl. There were other sounds that I could not identify and my imagination insisted on suggesting a variety of terrifying possibilities. As night fell, I settled down uneasily among the rocks to sleep.

I awoke sometime in the middle of the night with an uneasy feeling of being watched. The moon was hidden behind a bank of clouds and even the stars were veiled in the cloudy night sky. I looked around me, trying to scan my surroundings, but could see nothing. Then, as my eyes gradually adjusted to the darkness, I became aware of a form silhouetted vaguely above the rocks where I had been sleeping. I thought at first it was some great cat, a mountain lion perhaps, and then, as it leapt down from the rocks, there was a rustle of wings and I knew that it was some kind of enormous bird. Thinking that somehow the phoenix I had come to hunt had miraculously come to hunt me, I reached for the spear and stood up to meet it. The creature's eyes opened and it fixed me with a proud and haughty stare.

"*Would you hunt* me?" the creature asked, with a voice that seemed to come from inside my own head. Each word was weighted with menace and power.

"Are you a phoenix?" I asked out loud.

The creature snorted and I heard the echo of laughter inside my head. "*And if I were?*" it asked.

"Then I would. For I have promised to bring back both the feathers of a phoenix and the blood of a unicorn when I return."

"*If you do not even know what a phoenix looks like, then that was a foolish promise indeed,*" the creature said. "*And besides, if you need only a few of the phoenix's feathers, you would do far better to search for its nest and hope to find one or two stray feathers there. If you search for the phoenix itself, it will elude you forever.*"

I considered this. It seemed to me that finding a phoenix's nest might be just as difficult as finding the phoenix itself, but I supposed that at least the nest would not fly off before I could catch it. I recalled the red-and-gold bird with the long tail feathers I had seen as I climbed up the cliffs, and I realized that the creature in front of me was much larger. So if the creature I had seen above the cliffs was the phoenix, what was this?

"If you're not a phoenix, then what are you?" I asked, uncertainly.

"*Foolish human,*" it replied, its voice again echoing inside my head. "*Can you not tell a gryphon from a phoenix? How can you go hunting for something and have not the slightest idea of what it is you hunt? At this rate, you'll like as not return with pigeon feathers and the blood of an ass and count yourself a great hero. At least until you try them in your potion.*"

"My what?" I asked, feigning ignorance.

"*Your potion, little human. Do not try my patience. You are not the first would-be shape-shifter to come to these hills in search of phoenix feathers and unicorn blood. Nor will you be the first to perish if you persist in your foolishness.*"

"Why are you telling me all this?" I asked, puzzled.

"*I smelled the adder's blood,*" the gryphon answered, "*and came to see if it was injured. Its kind and mine have ever been at war, and I planned to finish it off if I caught it. But when I got here I found that the adder was long dead and, indeed, half-eaten, with you lying beside its remains, asleep, still smelling of the*

*adder's blood. Did you hope to transform yourself into an adder
by drinking its blood?"*

The idea shocked me. I had heard from the siren and Captain
Fleischman that a unicorn's blood could be used to make a potion
that would allow one to change shape, but it had not occurred to me
that this might be true of the blood of other animals as well. The
idea that I might go to sleep as a man and awake as a snake without
intending it was a terrifying one. Trapped as I was on this strange
world, at least I had my own body and my own mind. Who knew what
might happen to the mind of one who was forced to live his life as an
adder? Certainly I could never return home to my family in such a
form. Fortunately, nothing I had eaten thus far on this world had had
such an effect, but perhaps I needed to be more careful about what I
ate here on the Unicorn Isles.

"No," I said at last, "I was just hungry."

The gryphon made a sound that was a snort to my ears but sounded
like laughter in my head. *"But not hungry enough to finish it?"* it
asked.

I looked with distaste at the mangled, half-eaten carcass of the
snake lying on the ground. "Help yourself," I said, waving a hand at
it.

The gryphon leaped down from the rock where it had been sitting
and snapped up the remainder of the snake in its great eagle-like
beak. Now that it was closer I could see it more clearly, although it
was still hard to be certain what I was seeing in the nearly pitch-dark
night. The creature's hindquarters were shaped like those of a large
cat, a lion or perhaps a cougar, while the front half had the form of a
great eagle, but larger than any eagle I had ever seen. The head was
nearly as large as a lion's, with a great ruffled mane of feathers falling
to its shoulders. The chest too was covered in feathers and its front
feet were clawed like a bird's, sized for an ostrich perhaps, but sharp
as any eagle's.

The remains of the snake disappeared in an eye-blink and the
gryphon made a sound like a satisfied purr. *"Tasty,"* it said, speaking

inside my head again, *"though they are better warm. Let's see if there are any of his fellow vermin about to round out the meal."*

The gryphon began prying through the pile of rocks I had been using as my campsite, casually lifting huge boulders with its claws while it peered beneath for any snakes that might be hiding. I shuddered, both to think that I brashly proposed to hunt this powerful creature, thinking it was the phoenix I sought, and to think that having killed the first snake, I had then settled down to eat it and fallen asleep without thinking about whether any of its fellows might be hiding among the rocks. After a few minutes, the gryphon gave up its search.

"Alas, it seems that was the only one," it said, indifferent to my relief. *"Well, half a snake is a meager dinner for a gryphon, even if it suffices for you. So, it seems I must hunt for the rest of my dinner elsewhere. Unless, of course, I decide to eat you,"* it added.

I took a hasty step back and reached again for my spear.

"Only joking", the gryphon said. *"I wouldn't kill a fellow snake killer. Especially if he offers to share. Let me know if you come across any more of these tasties as you're wandering among the hills, and I may be able to help you out. You're on your own, however, when it comes to phoenix and unicorns. Quite indigestible, I'm afraid you'll find them."*

"How?" I asked, after I had caught my breath again. The gryphon's jest seemed none too funny to me, and all too reminiscent of a certain dragon who had seemed almost as interested in finding out how I tasted as in getting back the stone that the wizards had called the dragon's heart. "How will I let you know?"

"Just shout," the gryphon said, *"inside your head. Think of me, and perhaps this snake we've shared, so I'll know who is calling. And if there are snakes to be eaten, I will come and help you. But do not summon me lightly or for some other trivial purpose, or I may change my mind about eating you instead."*

And with that, the gryphon leaped into the air and flew off. I stared for some time in the direction it had flown but could see nothing except the blackness of the night. I settled back down eventually to sleep again, more uneasily even than I had the first time. Dreams of snakes and great flying monsters who wanted to eat me troubled my sleep, but though I woke several times, there were no other visitors that night.

When dawn came, I looked around, but there was no trace of my visitor of the previous night, not a footprint, not a feather nor a trace of fur. I began to wonder if I had perhaps dreamed the whole encounter, but I noticed that the snake was also gone, the only trace of its existence a small reddish patch of dried blood on the ground that the ants were already at work cleaning up. If I had dreamed the encounter with the gryphon, then the remains of the snake should still be there. And if I had dreamed both snake and gryphon then where had the little patch of blood come from? So, both snake and gryphon must have been real, as real as the little patch of blood on the sandy ground. But when it disappeared, who could say?

It occurred to me then, that I might expire here, leaving a similarly meager monument on this world if I spent all my time in useless musings. So, I munched a small bit of the yellowish seaweed and took a carefully rationed sip of water from my flask before setting out again, up into the mountains.

Hiking in the foothills was both easier and harder than walking through the grasslands below. On the one hand, I no longer had to push my way through the head-high grasses. On the other hand, it was all uphill and it seemed to get steeper with every mile, sometimes indeed with every step. By midmorning, I was well and truly into the mountains. Gone were the broad-leafed trees of the plain, and even the pines had begun to look stunted and sparser than the ones I had seen in the foothills below. From time to time I caught sight of a variety of small rodents hiding in the rocks. These animals were fatter than the chipmunks and squirrels I was used to at home. They were the size and shape of rabbits, but had shorter ears, like mice. I thought of trying to spear one and eat it, but like the rabbit I had seen the day before, they disappeared nimbly among the rocks, sometimes running easily up the nearly vertical rock faces that offered no purchase for my human fingers and toes. My stomach growled at the sight of escaping prey, but there was nothing I could do about it.

I had been walking for several hours and was just nearing the summit when I paused to catch my breath and saw in the distance a group of what looked like mountain sheep, skipping easily along the rocky face of the next peak in this range of mountains. As my belly began to rumble again, I thought wistfully of lamb chops cooked over an open fire, but even with wings, I doubt I could have caught them. An eagle soared lazily over the mountain peaks, in search perhaps of those rodent-like creatures I had seen earlier, but I had no further glimpse of the phoenix that day.

When I reached the top a short while later, there was little to see after all my efforts. The summit of the mountain was bare and windswept, with no sign of a nest of any kind, much less one lined with potent magical feathers. Indeed, it was hard to imagine that any kind of bird could nest in these inhospitable conditions. The chill wind cut through my robe, and I spent only a short time searching the peak for any signs of life before continuing down the farther side.

Surprisingly, I found that going down the mountain was no easier than it had been going up. While gravity was now on my side, I now had to worry about descending too quickly and ending up with a sprained ankle or worse. About halfway down, I came across a small stream where I stopped and drank. After two days of carefully rationing my sips of water, I was grateful to be able at last to drink my fill without worrying how long the water in my flask would last or what I would do when it ran out. I refilled the waterskin. I thought again of filling both of the leather flasks with water, but decided to still leave one unfilled against the unlikely possibility that I might be successful in my hunt for the unicorns. I had no idea whether being mixed with water might dilute or even destroy the magical properties of the unicorn's blood, but having risked my life on the chance that I could in fact find and kill one of these creatures, I did not want to risk lessening its magical potency, since it was precisely that magical potency I was counting on to get me back to my own world. I opted instead to follow the stream downhill and thus reduce the amount of water I needed to carry and to make it easier to refill my waterskin whenever I needed.

Dusk was falling before I reached the bottom of the mountain. By evening, I was back under the cover of the dense pine forest that grew at the base of the mountains. Reasoning that other creatures, some of whom I might not wish to meet, might come at night to drink from the stream, I left the streambed and walked a short way into the woods in search of a place to spend the night. There were plenty of trees, and I considered climbing one in search of whatever safety a roost in its branches might offer. However, the prospect of tumbling out of the branches if I shifted in my sleep persuaded me against this idea. I had just about decided to simply lean up against the nearest tree and hope for the best when I came to the opening of a small cave. I looked around the entrance to the cave for bones, paw prints, fur, or other signs of recent occupation by any large predator, but saw none of these, so I decided to chance my luck. Cautiously, holding my spear out in front of me, I advanced into the cave and looked around. It too, showed no signs of recent habitation. At least not by anything large and carnivorous. Remembering the snake that had surprised me the previous night, I probed with the tip of the spear among the rocks at the back of the cave. Nothing moved in response to my probing and there was no other egress from the cave that I could locate. Satisfied with my search, I settled down on the floor of the cave, ate a meager meal of dried seaweed, and sat thinking of home and family as the day's light faded from the surrounding forest.

What things crept by the entrance to the cave while I dozed I cannot say for certain, but I woke several times during the night, convinced I had heard something just outside the cave. Each time, I crept to the entrance of the cave, spear in hand, but each time I saw nothing. Once it seemed for an instant that I had seen a pair of large red eyes peering in at me through the mouth of the cave. But when I went to the entrance and looked again, they were gone. Had there been something there or was it just my overwrought imagination playing tricks on me? I had no way of knowing. I thought of the gryphon that had appeared to me the night before and then disappeared into the night again. Was there something just as fantastical outside the cave right now? If so, was it friend or foe? Such were the thoughts that danced uncomfortably in my head as I slept, or at least tried to sleep, fitfully on the floor of the cave. Eventually, my eyes closed and I let exhaustion claim its due.

Chapter Seventeen

Up and In

I awoke with the first light of dawn, stiff and cold from a night spent lying on the cave's bare stone floor, but otherwise unharmed. My belly rumbled with the memory of last night's meager supper, so I went in search of something to eat. After retracing my steps back to the stream, I drank my fill and refilled the waterskin. That done, I continued my trek downstream. As I approached the base of the mountain, the stream widened into a marshy area with trickles of free-flowing water separated by tiny islands covered with rushes. The water between the little islands was shallow enough that I could wade through it in most places. I crossed cautiously from island to island, using the spear to probe the depth of the water ahead of me as I went, since I had no desire to discover a hidden cave beneath the mud by falling into it, or disturb some large predator hidden beneath the water's surface. It was cold enough that I didn't think alligators or any of their cousins were likely to be lurking there, but who knows what sort of other creatures might live in the marshes above the Unicorn Plain? In places, the streams formed little pools that were deep enough to harbor small fish and even trout. I tried stabbing at these with my spear, but they easily eluded my clumsy efforts at spearfishing from the banks.

I spent most of the morning splashing about from pool to pool, scrounging for anything that looked vaguely edible. There were green leafy fronds that reminded me of fiddlehead ferns growing beside some of these pools. I was uncertain if these were edible, but with my growing hunger, I felt I had little to lose by trying them. To my delight, they proved not only edible, but quite tasty. I also found something that looked like watercress floating in some of the streams and, it too, proved edible. I might not have caught any unicorns or phoenix yet, but at least I was managing to fill my stomach with something other than raw bits of snake.

Late in the morning, I came across a small nest on one of the reed-covered islands. Not a phoenix nest, but one made by ducks or some related species of waterfowl, and to my delight, there were three small eggs inside it that completed my breakfast wonderfully. I ate them raw with great enjoyment, thinking that a few short weeks before I might have blanched at the thought of breakfasting on raw eggs and unknown fronds picked from a streambed, but those eggs now seemed a greater treasure than gold.

Three eggs later, my hunger satisfied for the moment, I set my eyes on the next peak in the island range, scanning the skies for the brilliantly colored red-and-gold bird I had glimpsed on my climb up from the siren's cave. Something that might have been no more than a glint of sunlight off an outcropping of rock near the summit caught my eye. I strained my eyes trying to discern whether it was the bird I had seen or merely some trick of the light, but it was gone. Feeling more hopeful than perhaps was warranted by that half-seen glimpse of golden color, I turned away from the streambed and began to climb again.

For the first two hours I walked easily up what seemed to be deer trails, but soon the trees became scarce again and the trail steeper, and I was forced to use my hands as well as my feet to climb. I had no rope to fasten a harness for myself (nor the skill to make one even if I had the rope), so I forced myself to go cautiously, testing each hand and foothold before I entrusted my weight to it. Several times I thought I saw the summit just above me, but each time when I reached it, it proved to be just a small shoulder on the face of the mountain, with a short ledge and then another steeper climb above it. Although the sun shone brightly, the chill mountain air cut through my cloak, and my fingers and toes began to ache with the exertion of pulling myself up over the rocks. Although the climb was not as sheer as the vertical cliff I had climbed up to reach the Unicorn Plain, it went on much longer. At last, when I thought I could go no higher, I reached a narrow ledge with a path that seemed to circle the top of the mountain, ascending slightly as it circled. I walked along it, trying not to look down at the great drop below me as I wound my way slowly across the face of the cliff.

When I began my ascent that morning, I had been in a small valley between the first two peaks of this range of mountains, but now the ledge had brought me around to the far side of the mountain, facing the sea. Looking out I could see the waves stretching out for miles to meet the horizon, while below me I could see nothing but a sheer drop down to the crashing waves. Ahead of me, about halfway around the mountain from where I had started, the ledge came to an abrupt end, blocked by a large boulder that had fallen across the path. I walked up to it and, holding on to the boulder, tried to crane my neck around it to see if the ledge continued on the far side of this obstruction, but try as I might, I could see no way past it. However, when I leaned back against the cliff, I saw that there was a narrow crevice between the cliff face and the boulder, that I could just wedge myself into, if I were foolish or brave enough to do so. Whether I could get out again was another question. Letting my hopes get the better of me, I decided that a crevice in a mountain top might be just the sort of place that a phoenix might like to build its nest. Of course, as my experience with the snake the other night had taught me, there could be other sorts of creatures hiding in there as well. I poked the spear in ahead of me, but no hissing serpents appeared to object to my intrusion. Having come this far I was not going to turn back now. I squeezed myself in through the crevice. When I did so, I was surprised to discover that the crevice opened into a twisting passageway. Unable to go any farther along the ledge I had been following, I decided to see where this passageway led. Within a few steps of the entrance to the passageway the light vanished, leaving me to grope forward in darkness. Keeping one hand against the wall, I used the butt end of the spear to probe the floor and walls ahead of me, wary of finding a sudden chasm or obstruction. A few yards into the cliff, the passageway began to climb, following the dark path up and into the mountain.

Groping my way forward, it seemed that every few steps a stalagmite rose up, or a low-hanging stalactite hung down from the roof of the passage to partially obstruct the way. In the darkness it was often difficult to tell one from the other, but by going slowly and tapping ahead of me with the spear, I was able to avoid most of these and did not sustain any serious injuries. I had been climbing up through the blind tunnel for some minutes when I saw light up ahead of me. Emerging from the tunnel, I stepped into a wide chamber lit at the far end by what appeared to be a window, or at any rate an opening in the wall of rock. The center of the chamber was filled with a pool of water that stretched to the wall on either side, leaving a small dry area where I stood at the entranceway to the passageway I had just exited. I could see marks on the walls that suggested that in the past the water level must have been higher and that water would have flowed down the length of that passage and exited from the fissure behind the boulder where I had entered. The thought occurred to me that if this chamber flooded regularly with melting snow or heavy rains then I might be washed out of this chamber, down the twisting pathway I had just ascended and spat out of the side of the mountain onto the rocky shoals below. It was not a comforting thought.

There was another dry space I could see at the far end of the chamber, just beneath the window-like opening in the wall of this cave. I thought that if I waded over to it, I could probably look out and get a better idea of where I was, and whether there were any possibility of ascending or descending from there, or if I would have to retrace my steps back through the passageway I had just exited. There was no way to gauge the depth of the pool from where I stood, and so, using the spear as a probe for unseen hazards beneath the water's surface, I began cautiously wading to the other side. I had taken no more than three steps from the edge of the pool when something large stirred beneath the water. Hastily, I started backing toward the shore, my spear held in front of me. A dark form surged beneath the water and I leaped back onto the shore. A second later the water erupted and a huge eel-like head rose from the depths of the pool and snapped where my feet had been an instant before. I stabbed down with the spear and gored one of its eyes. It recoiled, hissing. I backed into the mouth of the tunnel and darkness enveloped me again. From the chamber beyond came more hissing and the sound of something large and powerful slithering out of the water toward the tunnel. There was a glint of red from its remaining eye and a flash of white from its razor sharp teeth as it thrust its head forward, reaching for the spot where I stood in the mouth of the tunnel. I thrust again with the spear, goring its other eye. Blinded now, the creature roared with rage, snapping with its fishy jaws scant inches from my face. I backed down the tunnel as quickly as I could while still holding the spear out in front of me. The eel-like creature lunged again and again, forcing more of its bulk out of the water and into the tunnel with each lunge. It was pitch-black in the tunnel, so I had no way of knowing where the creature would strike next, but I could hear the clash of its great jaws each time it struck out. At last, I simply turned and ran blindly down the tunnel, a hand held out in front of my face to intercept any low-hanging stalactites.

When I reached the bottom, I could still hear the lunging and snapping of the great eel-like creature in the passageway above. Squeezing myself out through the opening, I backed cautiously out onto the narrow ledge that circled the mountain. With my heart pounding wildly, I held my spear at the ready, and waited for the creature's head to emerge from the entrance to the tunnel. A second later, it did, ichor dripping from its blind eyes. It opened its huge jaws and hissed with rage. As it did so, I thrust the spear into its open maw, past the rows of fearsome teeth, and up into the roof of its mouth. With a flick of its powerful neck muscles, it tore the spear from my grasp, then bit down hard, splintering the spear between its massive jaws. Terrified, I backed away farther.

Seeing the eel-like creature emerging from the side of the cliff, I remembered the snake that had emerged from the rocks where I was sleeping just two nights before, and how the gryphon had disposed of its remains in a single gulp. I wished desperately that someone or something could come along and rid me of this serpent-like creature as easily. As I backed my way around the ledge, the eel continued to slowly emerge from the crevice in the mountainside. At first I thought the weight of its head would cause it to come tumbling out in a rush and plunge down the cliffside, but when a few more feet of its neck emerged, it lifted its head above the rim of the ledge and began to slither toward me, blind eyes oozing, but still with massive teeth that I was powerless to defend myself against. I reached the end of the ledge and realized I did not have time to cautiously lower myself over the edge and looked around in vain for anything I could use as a weapon.

Before I could decide between the unwelcome alternatives of an uncontrolled slide down the side of the mountain or a suicidal rush at the blinded, but still deadly, giant eel, there was a flash of red and gold above me, and I saw the form of a great winged cat come plunging down the side of the mountain, its oversized eagle's claws spread wide before it. With a screech, it plucked the enormous eel, which must have been ten yards in length, from the ledge and soared into the air. The eel writhed, snapping at the gryphon, which released its hold.

The eel fell, plummeting down the side of the mountain, and crashed onto the rocks below, where the gryphon swooped down to finish it off. I watched as the gryphon slashed and battered its prey on the rocks till the giant fish stopped moving. Then as I watched, the gryphon began tearing great hunks of the eel's flesh off and devouring them raw. Though I had done much the same myself with the carcass of the snake I had killed two nights ago, the scale of the carnage was still appalling. With my heart still pounding from the nearness of my escape I sat down on the ledge and waited for my breathing to return to normal. It was several minutes before I could stop shaking and force myself to begin the long climb back down the mountain.

When I reached the bottom, the gryphon was still feasting on the last of the eel's carcass, ripping off pieces of its flesh with evident relish. "*Now here,*" said the gryphon, his voice, as before, seeming to appear magically inside my skull, "*is a meal more to my liking than the paltry worm you offered me the other day. You did well, luring it out of its nest like that. These young ones are nice and tasty, and they don't have all those indigestible scales. Not to mention the fire, of course. We should try that again sometime, sending you into a nest as bait to see if we can lure any more out. Though I suppose it could be hard on the bait.*"

"Please do not think me ungrateful for being rescued, but I think I will pass on your generous offer," I said, declining the chance to be used as bait on future eel-hunting expeditions. "But there is one thing I would like to know, if you are able to tell me."

"*Yes, and what would that be?*"

"What was it?"

"*Dragon-spawn, of course,*" said the gryphon between mouthfuls. Though the eel-like creature was almost three times its own length, the gryphon appeared determined to finish eating it at a single sitting. "*The larval forms are the best, before they get all that hard, scaly armor, though the juveniles can be quite good, too, if you can manage to pounce on one before it gets its head turned around to start spewing fire at you. And even I wouldn't want to try tackling one of the adults, of course."*

"Of course," I said, feeling somewhat confused. Then an odd thought occurred to me. "What do they look like?" I asked after a pause, "The adults, I mean."

"What do they look like?" the gryphon repeated, sounding puzzled. *"Surely you've seen dragons before? Big lizardish-looking things with wings, all covered with brightly colored scales."*

"Brightly colored, with wings," I repeated, feeling more confused than ever. "And the juveniles? What do they look like?"

"Much like the adults," said the gryphon, sounding amused at my ignorance, *"smaller, of course. Maybe twice the size of the larvae"*—here it indicated the rapidly diminishing corpse of the ten-yard-long "larva"—*"and no wings, of course. They don't get those until the last molt. Usually duller in color, too, sometimes green, sometimes brown. They blend in with the trees that way, makes them harder to catch. The adults, of course, don't have to blend in. Even I can't hunt them."*

"No wings," I repeated slowly, "and duller colors. Sometimes black, do you suppose?"

"I suppose," agreed the gryphon. *"Why do you ask?"*

"I met a dragon once," I said. "Back on the other side of the ocean. And it was black, with no wings, so I suppose it was a juvenile, although it certainly seemed big enough to me. The wizards said that if it got its heartstone back, it would take to the skies and seek a mate, so I guess they knew what it was, even if they didn't explain it to me."

"Get its what back?" asked the gryphon.

"Its heartstone," I said, and explained about the green stone that the dragon had "hired" me to find.

"They hid the dragon's heartstone?" the gryphon asked after I had finished my explanation.

"Yes," I said, "that way the dragon can never grow up and mate, so at least they are safe from the greater depredation that would come from having a whole swarm of dragons on their shores."

"*They think having a marauding juvenile dragon in their neigh-borhood is safe?*" asked the gryphon incredulously. "*It's the juve-niles that cause all the trouble. The adults eat almost nothing and generally leave any place they visit within a few days. They're only interested in finding a mate and a place to lay their eggs. Fools!*" it added contemptuously, but whether it referred to the dragons or the wizards, I could not say.

"What sort of a place would they look for?" I asked, "The dragons, I mean."

"*A pool,*" the gryphon explained, "*like the one in the mountain where you found this dragon-spawn. A place with fresh water, but no light. The eggs are translucent and the larvae are very sensitive to light, and quite tasty, as I think I may have men-tioned.*"

The eel-like form was by now stripped of its flesh almost complete-ly. Only the bones and a few bits of skin remained. Then I saw, lying against the vertebrae, just beneath the place where the head met the rest of the skeleton, a shining green orb, dark like jade-colored glass, but pulsing with an inner fire, although the dragon larva, if that's what the eel-like creature had been, was clearly quite dead. The gryphon saw it too and stretched out a long-taloned paw to seize the stone, snapped it up in its beak, and swallowed it.

"*That one is mine,*" it said, as if there could be any doubt after it had already eaten the heartstone. "*Not that it would have done you any good if you had taken this heartstone back to your black dragon. Only its own heartstone will allow it to mature into an adult. Though why one would want to keep a juvenile dragon hanging about in their neighborhood is beyond me. For one thing, it will keep growing. How big did you say your black dragon was?*"

"I'm not sure," I answered, "but I think it must have been at least three times the size of this larval one."

"That is big for a juvenile", said the gryphon, *"almost as big as some adults. Still, there's not much you can do about it over here, so I guess you will have to let the wizards figure out what to do with their pet. What do you propose to do now?"*

"I don't know," I said. "I had set out looking for a unicorn or a phoenix, but without my spear, there's not much I could do against a unicorn, so I guess I'll concentrate on looking for the phoenix."

"There's not much you could have done to a unicorn even with that puny spear," said the gryphon.

"Are they so powerful?" I asked, naively.

"It's not so much that they are powerful," said the gryphon, *"though they certainly are that. It's that they are so powerfully magical."*

"Of course," I said, "that's why I'm hunting them."

"But what you don't seem to have grasped yet is that if you are hunting a powerful magical creature, you won't be able to catch it unless you have powerful magic of your own," said the gryphon.

"You mean something like that green stone you just swallowed?" I asked.

"Something like that, yes," said the gryphon with a satisfied look.

"But then, how will I ever catch one?" I asked.

"You won't," it said.

"I won't or I can't?" I asked, hoping for a clearer answer.

"Exactly," said the gryphon.

I thought about that for a moment and then said, "I can't, but you could. You've just eaten the heartstone of that dragon, which you tell me has powerful magic, and you yourself are a powerful magical creature, so *you* could catch a unicorn."

The gryphon looked at me oddly for a moment. *"Perhaps I could at that. But I won't. After all, I have no particular quarrel with the unicorns, and no desire to start one just to appease your bloodthirsty friends. So I'm afraid, if it's unicorn blood you want, you'll have to get it yourself.*"

"But you just said—" I began.

"*I know what I said,*" said the gryphon, "*and it is true. In your present form, you will never catch a unicorn, because you are too weak and your present form has no magic of its own. But there are other forms you might take. If you ask nicely, I might help you.*"

"Other forms?" I said, startled at the thought. "But I thought the potion for shape-changing required unicorn's blood and phoenix feathers. And if I need to change shape to get those things, then it's hopeless."

"*Not at all,*" said the gryphon. "*Unicorn blood and phoenix feathers are used in some common recipes because both are powerfully magical and have transformative properties, but there are other ingredients with transformative properties as well.*"

"Such as?" I asked, skeptically, wondering what new quest or wild-goose chase I was about to be sent on this time.

"*You won't like it,*" said the gryphon.

"As it seems I have no choice," I said, stoically, "you may as well tell me. What do I need to look for now?"

"*I didn't say you needed to look for anything,*" said the gryphon, "*I only said you wouldn't like it. Dragon's flesh has a good deal of magic in it and the larval form is quite high in transformative nutrients, especially if it has been partially digested by a magical creature, such as myself. But I don't suppose that will make it any more palatable for you.*"

With that, it regurgitated a small piece of the dragon larva's meat into my lap, reminding me oddly of a mother bird feeding its young, though I had never stopped to think about how revolting it would feel to be in the place of those young birds.

"*Go on, eat it up,*" the gryphon commanded. "*It's a great honor, you know. Not everyone can claim to have been mouth-fed by a gryphon.*"

Struggling to control my revulsion, I picked up the slimy, fishy-smelling piece of flesh it had just spit up into my lap and placed it into my mouth. With an effort, I swallowed, and at once, I regretted it. My head began to spin, my vision blurred, and my stomach felt violently ill. I tried to stand and fell over on my side as the world spun around me.

"*Not yet,*" the gryphon cautioned. "*Wait till the transformation is complete.*"

I flopped on the ground, my body wracked by strange twisting and tugging sensations, and my head felt like it was trying to explode.

When the world stopped spinning, I blinked my eyes several times and then, cautiously, tried getting to my feet. When I did so, I noticed that my vision seemed oddly flat. There was no sense of seeing things in three dimensions, although I could see farther to either side than I ever could before. I had almost panoramic vision on both sides, but directly in front of me things lacked the sharp focus I was used to. I looked down at my feet and saw that they were not feet, but hooves.

"*You've turned me into a horse!*" I shouted inside my head, but all that came out was a whinny. "*Or a donkey, or an ass, or . . .*"

"*Not a horse or a donkey,*" answered the gryphon's voice inside my head, "*and no more of an ass than you were before the transformation. You are a unicorn.*"

"*A unicorn?*" I spluttered. "*But I was supposed to be hunting unicorns, not getting turned into one. I thought you were going to turn me into a gryphon!*"

"*A gryphon?*" said the gryphon, amused. "*You rate yourself too highly. You wanted to hunt unicorns for their blood but couldn't, because you had only your weak human body. I have given you a body that is the equal of a unicorn's, exactly. The males often spar in the breeding season and will occasionally gore one another. If you still want to hunt for unicorn blood, you now have a magical weapon on your forehead that is equal to the task. At any rate, it will be equal to the task if you are. If you've changed your mind, just wait, the spell should wear off in a day or two.*"

And now, if you have finished making ungrateful remarks, I have other business to attend to."

"*Wait!*" I shouted, as the gryphon prepared to launch itself once more into the air. "*The other unicorns, how do I find them?*"

"*So you're going to hunt unicorns, after all?*" the gryphon said. "*You're either braver or more foolish than I expected. They are back in the fields where you first came up from the coast. In your new magical form, you should see them plainly enough. Of course, they will also see you.*"

Chapter Eighteen

Hunting Unicorns

AND WITH THAT, THE gryphon flew away, leaving me to retrace my steps of the past two days and to learn if I, as a unicorn, could now hunt unicorns. The first challenge was what to do with the various possessions I had been carrying (all of which had fallen from my body during my shape-changing), since unicorns have neither hands to carry things, nor pockets to put them in. After a brief moment's hesitation, I decided to abandon them all, except for the single leather flask that I hoped to use to collect the unicorn's blood if I was successful in my hunt. The flask's leather carrying strap had allowed me to carry it slung over my shoulder while I climbed. Now I used the tip of my horn to flip it up over my head. I worked my head through the strap so it hung down like a St. Bernard's legendary miniature cask of brandy. It occurred to me that even if I were successful in my hunt, I would no more be able to fill the flask than a St. Bernard could fill a cask that hung from its own neck. However, the gryphon had said that the spell would wear off in a day or two, so perhaps I could fill it after I resumed my proper human form. My other possessions I gathered into a crudely wrapped bundle, using the tip of my horn to fold my robe around them, and wedged the bundle into a space between two rocks at the base of a tree. There was nothing of great value there, except perhaps the conch shell that the Sea King had given me, which in any event would not be of much use in hunting unicorns. In the unlikely event that I survived my first attempt at unicorn hunting, I could always return to this spot and retrieve it later.

I made my way back to the small cave where I had slept the night before, hoping to spend the night there again before I ventured back to the Unicorn Plain. Again, I searched the area around the entrance for signs of large predators. In my new form, I was both faster and stronger than I had been as a human, and the horn on my forehead would make a fearsome weapon if I had to defend myself, but somehow, as a large herbivore I now had the instinctive feeling that I was prey. Seeing nothing alarming outside I ducked down so that my horn could clear the entrance and ventured into the cave. In my new shape, I discovered that I could not easily look up at the roof of the cave, which made me somewhat anxious. There was a fluttering above me in the recesses of the cave that made me think of bats, but nothing dropped down on me from above, and happily it seemed that there were no predators inside the cave, lying in wait for passing unicorns.

I slept standing up that night for the first time in my life. Of course, it was also the first time in my life that I had been a unicorn, so a little strangeness was perhaps to be expected. The thought that I was now a unicorn who was hunting for other unicorns was even more strange. The same magic that I was seeking, now flowed in my own veins. And what of my fellow unicorns, were they all "real" unicorns, or were some changelings, like myself? If so, what did it mean for me to be hunting them? Might they, just as well, be hunting me? Was that what the gryphon had meant with his warning that they too could see me? I tried to put all of these thoughts out of my head and sleep, but sleep was a long time in coming. My hearing was now sharper than it had been when I was human, but that only meant that the nighttime noises that had worried me the previous night were even more terrifyingly alive to me than they had been before. The high-pitched squeaks that had been inaudible to my human ears, were now omnipresent in the cave, and outside the calls of birds and insects seemed startling in the loudness. My ears twitched with every owl's call that I heard and when, sometime in the middle of the night I heard the far-off call of a wolf, every hair on my hide seemed to stand on end.

When dawn came I felt, if not exactly rested, at least relieved to have made it through another night alive. The world looked odd to me when I stepped out of the cave and into the morning light. The world as I now perceived it was full of form and motion at the periphery, where I expected to see nothing, or at most hints and shadows, and yet hazy and out of focus if I tried to look directly in front of me. I found I could focus better on things if I turned my head and looked at them sidelong, or better yet, turned my head from side to side to take in the whole panorama before me.

I retraced my steps through the mountains, moving much faster on four legs than I had on two. I could not climb as nimbly as the mountain sheep I had seen the day before, but since I was not trying to reach the summit this time it did not matter so much and even going the long way round the mountain I could get there much faster than I had the day before. At length I found myself back at the wide plain I had seen the first day I climbed up from the siren's cave. At first glance, the plain was as empty of unicorns as it had been when I first climbed up to it, but as I turned my head from side to side, I saw that the air shimmered with a kind of energy and was filled with a strong, unfamiliar smell that made my pulse race. After a while, the unicorn part of my brain told me that it was the smell of magic. The grass on the plain, which before had seemed perfectly ordinary, now rippled with rainbow hues that had been invisible to my human eyes, like waves of heat rising from the hot sands of the desert. I stopped to graze and, as I did so, I could feel the magic within me growing stronger, fed by the magic stored within the rippling blades of grass. When I had eaten my fill, I headed down towards the cliffs where I had climbed up before. Although it had taken me an entire day to cross the plain in my human form, as a unicorn I could now make it in less than two hours.

As I neared the end of the plain, I felt a disturbance in the rippling energy fields that rose up from the grasses, and I came suddenly to a halt, looking around to see what had caused the disturbance. As I did, another unicorn stepped out of the grass, although I was certain he had not been there a moment before. This was the moment I had been waiting for. Whether I was hunting him or he was hunting me, or whether both of us had been brought there by forces beyond our control I could not say. But if I was going to be a hunter of unicorns, this was my chance.

The strange unicorn pawed the ground in front of him and lowered his head, challenging me. I did the same and we both stepped forward, like two fencers waiting for the signal to begin a duel. There was a bunching of muscles, both his and mine, and then we both sprang forward. As we met, our horns clashed and we reared onto our hind hooves, kicking and biting. His horn gored me in the shoulder, and I backed away and braced for another attack. Before I had time to catch my breath, we clashed again, and again the real unicorn's attack was swifter. His horn plunged into my flank on the other side, and I stumbled to my knees, dizzy with pain. Rearing, he used his hooves to batter my head till I began to see stars. I thrust at him with my horn again and again, but each time he leapt nimbly away and then reared to batter me again. When he paused, I sprang up and lunged at him with my horn, but he danced nimbly aside and then returned to battering me with his hooves. When he paused again, I got painfully to my feet, then turned tail and ran, while the real unicorn reared and brayed his triumph to the herd.

Ignoring the pain from the wound in my side, I ran until I came to the edge of the cliffs where I had first climbed up from the siren's cave and then, when I could run no further, I lay down, exhausted and bleeding. When I awoke, a strange sight met my eyes. It was the captain, and he had taken the leather flask from around my neck and was holding it up to the wound in my shoulder while pressing on it to force the blood to trickle out of the wound and into the leather bottle. My first thought was that he did not know me and might kill me for the sake of the magic in my blood. My second thought, even more terrifying, was that he did know me and might kill me anyway. After all, it was he who had given me the flask to wear around my neck. Perhaps this had all been some horrible trick. I tried to rise to fight him, or to flee, but I was too weak. I stumbled back to my knees and my vision swam with rainbow-hued shadows. The world spun around me, and I fell into a deep, deep sleep.

Chapter Nineteen

Up and Out

I AWOKE IN THE Siren's cave, lying naked, once more in human form, on the same little rocky beach that I had set out from four days earlier. At least I thought it had been only four days, although I realized I did not know how long I had lain there unconscious. It might have been a few hours or a few weeks, I had no way of knowing. The wounds in my shoulder and my flank that the other unicorn had inflicted on me while I was in my unicorn form were healed, but whether this was a beneficial side effect of the transformation spell wearing off, some special healing magic worked by the captain or his wife, or just the natural magic of the body's own healing powers and time, I could not say. I tried to sit up, but my head swam with dizziness and the aches in my body reminded me of the battering I had received from the other unicorn, so I lay back down on the sand.

A little way away from me, on the far side of the little beach, the captain and his wife, the siren (I could not recall if she had ever told me her name), were conversing in low voices as she sat, absentmindedly running her long fingers through the water at the edge of the shore. She was eating while they talked, like a human munching peanuts, but with a diet no human could stomach. Every minute or two, her hand came up out of the water with something small wriggling in it, sometimes a small fish, sometimes a small crab or a sea urchin. Whatever it was would then disappear into her mouth. Small details like bones, claws, and shells apparently did not bother her digestive system.

After a while, the captain glanced up and noticed me watching them. "Good, you're awake," he said.

"So it seems," I replied, sitting up painfully, "and back in my own form. Though I'm afraid I may be somewhat underdressed for the occasion," I said, opening my arms to point out my lack of attire.

He laughed. "Not to worry. I will find something for you from aboard ship, though it may not be as fashionable as the wizard's robe you were wearing when you set out from here last time."

"Whatever it is, I am sure it will suit me better than the unicorn's hide I was wearing when you found me. Or did I only dream of being a unicorn?"

"Nay, that was real enough," the captain said, "and more to the point, it was real unicorn's blood running in your veins while you were wearing your unicorn form, and the blood does not seem to have changed back to human's."

He held up the flask that he had apparently filled with my blood while I was in unicorn form, unstoppered it, and let a single drop fall onto the tip of his finger. It glowed with a pearly white light, like moonlight tinged with iridescence.

"Be careful with that," his wife snapped, "there's powerful magic in that blood, and I don't want you unleashing it with no thought to the consequences or the cost."

"The cost?" he repeated, puzzled.

"Your friend has paid dearly for that," she said. "After all, it's his blood."

"My blood," I said slowly, looking at the iridescent drop on the end of his finger, trying to imagine it running through my veins like quicksilver. It did not seem possible, but there it was, glowing with the same magical potency I had felt when I ate the grasses of the Unicorn Plain.

"Yes," said the captain, "your blood, but unicorn's blood nonetheless, since you were a unicorn when I took it from you. So, despite failing in your hunt for a unicorn, you have succeeded in obtaining the blood of a unicorn. Now all that remains is the phoenix feathers."

"The phoenix feathers?" I repeated, dully, my head still aching from my injuries and my long sleep.

"Yes, phoenix feathers," he repeated. "The other magical ingredient we need to work the shape-changing spell so you can go back to the Halls of the Sea King and rescue Greytail. Or had you forgotten?"

In truth, I had forgotten. Or, if not actually forgotten, put it so far out of my mind that it seemed like something from a distant dream or a tall tale, but now, it seemed, I was back in that tale, with the final chapters still to be written.

"Don't worry," he said, seeing the look of dismay on my face, "we're not leaving tonight. We'll wait until after breakfast at the earliest."

In the end, it was another three days before I felt ready to leave the cave. Whatever healing spell had cured me of the injuries inflicted by the unicorn, had left me feeling almost too weak to walk, and ravenously hungry. Though I could not digest shells and claws like the siren, I found that a diet of raw seafood restored my strength more quickly than I would have expected, though the salt water left me feeling parched after every meal. Since I was too weak at first to leave the cave, the captain brought back fresh water for me in a leather flask, like the one I had lost when the gryphon transformed me into a unicorn and I was forced to leave my belongings behind.

While I rested and then slowly began to exercise to regain my strength, the captain returned to the *Siren's Song* and brought back clothes for me, some of his and some that he had borrowed from the crew. My borrowed finery was none too fine, and the boots fit poorly. However, it would certainly be better than heading out in search of the phoenix dressed in nothing more than a smile. Even after three days, it was not so much that I felt ready for the task ahead, as knowing that my resolve would grow weaker and the task before me appear ever more daunting with each passing day that pushed me to set out before my courage failed completely.

We set out the same way we had before. After stopping to fill our flasks at the spring, we began the precarious climb up to the Unicorn Plain again. How the captain had made it down those cliffs carrying my unconscious body I could not imagine, though for a man who spent his days on the deck of a ship he seemed remarkably sure-footed as we made the climb up the cliffs. Even so, with my unicorn body it would have been impossible for him to carry me down those cliffs. I wondered how long he had had to wait for me to turn back to human form or if he had used some sort of pulley to lower me back down.

The trek across the Unicorn Plain to the base of the mountains was uneventful this time. No mysterious gryphons or even snakes, disturbed by our passage, appeared to enliven the journey, and of my erstwhile opponent, the unicorn there was no sign. Some part of me kept expecting him to reappear and finish the job he had started, so I was more than a little uneasy as we walked through the tall grass. But the unicorn and his herd seemed to have disappeared just as magically as they had appeared to me before.

I wondered why the captain had decided to accompany me this time and then, conversely, why he had not accompanied me when I went out to hunt the unicorn the first time. Perhaps, I thought, he had hunted unicorns before and thought little of my chances of finding one, or perhaps he and the siren had had some other secret engagement that he chose not to share with me. Whatever his motivations had been, he came with me this time, and had brought nets with which we hoped to trap the phoenix, although since I had only seen the phoenix once from a great distance I was not sure how useful these would prove.

We spent two days crossing the Unicorn Plain and another three exploring among the foothills of the mountains without any sighting of the phoenix, although we did manage to locate my clothes and other belongings, including the conch shell that the Sea King had given me, still wedged between the rocks at the base of the tree where I had been forced to leave them when I changed into a unicorn. Gratefully, I stripped out of my borrowed clothes and boots and back into my own familiar, if now rather travel-worn clothes and shoes. We camped that night on the far side of the mountain where I had had my encounter with the dragon spawn. We had taken the long way around, which added several miles to our trek, but I had no desire to try scaling those heights again. True, the dragon larvae had been removed from its cave lair, but I had found no passable way up to the summit, and no desire to go exploring in those caves again.

I woke the next morning to the sound of a high-pitched screech, somewhere off in the distance. I looked up at the mountains ahead of us, which were now shrouded in fog, seeking the source of that strange cry. I was sure I had never heard it before, and yet, somehow I was equally sure that it was the cry of the phoenix. Whether this was some residual effect of the magic that had coursed through my body while I was in unicorn form, or merely self-delusion on my part, I could not say, but the sense of certainty stayed with me as I strained my eyes for a glimpse of quarry amidst the fog-shrouded peaks. I had almost given up when suddenly I caught a glimpse of brilliant red and gold in the sky, near the top of the next mountain peak, perhaps half a day's walk from where we had camped for the night. As I watched, the phoenix circled the peak of the mountain and then disappeared from view. I shook the captain to wake him and pointed out the peak where I had seen our quarry disappear. He nodded and as quickly as we could, we gathered up the few things we had been carrying, putting them back into our packs and set out towards the mountaintop, eyes fixed on the location where I had last seen the phoenix.

This was a different mountain from the one where I had encountered the dragon-spawn, but part of the same chain that ran like a ridge of spines across the island's back. As we climbed up again through the foothills, the vegetation once more grew sparse, tall trees giving way to pines and then to scrubby bushes. As we approached the top, we began to see snow, even though we were still some weeks, or so the captain said, from winter. A cold wind blew off the top of the mountain and I wrapped the wizard's cloak tighter around me. The captain, for his part, wore an oilskin coat that would have withstood a gale aboard his ship like an otter's skin but seemed thin for a climb at this altitude. I could see my breath in the air before me and felt the shiver of the wind running down my neck. As we climbed, the ground grew slick with snow and the ascent became ever steeper, so that once again, I was forced to use my hands as well as my feet as we made our way up the mountain. At last we reached a sheltered spot where a large boulder blocked the path and it seemed we could go no farther.

The captain stopped, removed his coat, and began removing all of his clothing, seemingly impervious to the subzero temperatures.

"What are you doing?" I asked, as he stripped off his clothes.

"Changing," he said. "You take the gear. When the transformation is complete, climb on my back and hold tight. I won't be able to catch you if you let go."

I stared at him, dumbfounded, as he continued to strip off the remainder of his clothing. When he had removed the last articles of clothing, he took a small sip from a flask and then placed it back into a pocket inside his coat before pushing his bundle of clothing over toward me. I took the bundle from him, wondering if he had lost his mind.

"Put the clothes in my pack and put both the packs over your shoulders," he commanded. I stared at him for a moment, bewildered, standing naked in the freezing cold, then shrugged and did as he had ordered.

The captain shivered and sat down, naked on the ground. I wondered if he planned to just sit there until he froze and then strange things began happening to his body. First his eyes and then his whole head appeared to bulge and coarse hairs began to sprout from his body. He writhed on the ground, his legs twisting into new, unnatural angles and his hands and feet withdrew into his arms and legs as one nail on each hand and foot swelled to become a hoof. In moments, his metamorphosis was complete and I was standing in front of a large mountain sheep who waited impatiently as I strapped both of our packs on my back. At his invitation, I climbed onto his back and grabbed on as tightly as I could, burying my hands in the thick wool behind his neck.

I felt a bunching of muscles beneath me, and then we were airborne, springing up the face of the mountain as the boulder, which a minute before had seemed an impenetrable barrier to our progress, became a springboard launching us into a vertiginous series of leaps from boulder to boulder and at times up the sheer face of the mountain, the captain in his sheep's form finding toeholds where I saw only smooth rock above a long lethal drop. There were mists, or perhaps low-hanging clouds at the top of the mountain, so that at times it seemed that we flew through the air above the clouds as we leaped from crag to crag, the captain finding one invisible *point d'appui* after another as I hung on for dear life. It was probably only minutes before we reached the top, but each leap seemed a lifetime to me, as it felt each time that it might be my last. My heart was pounding when we reached the top, which proved to be a windswept crag bare of any vegetation or signs of animal life.

From the summit, I could see the entire island spread out in a panorama before me, my eyes traveling from peak to peak along the ridge of the island's spine. There were seven peaks that I could see, starting with the one where I had encountered the dragon-spawn, the one we were on now, and five more stretching away into the distance. The summit of each mountain could be seen rising up out of the mists like islands rising out of the sea, with the plains hidden in the mists below us. I scanned the clouds around us like a mariner searching for a diving whale. Then suddenly, rising out of the bank of low-lying clouds below us, I saw the phoenix again, a flash of red and gold, breaking through the hazy white of the clouds. I raised a hand to point, and regretted it instantly, because the captain, in his mountain sheep's form, leaped suddenly from the crag where we had been standing into the clouds below. I thought we would plunge to our deaths, but no sooner had we entered the clouds than his feet sprang off some invisible (to me) rocky crag and we were airborne again. We flew in a series of sudden lurching movements through the clouds, like a ship tacking first this way and then that, but always pursuing a single objective. At times I caught glimpses of our quarry, and at others I could see nothing but clouds and mist as we sprang from one invisible outcropping to the next below the summit.

Then suddenly we were in the open again, a patch of blue sky and sunshine appearing out of the mists, and the phoenix directly in front of us. The mountain sheep's great leap brought us within an arm's reach of the bird. There was no time to throw the net, so I reached up and grabbed for the bird, hoping to seize hold of its tail. Instead, I found myself lifted from the sheep's back, dangling in midair, hanging on to one of the long tail feathers of the magical bird. There was a flap of wings and the phoenix soared higher, lofting me high above the mountain summit. I looked down and saw the captain, still in sheep's form, staring up at me from the rocky crags below. The phoenix flew higher still and I lost sight of the captain in the swirling clouds.

With mighty strokes of his wings, the phoenix soared ever higher. The air grew colder and thinner than it had been even on top of the mountain, and I was wondering if I would freeze to death, suffocate from lack of oxygen, or lose my grip and be shattered on the top of the mountain below, when the phoenix dove, plunging us back down into the clouds. I hung on for dear life as the phoenix began to turn from side to side while diving, like a fish caught on a line. With each turn I feared I would lose hold and be flung off into the clouds or smashed against some unseen precipice. I closed my eyes and hung on.

When I opened them again several minutes later we were far out over the ocean, the Island of the Unicorns and its mountains far behind us. The sun was setting in front of us, its reddish glow spread across an unbroken horizon. I was holding on tight to the magic feather, hoping that we would not plummet down to the sea below us, when the phoenix gave a sudden jerking motion and shot skyward. The tail feather I had been holding pulled away from the bird and I hung, suspended in midair, holding a single magical feather in my hands.

Chapter Twenty

Adrift

How long can you hold on to a feather? This might not ordinarily appear to be a question of utmost importance, except that in the present circumstance, my ability to keep hold of the phoenix's magical feather was all that lay between me and a sudden plunge of several hundred feet ending in a splash for me and a meal for the sharks. So I held on. The sun set and I drifted through the night, grasping tight to the magical lifeline that kept me suspended far above the tossing waves below. I watched the stars come out. There was little else to do there, suspended in midair, so I looked for familiar constellations. I found the Big Dipper, and I think the North Star, and with that as a reference point noted that I seemed to be drifting slowly (or perhaps not so slowly, it was difficult to gauge distance with only the uncertain height of the waves below for comparison) westward.

How long can you hold on to a feather? I tried not to think of the obvious answer to that question: until you let go. The sky lightened and still I hung there as the rosy light of dawn spread out over the water's surface, turning it from black to rippling shades of green and grey. I waited, watching the clouds drift by overhead, wondering if the prevailing winds would eventually blow me to shore or if I would simply hang there until I grew too weary to hold on any longer and then plunge down into the waiting embrace of the sea. Once I saw a bird, an albatross I think, and I marveled to see it so far from any shore, gliding effortlessly, carried on invisible currents high above the waves to some unknown destination. I wished my own flight were as swift and certain. I thought longingly of the little harbor we had set out from all those weeks before and wondered if I would ever see it again. I thought, too, of Elizabeth and the children, whom I had not seen now in several weeks. What were they doing? Were they searching for me? Or did they grieve, thinking me dead? And if the little harbor I had set out from with Greytail seemed impossibly far away, how much farther were those I had left behind in another world? My thoughts turned useless circles as I hung there, holding on to the feather for dear life. For muse as I might, I could not let my concentration waver for even a moment if it meant losing hold of the magic feather that kept me aloft. Nor did I dare to sleep. For fear that sleeping I might lose hold of that precious talisman and wake to find myself falling into the sea. So, I forced myself to stay awake, singing songs to myself, telling myself stories that I remembered from my childhood, and making up new ones when I could recall no more. Anything to keep myself awake and keep my grip on the feather.

By the third day my arms ached and my skin felt raw from the sun and the wind despite the wizard's cloak that kept my exposed areas to a minimum. My mouth was parched and my head swam with fatigue, hunger, and dehydration. I wondered how long it would take before I slipped into delirium. In the distance, I could hear the cries of gulls, and I knew that I had blown closer to shore. I wished again for the tiny port I had set out from, and it seemed as if I picked up speed, the feather's magic answering my unspoken plea.

In another hour I could see land, a long narrow island jutting out into the ocean with a sheltered bay behind it. I saw ships, some with two masts, some with three, smaller fishing boats with just a single mast and dinghies weaving in and out among the larger vessels. The harbor looked remarkably like the one I had left a few weeks before. And then, we were coming into the harbor, the feather and I, and I recognized it as the one I had been wishing for, the same one I had left those many weeks ago. I thought of going back to the Pickled Parrot and trying to persuade the captain's daughter to take me, or find someone to take me, back to the wizards' castle, and then I wondered if I could will the feather to carry me there directly. After all, with thousands of miles of coast where I might have blown ashore, I had managed, with only an unspoken wish, to come ashore at precisely the location where I had set out all those weeks ago. I looked down at the landscape spread out before me and saw the promontory where the wizard's castle stood. I pictured myself landing softly in the courtyard of the castle and, though there was no change in the wind, we began to drift away from the harbor and up toward the Castle of the White Wizards.

Chapter Twenty-One

Is Anybody Home?

I SPIRALED SLOWLY DOWN, the towers of the wizards' castle appearing to me first as white pinpoints set amid the green of the surrounding forest, then the castle seemed to swell beneath me as I drifted downward so that it looked like a doll's house, then a child's fort, and finally it assumed its full proportions. From above, I could see the layout of the buildings that had been obscure to me during my earlier stay there. The castle was arranged as an asymmetrical, squared-off figure eight, with two courtyards and eight towers. There were towers at each of the four corners, one at either end of the row of buildings that separated the two courtyards and two more in the larger half of the figure eight. The stables and the well stood in the larger of the two courtyards, and I found myself drifting slowly down toward that part of the castle. My feet touched down, not as lightly as a feather perhaps, but softly enough that though I tumbled to the ground, I did not seem to have broken any bones.

I lay there a long moment, breathing heavily, trying to make sense of what had happened. I was exhausted, my arms ached, the inside of my mouth felt as dry as a desert, but, somehow, miraculously I was on this side of the ocean and alive. I tucked the feather into my pack, beside the Sea King's conch shell, and only then realized that I still carried, not just my own pack, but the captain's as well, including the flask of mysterious liquid that he had drunk to transform himself into a mountain sheep, back in some other life on the far side of the ocean. Did he need it to change back, I wondered, or would the transformation wear off, like the spell that had changed me into a unicorn? I had no way to find out and no way to return the flask to him unless I wanted to chance another voyage across the ocean suspended from a magic feather which, I assured myself and the feather, I most certainly did *not* want to do.

After I had caught my breath and my head had cleared at least a little, I got up and began to look around. Surprisingly, no one came out to the courtyard to ask me what I was doing. There was a well in one corner of the courtyard with an old-fashioned crank handle. I walked over to it, raised the bucket and drank deeply, straight out of the bucket, and felt some of the weariness wash away from me. Still no one came out to question what I was doing.

I looked into the stables. They were empty, with not even a trace of horse droppings on the ground to indicate recent habitation. Curiouser and curiouser, I thought. I went back to the guard's room where I had entered the castle the first time, but it too was empty, save for the small pillow on the doorkeeper's wooden bench. Whether he had stepped out a moment ago or had been gone for weeks I couldn't say. Puzzled, I began to explore, first the two courtyards and then the various halls within the castle proper. I spent several hours wandering about the different levels of the castle, from battlements to basement, even venturing into some of the tunnels I had explored before, but there was no sign of life, human or otherwise. Puzzled, hungry, and exhausted, I sat down on the ground in the inner courtyard to think.

Where could they all have gone? They might, I supposed, all be out looking for the missing Greytail. Though since our hunt for unicorns and phoenix feathers had been expected to take several weeks, it seemed unlikely that they would even know she was missing. Perhaps the Sea King had somehow gotten word of the missing pearl's whereabouts and sent a ransom demand to the wizards? Possibly, I admitted to myself, but that still didn't explain why there was no one left in the entire castle. Was everyone who lived and worked in the castle a wizard, I wondered, and how many wizards were there? I thought back to my first visit. Now that I thought about it, even at that time, the castle had seemed mostly deserted. How many people had I actually seen? There had been the guard who first let me in, the wizard I had met in the tunnels, and Greytail. That was it. In the entire castle I had seen only three people. It seemed likely that there had been more people I had not seen, but perhaps only a handful. So, maybe they really had all packed up and gone off in search of the missing wizard. After all, it wasn't as if they needed to leave a company of guards behind. Who would try to break into a castle, especially a castle that belonged to a bunch of wizards? If I hadn't had the phoenix's magic feather to float me in, I could have sat outside the walls for a week and had no idea whether there was one person inside or a thousand or, as it now appeared, no one at all.

My belly rumbled, reminding me that it had been three days since I had eaten. Traveling by magic feather might be faster than sailing, but the meals and accommodations definitely left something to be desired. I went back into the larger courtyard in search of food. In the tower nearest the stable, I found the kitchens, and more importantly, storehouses full of supplies. There was no means of refrigeration that I could see, but I found cupboards full of grains and barrels with apples and baskets with several kinds of nuts. I sat eating apples and cracking nuts with my hands against a rough stone counter until my hunger was sated. Then I went out into the courtyard and drank some more from the well.

I began to ponder my next moves. I could simply wait here, helping myself to the wizards' larder until they returned and then explain to them what had happened to Greytail and hope they would not hold me responsible for her capture. Or, I could take advantage of the wizards' absence to hunt for the pearl. This was, of course, a riskier proposition, since if the wizards returned and found me rummaging through their treasures they would, quite rightly, be likely to take it amiss. There was also the possibility that even if the wizards were gone, they might have left some sort of protective spell guarding the pearl that could prove fatal to me even in their absence. On the other hand, if I found the pearl, my negotiating position with the Sea King would be greatly improved. What to do?

In the end, curiosity got the better of me. I spent the next several days exploring the castle from top to bottom. In doing so, I confirmed the complete absence of any inhabitants (unless they were hidden in some sort of secret passage that I could not find), but came no closer to discovering the pearl's whereabouts. Scrolls, papers, and manuscripts, both bound and unbound, were in evidence in several rooms, as was a great deal of dust that had gathered under the many beds I found. But there were no secret treasure rooms (or none that I could find). Indeed, few luxuries of any kind were in evidence. The furniture tended toward the utilitarian, wooden tables and benches being far more common than the stuffed chair where I had found the old wizard that first night. Dishes were wood or pottery, not metal, and the silverware all seemed to be of pewter, not actual silver. What richness there was I discovered only in the libraries, of which there were several, with volumes in several languages I did not know, so how or if they were organized was a mystery to me. Of these, the messiest by far was the one in the basement where I had met the old wizard and his rat, Matilda. Books, papers, and dust were still there in abundance, but if any treasures were hidden there, they eluded me. Even the rat seemed to have disappeared.

I had feared that some kind of magical warding spell might strike me as I rummaged, but it appeared that the wizards' best defense against thievery was the lack of anything that a thief might want to steal. Aside from the one book I needed, the book that had brought me here (which, as far as I knew, was still safely in the dragon's keeping), none of these books were of any use to me. I thought of taking one or more books that I might be able to barter when I left the place, but the prospect seemed to amount to a kind of desecration, and I could not bring myself to do it.

I pondered what I should do next. I still had the phoenix feather. I didn't know if its magical lifting abilities would work for me again or, if they did, how long they would last. It would be extremely unpleasant to find out halfway across the ocean that its magical batteries had run down. I also had the Sea King's conch shell, though calling him before I had found the pearl seemed an unwise choice. I even had the captain's leather flask and the remains of the potion he had used to transform himself into a mountain sheep, although what good such a shape-change would do me, I couldn't fathom. Certainly, as a sheep I could travel faster than I could as a human, but where would I go?

I set the three objects out in front of me: feather, flask, and shell, and contemplated my options. All three were imbued with powerful magic, but all three seemed equally useless in my present predicament. Perhaps if there were some sort of magical flea market I could trade them for a magical book of maps, although I had no idea of what the exchange rate would be. How many magical feathers or shape changing potions was a book of maps worth? And to whom? The dragon, of course, still had the original book of maps, or so I hoped, but since none of these magical objects was the dragon's heartstone, it seemed unlikely that he would accept one of them, or even all of them as a substitute. The same, of course, was true of the Sea King's missing pearl and in all my searching I had seen no sign of either pearl or heartstone.

As I sat there, looking at the three objects, something about the feather caught my attention. It still shimmered with the red and gold brilliance of the phoenix. Despite being grasped in my hands for three days during our voyage across the ocean, it looked none the worse for wear which was surprising enough in and of itself, but there was something else odd about its appearance. If I looked at it, I could see the feather itself in all its fiery glory, but if I looked through the feather, it seemed as if I could see through the floor of the room where I stood, into the room below, and as I peered closer, I realized that it was not a room that I saw, but a forest.

I looked up. The room seemed as solid as it had a moment before. I looked back at the feather and then through it. Again, I saw what looked like a forest spread out below me. Was this a window into my own world, where the Castle of the White Wizards did not exist? Or perhaps a window into some other world? I picked up the feather and held it up to my eyes. Peering around the room, or what had been a room before I looked through the feather, in every direction I saw the leaves and branches of a dense forest extending above and below me. I looked down at my feet and saw that I seemed to be standing on a branch of a great oak tree with a drop of perhaps thirty feet to either side. Hastily, I removed the feather from my eyes, and the room reappeared.

I swallowed and a wave of vertigo passed over me. Having spent three days suspended over the ocean, I had no desire to find myself falling to my death from a tree, even though in comparison, the height of the tree seemed negligible. Breathing heavily, I set the feather down and thought. What did this mean? Looking through the feather, I could see into another world, a forested world apparently, where the Castle of the White Wizards did not exist. Was it my own world, or some other? How could I find out?

I picked up the three magical items and placed them back into my pack. Slowly, carefully, I walked out of the room where I had been searching, down the stairs, and out into the courtyard below. The castle walls seemed as solid as ever, though when I had looked through the feather they had melted into nothingness, and it had seemed as if I stood perched on the limb of a great tree. Which was real? Or was neither vision real and all my adventures of the past several weeks the fevered dreams of a self that lay far away, perhaps in a hospital bed, in a world devoid of magic? How could I tell?

I took the feather out of my pack and held it cautiously up to my eyes. As I looked through the feather, the entire castle seemed to disappear. My eyes told me that I was in a small clearing in a forest, surrounded by a dense circle of tall oak trees whose trunks rose perhaps sixty feet or more into the air. Was this real or some kind of optical illusion? Holding the feather in front of my face, I walked forward, my other hand held out in front of me in case I should suddenly bump into the now invisible walls. I didn't. Instead, I stepped cautiously between the closely spaced trunks and out into a clearing by the edge of the large rock formation where the castle had sat a few moments before. I looked down over the edge of the rocks. Below, in the distance, I could see the harbor town I had sailed from a few weeks before. It looked unchanged. I turned around to face the area where the castle had stood and still saw only trees. I lowered the feather from my eyes, and the castle reappeared.

I walked back towards the castle and put my hand against the wall. It seemed solid enough. I pushed on it and nothing happened, which was perhaps not surprising, given that this was a solid stone wall—except that I had somehow just walked *through* that wall. I put the feather back in front of my eyes and the forest reappeared, and my hand was pushing on the bark of a great oak tree. I shook my head, trying to figure out what this might mean. Did the forest and the castle exist in one world or in two? If it was one world, then which one was real? If two, how did the simple act of holding the feather up to my eyes allow me to see, and apparently step, between them?

No answers came to me. I put the feather back up to my eyes and stepped back between the trees. I wondered, briefly, what would happen if I were to lower the feather at the precise moment that I was crossing through one of the walls. Would I be killed, half of my body left on one side of the wall and half on the other, or would I be trapped like a ghost within the wall itself? I decided not to chance it.

Back inside the circle of trees, I looked around. The pattern of the tree trunks roughly followed the outlines of the castle that I had seen from the air, with two large clearings where the courtyards had been, separated by a wall of trees. I was standing in what had been the larger of the two courtyards, where the stables and the kitchen had been. The library and most of the sleeping quarters had been in the towers off of the second, smaller courtyard. There was a strange half-familiar scent coming from that direction. I looked over towards the smaller courtyard, trying to identify the source of that strange scent and saw that there was a bluish light coming from one of the trees. I walked over towards the tree that the light was coming from and breathed in deeply. When I did, I recognized it instantly as the scent I had smelled from the grasses on the Unicorn Plain. It was the smell of magic.

The tree with the mysterious blue light was on the far side of the ring of trees that made up the walls separating the two courtyards. Stepping carefully between the closely spaced trees and keeping the feather pressed tightly to my eyes, I made my way into the smaller courtyard and then over toward a tree, standing in one corner of the clearing that seemed to be the source of the odd light. Looking up, I saw that the light was coming from a knothole about halfway up the tree. It occurred to me that this was just the sort of place where a squirrel might store its nuts for the winter, and perhaps other treasures as well.

I stepped back into the clearing and took the feather from my eyes. The castle reappeared, and the blue glow that I had seen coming from the tree vanished, along with the rest of the forest. Interestingly, not only did the light from the tree vanish, but the scent of magic that I had noticed a minute ago seemed to disappear as well as soon as I removed the feather from my eyes. The blue glow I had seen earlier had been coming from a spot that was now midway between the second and third stories of the building, hidden somewhere in the third-story floorboards, or perhaps behind a removable panel in the ceiling of the room below. I had searched those rooms carefully, more than once in the preceding days and seen no sign of a trap door or hidden recess, but perhaps the hiding place was only visible to someone looking through the magic phoenix feather, or whatever equivalent the wizards used. I thought about going up and using the magic feather to search both those rooms again. The problem was, when I looked through the feather, not only the image, but the substance of the castle seemed to disappear, and I might find myself suddenly plummeting thirty feet to the ground below.

I took off my pack and began to rummage through it. I found a small leather strap and used that to tie the feather firmly in front of my eyes, then looked up at the newly visible forest. I could still see the blue glow emanating from one particular tree, about thirty feet off the ground. I walked over to the tree and began to climb. Greytail, I'm sure, could have scaled it in the blink of an eye, but for me it was slow going. My recent practice at finding hand and toeholds among the rocks on the Unicorn Isles seemed to help, as I had never been much good at climbing trees before this adventure, but helped by the closely spaced branches on the tree, I managed to make my way up, steadily if not swiftly.

I reached the place about halfway up the tree, near a fork in the main trunk, where the blue glow pulsed from its knothole, and the heady scent of magic wafted over me. I hesitated before reaching in, wondering if I would get bitten or stung by some unseen guardian. It would be just like a wizard, I thought, to put her treasure in a knothole with a bee's nest or a family of sharp-toothed possums for company. Or perhaps there were magical guardians with worse than bee stings to offer for unwise burglars. I looked again at the little knothole. There were no bees or other flying insects coming out of it, and no sharp toothed denizens that I could see. I took a deep breath, then closed my eyes and reached in. My hand closed around a smooth globe the size of a grapefruit. I brought it out and stared. It was a pearl, with a size and luster even greater than those I had seen in the Sea King's crown, and it pulsed with magic: the Sea King's pearl.

Chapter Twenty-Two

Acquaintances Renewed

Tucking the pearl as carefully as I could into my pack, I made my way cautiously back down the tree. I stepped back into the clearing that had been the castle courtyard and removed the feather from my eyes. Nothing happened. The clearing stayed a clearing and the forest stayed a forest, with no magic castle appearing out of thin air. Why this should have surprised me so much, I cannot say. After all, in my world, when you look at a forest, you expect it to remain a forest and not have castles suddenly appearing from nowhere. Nonetheless, I was deeply puzzled. All that morning, every time I had looked through the feather I had seen into what seemed to be a different world, one where the Castle of the White Wizards was replaced by virgin forest. And when I took it away, the castle reappeared. Now, it seemed the castle was gone. Gone for good or just waiting to reappear? I couldn't say.

I stood for a moment looking around at the trees surrounding the clearing. They continued to look like trees. After several minutes in which nothing happened, I put the feather back in my pack and headed out of the clearing. I had a moment's trepidation as I crossed the line of trees that marked the edge of the clearing, wondering if they would suddenly turn back to stone walls, trapping me inside them, but they stayed trees and I passed by with no more resistance than the brush of leaves against my cloak.

I walked out to the edge of the tall rock formation where the castle had stood and looked out at the town below. It, at least, seemed unchanged. I sat for a long while contemplating my options, once more. I now had the Sea King's pearl in my possession. With it, I could go back to the Halls of the Sea King and ransom Greytail—if I could figure out how to get there. In truth, I had no more precise idea of where the Halls of the Sea King were than somewhere under the Atlantic Ocean which, to state the obvious, is a very big place. And without the siren's help, I had no way to breathe beneath the waves.

I also had the conch shell the Sea King had given me. *Blow it, wherever you are, I shall hear it, and answer your call,* he had said. Would he hear it now, I wondered, if I blew it from the top of this cliff? And, if so, how would he answer? I decided that if I were going to call on the Sea King, I should probably do so from the shore. That way, he could be in his element and I in mine, and we could negotiate Greytail's release. What Greytail would say about the disappearance of the castle, I did not know, much less what her fellow wizards would have to say about it. Exactly what their reaction would be I couldn't predict, but I imagined they would be none too pleased. Fortunately for me, none of them had been in evidence the whole time I had been here. Probably the best thing to do would be to work on getting Greytail out of that giant oyster shell. After that I could sort things out with Captain Fleischman and the siren, and then maybe I could talk to the wizards about figuring out a way to get me back to my world, assuming they didn't just turn me into a toad or something because I had made their castle disappear. All in all, getting back home seemed a rather daunting prospect.

I had begun looking for a way down from the top of the cliffs, when I saw something that made my heart almost stop. Climbing up the sheer rock below me was the Black Dragon. Just in case I didn't have enough problems, I thought. What to do? I could run back to the castle, except that there was no castle anymore. I could try to hide in the woods, but I suspected that since the dragon was now, apparently, able to cross over into the territory of the White Wizards, it would have no trouble finding me anywhere in these woods. Run down to the village? The paths I could see leading down from the summit all looked rocky and steep, and the dragon seemed far more sure-footed than I was.

There is Zen koan that says, "The emperor commands that if you speak, you shall be put to death. The emperor further commands that if you do not speak, you will be put to death. What should you do?" I sat down by the edge of the cliff and waited.

In a short moment, the dragon completed his ascent, and climbed up onto the summit beside me. He was as big as I remembered. His claws and his teeth were also as big as I remembered. The dragon peered at me, eyes glittering over his long thin snout, and seemed to smile. I thought about the Zen koan and smiled back at the dragon.

"Welcome back," said the dragon. "Congratulations. I see you have been successful."

"What do you mean?" I asked.

"In your quest," he replied, "to find my stone."

"Why do you say that?" I asked.

"It is obvious. The castle is gone. So the spell that maintained that illusion has been broken, from which I infer that you have plucked my heartstone from out of their web of magic entanglements, allowing the rest of the edifice to collapse. Neatly done. And now, to complete our bargain . . ." The dragon held out a clawed forelimb to me.

"Not exactly," I said.

"What do you mean, 'not exactly'?" asked the dragon.

"I mean that it was not your heartstone that I removed from the wizards' web. It was something else," I replied.

"What sort of a 'something else' did you remove?" he asked. "What else could be so powerfully imbued with magic that its removal would cause the entire castle to disappear?"

"This," I said, holding up the glowing sphere, "the Sea King's pearl."

The dragon looked at it, his eyes narrowing greedily.

"And do you offer me that, in place of the green stone, to fulfill our bargain?" he asked, somewhat too casually.

"I can't," I said.

"Can't?" said the dragon, "or won't? Think carefully before you say '*can't*' to a dragon, little human."

"I need to give this back to the Sea King," I said, "to ransom Greytail."

"And who would that be?" asked the dragon.

"A wizard," I said, "or a squirrel. Or a wizard who is sometimes a squirrel."

"And what does this wizard or squirrel or whatever he is have to do with the Sea King's pearl?" asked the dragon.

"She is shut up inside a giant oyster in the Halls of the Sea King, being held for ransom by the King," I explained.

"Is she, indeed?" said the dragon. "And so you propose to return this pearl to the Sea King, in order to free the wizard, Greytail, is that correct?"

"Yes," I said, simply.

"And having done that," he asked, "How do you suppose you will fulfill our bargain? Or had you forgotten about that?"

"I haven't forgotten," I said. "I just need a little more time."

"More time?" the dragon laughed. "And what will you do with a little more time, if I allow you to keep living? You haven't the faintest idea of where my heartstone is, do you?"

"Actually," I said, "I do."

"And where would that be?" asked the dragon, edging closer.

I took a step back, and then realized that if I kept backing up I would soon find myself tumbling backward over the edge of the cliff.

"In a siren's cave," I said, "on the far side of the ocean, at the base of one of the Unicorn Isles."

"Indeed?" said the dragon. "How inconvenient for me. And for you, I would imagine. So, how do you propose to get it? Or do you bring this up merely to say that it is far away and thus, beyond my grasp?

I warn you that even if the heartstone is beyond my grasp for the moment, you, most assuredly, are not."

The dragon held up a large clawed forelimb, reminding me vividly that I was between a very large dragon and the edge of a cliff.

"I can get it," I said quickly. "Once I have freed Greytail, I am sure I can persuade her to help me get the heartstone back from the siren and Captain Fleischman. She'll be in my debt after all, and if she repays her debt to me by getting the heartstone back, then I can give it you, fulfilling our bargain."

"Very neat," said the dragon, "but a tad uncertain for my taste. It would be simpler, I think, to return the pearl to its rightful owner."

"But I just said I was going to return it to the Sea King," I protested.

"So you did," said the dragon, "but he is not the rightful owner of that pearl. Or did this siren you speak of not tell you that the pearl was stolen by the Sea King himself from the Siren Queen?"

"She did," I said, "but I wonder that you know of it, for I am sure I have not yet told you that part of the tale. And as to returning the pearl to the Siren Queen, she is either dead or imprisoned somewhere in the Sea King's dungeons, and thus beyond my help."

"Perhaps," said the dragon. "And perhaps not. She may be closer than you suspect."

"What do you mean?" I asked.

"I mean, that you had no need to tell me that part of your tale. Indeed, I know it far better than you, little human, since it is my own."

"What?" I said, bewildered.

"The Siren Queen is neither dead nor imprisoned in any dungeon belonging to the Sea King," said the dragon, "Unless you count this dragon's form as my dungeon."

I stared at the dragon, mystified.

"When he stole my pearl," the dragon went on, "the Sea King used its powers to transform me into a dragon and banished me to these desolate shores, cut off from any aid from my daughters. But now you come, mysterious other-worlder, and pluck that same pearl from out of the wizards' magical webs and hold it out to me, little guessing of its worth and import to me. Or would you deny it to me still, having heard my tale?"

I hesitated for a moment. "I will give it to you," I said, "On one condition."

The dragon held up an enormous clawed forelimb. "Think carefully," she said—and I realized that I was now thinking of the dragon as "she," and thus that I had, at least implicitly, accepted what she said as the truth, and that whatever her current form, the being before me was none other than the missing Sea Queen—,"before making your demand. Remember that I am still a dragon and could take it from you easily if I chose."

"Perhaps," I said, "and perhaps not. In any case, my condition is this. When you have it, you will go to the Halls of the Sea King and ransom Greytail yourself and see that she is returned safely to these shores. Can you do that?"

"I can, and will do it most willingly. There will be words, and more than words, between myself and my Lord, the Sea King. He will find that his Queen is not so easily dismissed. A reckoning between us is long overdue. And having settled my affairs with the Sea King, if Greytail, as you name her, still lives, I will most happily return her to these shores. But come, we must get to the coast before I make the transformation."

The dragon stood up and began walking towards the far side of the hill. Having agreed to my bargain with the dragon, there was little I could do but follow. She led me down the back of the hill, not trusting, wisely, in my abilities to descend the vertical cliff she had just climbed up. The path she chose was more direct than the one I had followed with Greytail, a linear approach made possible by her ability to uproot any obstructing brush or vegetation with a swipe of her massive claws. I followed along behind, stepping over the remains of mountain laurel and even small trees as best I could. We came to the place where Greytail, or someone, had staked a rope across the little river at the base of the cliffs. The dragon simply leaped over the river in one mighty bound. I thought about trying to run across the rope as Greytail had, but settled instead for wading through, clinging onto the rope with one hand and trying to keep my pack out of the water. I was soaked through by the time I got to the other side, but at least the dragon had not made me strip off my clothes and submit to an all too intimate inspection before I crossed.

We followed the river down towards the town, using the same take no prisoners approach to obstacles that the dragon had used coming down the hill. It was somewhat slower going than drifting down the river, but certainly faster than I would have gone on my own.

Presently, we came to the town. There was a thick stone wall surrounding the town on the side that faced the forest and a heavy wooden gate that was closed when we came to it. I had thought we might turn and go around the town wall, but instead the dragon marched boldly up to the gate and throwing her great weight against the wooden gate, proceeded to tear it off its hinges, flattening it to the ground. I thought the sound of the gate crashing might bring archers and pikemen running to defend their town, but showing perhaps more wisdom than courage, no one came out to challenge the Black Dragon and we strolled unchallenged through the main streets of the town down towards the harbor.

We stopped outside the Pickled Parrot, and the dragon trumpeted a roar that left no doubt as to who had come calling. Again, I looked around to see if any armed defenders of the town would appear, and wondered if I would end up getting caught in the crossfire, but to my relief none appeared. Instead, after a moment, the door of the inn opened and a young woman stepped out. It was the same golden-haired, gray-eyed young woman I had seen when I dined there before setting out with Captain Fleishman all those weeks before, the Captain's daughter, Alicia.

She looked calmly up at the dragon and then at me, eyebrows raised questioningly. Certainly, she was calmer than I would have been under the circumstances. Since the dragon had said nothing to me about stopping at the Pickled Parrot before proceeding to the harbor,

I was unsure as to her intentions. Alicia, however, seemed unfazed by the appearance of the fearsome creature outside her door. I started to say something to Alicia, but the dragon cut me off, mid-syllable.

"I would have words with my granddaughter before I go," said the dragon. "You may wait here."

It was a command, not a request. Whether she spoke as the Siren Queen or simply as a large and powerful dragon, I did not know, but her tone left no room for discussion. I waited.

I followed them with my eyes as they headed down to the docks. They stood talking for a long while at the end of one of the piers, but what they spoke of, I could only guess at. I had been startled to hear the dragon claim Alicia as her granddaughter since I had said nothing to her about that part of my story, but perhaps she had known of the circumstances surrounding Alicia's birth before she had been changed into a dragon. And if the Siren Queen was now returning to her own realm, what did that mean for Alicia? I had no idea. Perhaps she herself did not know.

After a while the young woman beckoned to me. I hurried down to join them at the dock.

The dragon turned to me and held out one of her large, clawed forefeet, "I will now require that pearl of you."

"And in return?" I prompted, perhaps unnecessarily reminding her of her earlier promise.

"And in return, I will return the wizard Greytail to these shores, alive and unharmed, at least by my hand, or else her remains, if she be already dead," the dragon promised.

This last possibility was one I had been trying to avoid thinking about, but if she were dead, I would rather know. I was still unsure if this was the right choice, but there was no going back now.

"Agreed," I said, and took the pearl out of my pack and handed it to the dragon, who took it, almost delicately, between two claws of her right front foot.

She took the pearl, which still glowed with a pulsing blue light, and held it up to her eye. Her claws closed slowly over it, shutting off its light, and then there was a burst of blue light, brighter than any lightning bolt, and a sound like thunder that knocked me back on my feet. When my eyes cleared, I saw the Siren Queen in her true form. She was on a scale to match the Sea King, at least twelve feet from the top of her head to the end of her fishlike tail, but where his lower half seemed to come from some member of the sea mammal family, an oversized walrus perhaps, hers was covered in scales, like a fish. Like her daughter, in place of hair she had a mass of silver-and-grey fronds that fell over her shoulders. She had a crown of braided silver set on her head, in the center of which shone the blue pearl, its single, perfect ornament.

I had thought the Captain's wife majestic when I saw her, but her mother had an even greater aura of power in her vivid purple eyes. This was the goddess for whom men smashed their ships against the shoals, willingly, and I knew that if she called, I would jump now into the water with her and drown.

"Wait here," she commanded. "Within three days I shall return your oyster-eaten wizard to you, or her remains if she be dead, and by my deeds you shall know the worth of the Siren Queen's word."

Then, turning to Alicia, she added. "You too, granddaughter, will remain here, at least for the time being. Think well on what I have told you. When I return, I shall expect an answer."

With that, she dove into the water and disappeared from view. I walked back to the Pickled Parrot with the Captain's daughter, Alicia. As we walked, I could see people peering out of shuttered windows at us, but no one came out to challenge us or question us about the mysterious dragon who had just changed into a siren and then disappeared. No doubt the whole town would be buzzing with gossip and questions about today's strange events for days, if not years to come, but not knowing when the dragon might choose to reappear, they no doubt judged it safer to leave us in peace at least for today.

I had thought to question Alicia about what the dragon had said to her while they spoke together on the dock, but she would say nothing of the matter. However, to my relief, Alicia let me stay free of charge at the inn while I waited for her grandmother to reappear. Despite having given up my greatest treasure to the dragon, I still had some valuable items in my pack, the phoenix feather and the captain's flask of shape-changing potion not least among them. What I didn't have was any coins. I wasn't entirely sure if Alicia gave me room and board out of her own generosity or at her grandmother's urging, but I didn't question my good fortune.

The weather changed that night. A big storm blew in from the ocean and began to pound the town with high winds and heavy rain. I sat in the little attic room that Alicia had placed me in and listened as the rain lashed the wooden shutters and the sounds of thunder boomed in the night sky above the inn. As I listened to it, I wondered if the change in weather were coincidence or if the storm we were experiencing was the echo of some fearsome battle beneath the waves. I thought, too, of the storm that had assailed my own home, now worlds away, the night that I first encountered the dragon's magic book. That storm, I now understood, had been of the dragon's making. An advertisement, if you could call it that, that I had unknowingly answered by opening the book. Was this storm, too, of the dragon's making? Or perhaps I should say the Siren Queen's since they were now revealed to be one and the same? Or was it the Sea King's? He, too, was a master of storms, I knew, so this could well be his work. Or perhaps the two of them contended magically, as Greytail had tried to do by calling up her own storm to fight the one the Sea King had used to pull us down into his realm, and the wild chaos that raged above our heads was the echo of their marine warfare. The Siren Queen, now that she was back in possession of the pearl, would, I had no doubt, prove a more worthy opponent for the Sea King than Greytail had, but was she strong enough to defeat him? I had no way of knowing.

Each day I ventured the short distance from the Pickled Parrot down to the docks and stood peering out across the waves, looking for any sign of the returning siren or of Greytail, but there was nothing but the gray sky roiling with clouds, the storm-tossed waves that crashed up over the docks, and the pounding wind and rain. After a short while, drenched through and shivering from the cold, I would retreat back to the shelter of the Pickled Parrot, where I would sit by the fire until I dried.

I suppose if there had been more paying customers, Alicia might have shooed me away from my place by the fire. But between the foul weather and the fear that the dragon's sudden appearance outside the inn had provoked amongst the townspeople, paying customers had become scarce these past few days, so I was free to sit by the hearth and wait, while we waited for the storm to abate.

"Patience, master wizard," Alicia said to me. "The queen will soon return with your friend."

"How can you be so sure? Didn't the Sea King defeat her once before? What if she, too, is now locked away inside some giant oyster, or worse?"

"She is the Siren Queen, and she wields the power of the pearl. She will be victorious."

"I suspect that you are only saying what you wish to believe, because you are her granddaughter."

"That may be so," she admitted. "But that does not make it less true. Now, hush and let me listen to the sounds of the sea. I would hear what news is in the wind and the waves."

She held the Sea King's conch, which I had lent her, up to her ear and seemed to listen intently. Whether she could in fact, hear voices speaking to her from the sea or whether she wished simply to be alone with her own thoughts, I could not say, but I shared her desire for silence, so we sat, listening to the wind and the rain that howled outside the inn, wondering what the morrow would bring.

CHAPTER TWENTY-THREE

HOMECOMINGS

ON THE THIRD DAY, the weather changed again. I could feel it in my bones even before I sprang out of bed and opened the shutters. I poked my head out and saw that the pounding rain had given way to clear skies. Alicia and I walked down from the Pickled Parrot and sat on the wooden docks, watching the dawn sun rise into the sky and waiting. The wind and the waves had died down and a pale-yellow sun was rising over the surface of the water. We had been sitting there for a little over an hour and the sun was now fully up when we saw a ripple in the water like a shark's fin cutting through the waves and, as we watched, it moved swiftly and surely toward the shore.

The ripple grew larger as it approached land and then the water exploded like a geyser in front of me and I beheld the Siren Queen again, now in her own element, water cascading from her silver pearl-adorned crown down over her face, bare shoulders and breasts.

She was beautiful and terrible, her purple eyes alight with power and her face flush with the joy of victory. In her hands she held a limp form that beside her appeared no bigger than a child's doll. The form was a woman's, wrapped in a wizard's cloak, the twin of my own, and I feared that Greytail was dead.

"Fear not," said the Siren Queen, "your friend lives, though it will be some time before she is fully recovered from her time inside the oyster. Take her, and by this I account my debt to you repaid."

And with that she threw Greytail's body up onto the dock. There was a *whuff* of expelled air when Greytail landed on the wooden dock, but she did not cry out or even open her eyes. I rushed to her side. I saw her draw in breath and when I looked more closely I could see that there was a steady pulse at the base of her throat. It was as the Siren Queen had said: she lived.

"And you, granddaughter," said the Siren Queen, turning to Alicia, "have you made your choice?"

Alicia paused, took half a step towards the edge of the dock, then stepped back and raised her head to meet the Siren Queen's eyes.

"I have," she said, "and I choose the land."

The Siren Queen gazed at her silently, her purple eyes fixed on Alicia's grey pupils, for perhaps thirty seconds, seconds that seemed to drag on into hours, as I watched, waiting to see what her response would be.

Finally, she nodded. "So be it," she said, and turned from us, her huge form vanishing beneath the waves. There was a splash and a silver flash of her tail and she was gone.

Alicia stood mutely, watching as the ripple of the Siren Queen's passage flowed out across the harbor into the Sound until it was lost from view. There might have been a tear in her eye as she turned back to face me, or it may have been only the reflection of the sun on the waves that I saw in her eyes.

Alicia and I helped Greytail rise unsteadily to her feet. She sucked in a great rasping breath, coughed, and then slumped down limply again in our arms. Seeing that she would not be able to make it up the hill on her own, Alicia and I each draped one of Greytail's arms over our shoulders in a sort of fireman's carry and half-dragged, half-carried her back up the hill to the Pickled Parrot. Inside, Alicia laid Greytail's inert form down on the flagstones in front of the fireplace and waited till she was strong enough to sit up before offering her something to drink. First water, and then a clear broth. Greytail drank the water avidly, as if the time she had spent imprisoned inside the giant oyster had saturated not just her robes, but her body too with a salt brine that needed to be rinsed out of her. After a few sips of the broth, she pushed the spoon away and would take no more. It took both of us to help her up the stairs to one of the bedrooms on the upper floor of the inn, which was awkward since the stairs were narrow and twisty, but she was small and limp enough in our arms that we could carry her without too much difficulty. When we laid her down on the bed, she fell into such a deep sleep that I feared she might never wake, but her breathing was steady and her pulse was strong and regular.

For three days, we nursed her back to health, starting with clear broth that we fed to her with a spoon, then advancing to fish chowder and finally to solid food. Even when she was restored to herself, Greytail would say nothing of her time inside the oyster beyond, "It was dark." Likewise, she claimed to remember nothing of how she had been rescued from the Halls of the Sea King by the Siren Queen.

On the morning of the third day, when she finally felt well enough to make it down the stairs, we walked outside the front door of the Pickled Parrot and turned, looking up at the hill where the Castle of the White Wizards had stood. I had told her that when I removed the Sea King's pearl from its hiding place the castle had disappeared, but she wanted to see it for herself.

"It's gone," she said, looking up at the now featureless hilltop.

"Yes," I said. "I'm sorry. I didn't know that would happen."

She looked at me oddly. "And if you had? Would you undo the act? No matter, what's done is done."

We stood looking up at the hill in silence for a few moments while I pondered what I had done and what it might mean for my chances of ever getting back to my own world. What thoughts went through Greytail's mind I could not guess.

"What will they do when they find out?" I asked at length.

"When who find out?" she asked.

"The other members of your order. The White Wizards."

She looked at me oddly for a moment and then began to laugh very softly. She took in a deep breath and then let it out slowly before answering me. "There was only ever one White Wizard," she said, "and you are looking at her."

I stared at her, puzzled, for a moment before the meaning of her words sunk in. I thought of the different people I had seen at the castle. There had been the guardian by the river, the guard at the door, the old wizard who had spoken to me of making a new map, and Greytail herself in her squirrel form. It occurred to me belatedly that I had never seen more than one of them at a time.

"Everyone I saw in that castle was you?" I said.

"Of course," she replied.

"But why?" I asked. "Why all the different forms, all the charades?"

"What is the point in having a castle," she asked rhetorically, "if you're just going to be a squirrel and eat nuts all day? I enjoy wearing my different human forms. And besides, if you are facing a large and voracious dragon as an opponent, it is far better to be thought an army of White Wizards than just one small squirrel."

"So, the squirrel is your true form?" I asked.

"You are looking for something which does not exist," she said. "Yes, the squirrel is my true form, my first one as it happens, but the form that I have now is just as much my true form now as the squirrel body I was born in, as is the old man, and the otter. They are all me, and I am them when I wear those forms."

The idea was more than a little disturbing. I told her so.

"Why does this bother you?" she asked. "You have been a shape-shifter yourself, have you not? When you were a unicorn, was that not your true form? If not, how could your blood have acquired its magical properties?"

And that idea was more disturbing still. Who or what, exactly, had I become when I transformed, I wondered? And, more importantly, who was I now?

"You are too caught up in appearances," she said. "Focus on what is."

"What do you mean?"

"Focus on now. What is it that you want to do now?"

"I find myself uncertain," I said after a long pause. "For the past several weeks, everything I have done was focused first on getting back to my own world and then on getting you out of that oyster shell. The one has been accomplished by the Siren Queen, but the other now seems impossible."

She tilted her head to one side and looked at me, a little oddly.

"It seems to me that for a man who has been in the Halls of the Sea King, transformed into a unicorn, and floated across the ocean holding on to a feather, you are awfully quick to say 'impossible' before you have even tried."

"How did you know about all that?" I asked.

"I'm not deaf," she said. "You've been boasting about your exploits to Alicia for the past three days, while pretending to look after me."

"I wasn't boasting," I protested. "I was telling her what happened so she would know how I left her father, and ended up back here beside her grandmother, who had apparently been transformed into a dragon, which I would think might have come as something of a shock to her. And besides, we *were* taking care of you."

"As you say," she said with a smile.

"So," I said, after a pause. "If you think it is not impossible for me to return to my own world, how would you suggest I begin? I have the phoenix feather, and while I do not have the unicorn blood, I do have the flask of the magic potion Captain Fleischman used to transform himself into a mountain sheep. Do you think those could be used to make a new magic book?"

"They might," she said, "with a great deal of effort and luck. It would help too if I had all of my books and the power of the Sea King's pearl at my disposal to aid in my spell making, but there is no use in dwelling on what is past. As you say, you have the phoenix feather and the potion, and those are not insignificant. But why do you assume we need to make a new magic book in order for you to return to your world? Would it not be simpler to start by looking for the old one?"

"And how would you suggest I do that?" I asked, "Or did you forget that the dragon who took the book from me has transformed herself into the Siren Queen, and is now who-knows-where under the sea?"

"I most certainly have not forgotten that the Siren Queen has gone back to the ocean. If she had not, I would not be here now. But more to the point, she is not here now, which makes this the perfect time to see if we can find where she has hidden the book. From what I overheard of what you said to Alicia, from the moment you revealed the pearl's existence to the dragon until the time she resumed her siren's form, you were with her the entire time, yes?"

"I was," I said.

"And when she resumed her siren's form, was she carrying anything on her person?" she asked.

"Only the crown on her head," I answered.

"Which means she did not take the book with her. Ergo, this is the perfect opportunity to look for it."

"And how do you propose to do that?" I asked.

"The same way you found the pearl," she said. "With the phoenix feather. That is its property after all, it cancels out magical energy, such as that used in making concealing spells."

"It cancels out magical energy?" I repeated, puzzled.

"Of course," she said. "That is why you were able to float over the ocean while holding onto the feather. It canceled the magical property that causes things to fall."

"You mean gravity?" I asked. "But gravity isn't magic."

"If by 'gravity' you mean the property that causes things to fall, it most certainly is magic. If it weren't, how could the feather have allowed you to float back across the ocean?" she asked. "But perhaps they have another word for that kind of magic in your world."

I had no answer to that, though I had the feeling there was more to it than that. The feather hadn't just canceled gravity. It had seemed to read my thoughts and then taken me to precisely the place I had been thinking of. Whatever it was, this process seemed to be more complex, more *alive* if you will, than a simple canceling of some magical force field, but it didn't mean I could explain it.

"And of course, it canceled the illusion spells I had used to create the castle. You must surely have noticed that. In fact, I heard you describe it in great detail to Alicia."

"Yes, but as soon as I took the feather away from my eyes, the castle came back."

"Of course," she said. "The effect is only temporary. What do you think would have happened if you had let go of the feather while you were over the ocean?"

"I would have fallen?"

"Exactly, the force that causes things to fall, which you call gravity, would have re-exerted its magic hold over you, just as the illusion spell re-exerted its spell on you when you took the feather away from your eyes."

"So, gravity is a kind of spell?"

"That which you call gravity is a magical force, which is canceled by the effects of the phoenix feather."

"I see. So where do you propose we should look for the book?" I asked.

"You could let the feather decide," she answered.

"What do you mean?"

"What did you do to return here?" she asked.

"Nothing, I just held on to the feather."

"Nothing more?"

"I held on to the feather and wished that I were back here."

"And when you wished, did you wish generally that you were somewhere safe, or did you picture it as a specific location?"

"I guess I thought first of the Pickled Parrot, and then when I saw that it was actually taking me here, I changed that wish and thought of the castle."

"And the feather brought you there."

"Yes."

"Then that is what you should do to look for the book. Hold the feather up to your eyes and picture the book in your mind's eye and, with luck, the feather may lead you to it."

A strange thought occurred to me just then. What if instead of thinking of the Pickled Parrot I had thought of home? Would the feather have taken me out of this world and back into the one I belonged in? More importantly, would it do so now?

Without a word I raced back into the Pickled Parrot and up the stairs to my room in the attic. I grabbed my pack and then ran back downstairs and outside to where Greytail was standing. I pulled the magic feather out of my pack, held it up to my eyes and wished with all my heart that I was back in my own house, with Elizabeth, John, Ruth and Helen. Nothing happened. I pulled the feather away from my eyes, dejected. Apparently whatever powers the feather had did not include returning me to my own world like a click of the heels of a pair of ruby slippers. Or perhaps I had used up its powers when I crossed the ocean and returned here. The thought washed over me like a wave of guilt. Had I been given one magic wish and wasted it? Had I thrown away my only chance of returning home?

"What are you doing?" Greytail asked.

"Looking through the feather."

"And did you picture the book?"

"No," I admitted.

"Then what did you picture?"

"Home, my home, in the world I came from."

"I see. And what was the result?"

"Nothing."

"Interesting. Perhaps that particular property only applies when you are floating from the feather. Do you think you could float to your world with the feather?"

I thought about that for a moment.

"I don't think so. When I came into this world, it wasn't so much that I moved. In fact, I didn't even stand up. It was more like the world moved around me and I arrived."

"So, you were re-born into this world?"

"No, I don't think so. I mean, I wasn't a baby or anything. I was the same me I've always been, but the world had changed."

"So, in some ways, the opposite of what happens with the shape changing potion?"

"I suppose so."

"And where exactly were you, when you arrived in this world?"

"Near the base of that other cliff formation," I said, pointing. "It was labeled 'Cliffs of the Black Dragon' on the map, though I don't know what it might be labeled now."

"Then that is where I suggest we begin our search," she said.

We said our farewells to Alicia later that morning. Packing took no time at all. I still had my small pack with my assorted magical treasures and the one with Captain Fleischman's clothes. Both were light enough that I could carry them comfortably slung over one shoulder. Greytail had only her cloak. What had become of her staff on the Sea King's halls neither of us knew, but by the same token, neither of us was in a hurry to go back and ask for it. Neither Greytail nor I made any promise to Alicia of when we might return, though perhaps, as an innkeeper, she was used to that.

The walk to the base of the other cliff formation proved shorter than I remembered. Whether that was because I was now fitter than I had been when I arrived in this world, or because with a wizard-squirrel as my guide, even in human form, our path was truer than the one I had first taken, I could not tell. In any case the walk that had taken me all day when I first arrived in this world, we now accomplished in a little under two hours. The woods may have been the same as when I arrived, but I was not.

The burned out houses I had passed on the way to the castle were still there. But with the dragon gone, the terror they inspired was greatly lessened. Of the dragon's mysterious servants we saw no sign. Whether they had been released to return to their old lives when she transformed into the Siren Queen or had followed her to their deaths or some new life beneath the waves, I could not say. As it was, we arrived at the Cliffs of the Black Dragon easily and soon thereafter located the remnants of the huge fire pit I had first seen on arriving in this world. The fire had long since burned out and autumn leaves were already beginning to cover over the ashes. I found it hard to believe that a few weeks ago I had sat face to face with Siren Queen in her dragon form in this very spot.

"Get out your feather," Greytail commanded.

I did as she suggested and placed the feather over my eyes and then, impulsively, turned to look at her, half expecting to see a small squirrel standing in front of me on the forest floor. Instead, I saw the same young woman in a wizard's robe that I had seen before I put the feather up to my eyes. She smiled at me, somewhat ruefully.

"I told you," she said. "This is my true form just as much as the other forms you have seen me in. Did you doubt it?"

"I wondered," I admitted.

"Enough of your wondering. If you are going to find this book before winter sets in you will need to start looking."

I put the feather back up to my eyes and began to search the area. My search was surprisingly short. There was a blue light pulsing from beneath one of the rocks that made up the ring of the fire circle, not unlike the one I had seen coming from the tree where Greytail had hidden the pearl. I ran over to it.

"Do you see it?" Greytail asked.

"I do," I said, upending the rock and pulling out the book.

I clasped it to my chest and felt a flood of emotions wash over me, relief and hope mixed with the fear that now that it was in my possession, the pages would prove as stuck as when I had first looked at the book and having come this far I might still be unable to use it to return home. I removed the feather from my eyes and looked back at Greytail. She regarded me calmly.

"You mean to return to your world, if you can?" she asked.

"I do," I said. "*Thank you* does not seem like enough. How can I ever repay you?"

She tilted her head and eyed me speculatively.

"Well, since you ask," she said. "You do have one or two magical items that might be of use to a wandering wizard. The phoenix feather, for example, will you have need of it in your world?"

"I suppose not," I admitted.

"Excellent," she said, "and the flask with the captain's potion? And the conch to call the Sea King?"

"If this works," I said, "you can have all of them, even the book."

She reached out and took the feather and the captain's pack from me. She started to reach for the book but then hesitated.

"The book I think you should keep. In case you decide to come visit me again."

"As you say," I agreed and opened the book.

Chapter Twenty-Four

Happily Ever After?

I SAT CROSS-LEGGED IN front of the dragon's abandoned fire pit and opened the book in front of me. It fell open to the pages I remembered. The labels proclaiming "Cliffs of the Black Dragon" and "Tower of the White Wizards" were gone, but the map looked the same. I turned back one page and found myself back in my living room. It was nearing dawn, and there was light coming in from the window. It seemed no time at all had passed since I had left. I looked back at the fireplace, and the book I had been looking at was gone. I hadn't set it down anywhere. I did not notice a flash or a loud pop as it disappeared. It was just gone, as if it had never been there at all. I looked around, but saw no trace of it, only the furnishings of my own living room. I felt dizzy for a moment, looking around at these familiar surroundings, and began to think that perhaps all of my adventures of the past several weeks had been but a dream. Perhaps, I hoped, I could forget all my wild imaginings of wizards and dragons. Perhaps none of that had been true, and I was really and truly safely back in my own world.

Or was I? The fireplace did not look exactly as I remembered it. I was sure that when I picked up the book, the fireplace in our house was an open wood-burning one, but what I saw now was a gas-burning fireplace fronted with glass. More worrying still, on the hearth of the fireplace there were two porcelain boxes. Each box had the name of one of our beloved dogs. I looked inside. In each box was a plastic bag, filled with ashes. I began frantically searching the living room. Aside from the two boxes on the mantle, there was no sign of the dogs. I paused in my search to look at a photo on the piano. It was a picture of a young man and two young women who bore more than a passing resemblance to John, Ruth, and Helen. Beside them in the picture were a middle-aged couple, who looked not unlike Elizabeth and myself. Was I back in my world, or had I slipped sideways into some other near-matching one? How could I tell?

I went out of the living room to the kitchen and looked out the back door. There was a squirrel sitting on the back porch looking in at me. We looked at each other through the glass door for a few moments. Greytail, I wondered, or just some other random squirrel? Neither of us spoke. She turned and scampered away through the yard, disappearing over the back fence into the woods beyond. I stood looking after her for a long time, a thousand strange thoughts running through my head. Was I back in my old world, or some strange new one? I had no way of knowing.

From upstairs I could hear the sound of voices.

"Again, read it again." It was the sound of the voice I remembered. The one I had been longing to hear all these weeks. Or almost. There was something subtly different about the voice. Was this my world or wasn't it? I had to know.

I walked quietly up the stairs, longing to race up them, but not wanting to frighten the child, whichever child I had heard.

I peered into the bedroom, Helen's bedroom, or so I thought. There was a young woman sitting cross-legged on the floor with a picture book held open, pages turned towards the two small children who sat at her feet. The young woman had my daughter's face. Not the face I remembered, not exactly, this was a young woman, a mother not a child, but it was recognizably hers.

"Helen?" I asked, uncertainly.

"Dad?" she asked, with equal uncertainty.

"I think so," I said, slowly.

The page turned and I was home.

ACKNOWLEDGMENTS

This book began many years ago as a writing prompt from my son, James, then age ten, "you find an old book that sucks you into an adventure." Over the years it has grown into the book you now hold before you. As C.S. Lewis said in the dedication of *The Lion, the Witch, and the Wardrobe*, "when I began it I had not realized that girls [and boys] grow quicker than books." And so it has proved with this book. Thank you to all who have helped it to come to fruition. First and foremost to my family: my wife Anne, and our children, James, Abigail, and Caroline, who have been my inspiration, my emotional support, and my tireless editors and proofreaders throughout its endless iterations. To my dear friend and copy editor, Christopher Caines, who encouraged me to pursue this project and taught me at least a little something about what a professionally edited manuscript should look like. To Maris Parker for advice on manuscript formatting and cover design, to Josephine Queen for bringing a fiction writer's eye to proofreading the final version of the manuscript, and to Rachael Clarke and the other members of the Write State of Mind for many helpful tips and conversations about the joys and perils of becoming a self-published author. And finally, to my colleagues and our patients here at Connecticut Mental Health Center for reminding me that there is more to life than books.

About Author

Robert Beech is a psychiatrist at the Connecticut Mental Health Center and a faculty member at the Yale School of Medicine as well as a sometime author of odd bits of fiction. His work has been published in 365Tomorrows, Everyday Fiction, Potato Soup Journal, StarShipSofa and a variety of boring professional journals.

He has lived in several places across the globe including Calcutta, New York, Paris, and Oak Park, Illinois. He currently lives in New Haven, Connecticut with his wife, their oversized pandemic puppy, and a small horde of cats. When not working or writing he enjoys running long distances (slowly), playing the French horn, and reading books in French and Spanish. His dream is to open a foreign language bookstore-café and sell as many books as Aziraphale.